THOUGHTS
TO DIE FOR

C.G. ROUSING

FOR FOREST

.

CONTENTS

C. G. Rousing

ACKNOWLEDGMENTS

Inspired by Forest

Cover art, illustrations and map by Jeremiah Humphries

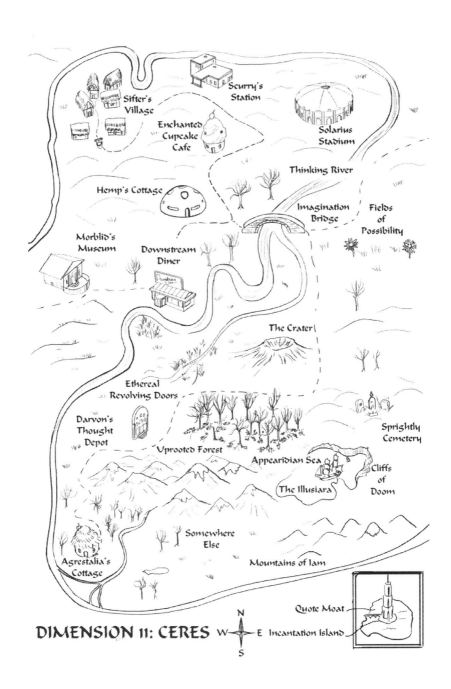

Sifter's Village

Scurry's Station

Enchanted Cupcake Cafe

Solarius Stadium

Thinking River

Hemp's Cottage

Imagination Bridge

Fields of Possibility

Morblid's Museum

Downstream Diner

The Crater

Ethereal Revolving Doors

Darvon's Thought Depot

Uprooted Forest

Sprightly Cemetery

Appearidian Sea

Cliffs of Doom

The Illusiara

Somewhere Else

Mountains of Iam

Agrestalia's Cottage

DIMENSION 11: CERES W E N S

Quote Moat

Incantation Island

C. G. Rousing

CHAPTER ONE

THE INVITATION

My hands trembled from a combination of fear and excitement. The instructions were simple. I was to burn it and go to bed as usual. It didn't make sense but neither had my fifteen years of life thus far. Since I felt I had nothing to lose, and being that I was beyond curious, I filled the sink with water, lit a match, and held the flame against the parchment paper. Pulling the flame away I read it one last time.

To: Levi Levy
From: The Interdimensional Council of Cognition

Congratulations, Mr. Levy! You've been chosen as a participant in the *Selective Thought Studies Program*, a 2-year inter-dimensional program at the Universe City of Ceres, Dimension 11. Should you wish to participate simply burn this invitation at precisely 11:11 on the evening of November 11th then off to bed as usual. Sweet dreams. Enjoy the ride.

The Honorable Elton Hemphelius III
Director of Dimensional Transference

Everything about the invitation was strange. Universe City? Is that a college town? Odd spelling. I'd never even applied to college. I was fifteen and a sophomore in high school. But, for as strange as this was it was incredibly exciting.

There were only two possibilities as far as I could see. At worst, I'd burn the invitation, nothing would happen, and I'd resume life as usual. At best, I'd wake up somewhere else as a student in the Department of *Selective Thought Studies* (whatever that meant) at the Universe City of Ceres in Dimension 11 (wherever that was) and get to skip two years of high school. The possibility of being released from the academic meaninglessness that surrounded me five days a week – all but a few months of the year – would make risking an unknown future worth it. It was an offer I couldn't refuse.

I lit another match and pressed it against the parchment paper. I watched the orange flame devour words. Charcoal flakes fell and turned the water grey. Panic and wild anticipation rushed me. There was no turning back. Burning the invitation meant I accepted the offer and ready or not it was going to happen. Whatever *it* was.

The hardwood floor squeaked beneath my bare feet as I crept down the narrow hallway to my bedroom. I could hear my heartbeat through thick silence. I caught a reflection in the trophy-lined cabinet and raised a hand defensively before recognizing myself. Matted golden curls dangled like dirty carpet fringe over cavernous emerald eyes that seemed to belong to someone else. Staring at my reflection I couldn't help thinking that maybe the school psychologist is right. Maybe there is something wrong with me. Maybe I'm imagining all this. But what about the invitation? Surely that's real. I held it. I burned it. It had come to me through a dream. I awoke with it crumbled in my hand beneath my pillow.

At first I thought my brother, Darryl, had played a joke on me but I realized he couldn't have known about my dream. Hard as I tried I could find no logical explanation for the existence of this strange otherworldly offer.

I questioned my sanity on more than one occasion. The only thing that kept me from feeling as if I were completely mad was my Yorkshire terrier, Alphia. Each night before bed I'd present her with the invitation. Each night she sniffed, barked and licked it. The fact that she could see it proved to me it was real.

More bizarre than the existence of this invitation is the fact that every time I touched it I felt a current travel through my body. It was a mildly shocking sensation that made me feel as though half of me were here and the other half somewhere else. I'd never felt that way before and honestly - I liked it.

I told the school psychologist, Dr. Oblivia, about it but I hadn't shown it to her. I tried to bring it to school but each time I walked down the driveway the thing would squirm out of my back pack and explode. Poof. Up in flames before my eyes.

The first time this happened I was quite upset because I thought it was gone forever. I felt as though I'd lost the only key to a parallel world I'd never know. That was *the* most stressful day of my life but when I returned home from school that day the invitation was on my nightstand. I didn't know how it got there but I cried tears of relief when I found it. It was at that moment that I realized how important it was to me. Not so much the invitation itself but what it stood for. I always felt there was something more outside the scope of the seemingly meaningless routine that had become my life.

I couldn't help wondering if Dr. Oblivia would have diagnosed me differently had she actually seen the invitation as opposed to my just telling her about it. Paranoid and delusional was a bit harsh.

Of all eleven sessions I'd had with her one in particular stood out. It happened the last Tuesday in October. At the end of our session as I approached the doorway she placed her hands on my shoulders, looked me square in the eyes and said, in her usual irritatingly, nasal voice, "I realize being an adolescent is stressful. There are all sorts of pressures kids your age must deal with. Sometimes we create imaginary friends to help us handle stress and sometimes we create worlds where we can escape. But Levi, please remember none of this is real. Other worlds simply don't exist."

My jaw stiffened as I gazed into her shallow eyes. I could hear the faint grinding of my teeth inside my head. Her condescending tone and coffee breath grated on me like nails on a chalkboard. I left her office and began to walk down the empty school corridor hearing only the squeak of my sneakers against the polished floor. After a few steps I stopped and turned back toward her. She was still standing there looking perplexed.

"I see you wear a symbol around your neck," I said, pointing to a sparkling piece of metal resting against vampire-white skin. My words echoed.

I watched her hand search her neck and throat for the silver, rhinestone encrusted cross as though she'd forgotten she were wearing it. When she found it she held it and rubbed it between her thumb and index finger.

"You probably believe in things like heaven and hell since you're wearing that," I whispered, as I jammed my notebook into my backpack. I had no interest in religious debate. I only wanted to seize what seemed the perfect opportunity to make a point.

She lowered her chin to look at the cross then looking up at me whispered, "I do - believe."

"So, when you say other worlds don't exist what you really mean is other worlds don't exist outside the ones you believe in."

Our eyes locked as I said this.

She opened her mouth twice to speak but only silence spilled from her lips. It was as if my words were churning through her head challenging her deepest beliefs.

Satisfied at seeing doubt transform the wrinkles on her face I considered the possibility that we had something in common – the diagnosis. I also considered the possibility that the worlds we each believe in really do exist.

CHAPTER TWO

THE ANNOUNCEMENT

Thirty minutes and three seconds had passed since I burned the invitation. Would sleep ever come? As I lay in bed waiting, adrenaline whizzing through my veins, my mind wandered to the dream in which I'd received the invitation.

Here's how I remember it happening. There was an elfish creature about as tall as a doorknob standing on a street corner in front of the *Don't Believe Everything You Read* newsstand. It held an *Almost True and Good Guess* newspaper open at arm's length. I remember the titles because I thought they were funny in a very true sort of way. The creature's glow was so vibrant that I had to shade my eyes. Seeing me do this caused it to apologize at once and its glow diminished as if on a dimmer switch.

"Greetings! I'm Sner," it said, practically beaming.

Hearing it speak without seeing its lips move was strange but stranger still was how, when it extended its hand for a shake, my hand passed through it the way shadows cross on a sidewalk.

"Sorry — my mistake. Can't touch in the in-between-dream dimension. You know, the half dimension," said Sner.

I didn't know what a *dimension* was let alone a half dimension. I stared at Sner's motionless lips as words echoed through my head.

"Dimensions are like radio stations. You have to be on the same frequency to hear the broadcast."

Sner could hear my thoughts and it made me uncomfortable.

"Everyone's telepathic in the in-between-dream dimension. That's why you're here. You heard our announcement. We heard your interest!"

"What announcement?" I asked, noticing how the gravel sparkled beneath my feet.

Sner tossed the newspaper into the air and spun in a circle fast enough to catch it.

"*THE* announcement. The one where we searched the dimensions' high schools for thought sifters."

I couldn't recall having ever heard such an announcement.

"What's a thought sifter?" I asked, as I watched Sner search the depths of its kangaroo-like pouch.

"You're a thought sifter."

"I am?"

"Yep. The Earth experience makes you forget who you *really* are. Dimension 11 will help you remember."

For the first time ever I wondered who I *really* was.

"Sifters know the power of their thoughts and choose them wisely," said Sner. "They understand that their thoughts and emotions create their experiences. Problem is they're a bit rusty around the edges. It's understandable. Sifting isn't taught in all dimensions - yours being one of them."

Staring at this strange little creature I tried best I could to absorb what it had said. As I watched it search its pouch a second time I wondered if it was male, or female.

"Male," said Sner, as several photos fell from his pouch. "I have something for you. I know it's here. I put it in here this morning," he said, frustrated.

"What's that in your hand?" I asked, pointing to an envelope he'd switched between his hands while searching his pouch.

"Hmm - there it is," he laughed, as he bent to pick up photos.

I tried to help but my hand passed right through them. As I looked more closely I couldn't help noticing that one of the photos was of Alphia and me playing sock-toss in my backyard. Before I had a chance to ask him about the photo I felt myself being pulled out of the dream as though I were a bit of thick milkshake being sucked through a very long straw. When I awoke I found the invitation crumpled in my hand.

Now, it's gone forever. All my proof up in flames. I tried to take a picture of it before I burned it but there was just a purple blur where the invitation should have been.

An hour passed since I'd burned the invitation. I was still awake, unchanged and definitely not in the 11th Dimension. Waiting is hard. The mind wanders. I started to worry about, well, every horrible possibility. The invitation had mentioned something about enjoying the ride. *What ride? What would Dimension 11 be like, if it really existed? Can I come home if I don't like it there? Am I really a thought sifter and how powerful can thoughts be? Will I miss my family? Will they miss me?*

I hadn't yet said goodbye to my family. In all the excitement I'd actually forgotten about them. Hmm. What does that say about me? About them? About us?

Tossing aside my ocean blue, 100% cotton sheets I made my rounds starting with my brother. I paused outside Darryl's bedroom.

With his eyes affixed to the televised championship wrestling match Darryl said, "I know you're there. I can hear you breathe little bro. Where's mom?"

"Working late as usual," I answered. "Oh, she called earlier. She said there's a frozen dinner – in the freezer – if you're hungry."

"Oh. Thanks," said Darryl, burping loudly. "Good thing she said it's *in the freezer*. I'da never found it."

I grabbed the black rubber handles of the steel pull-up bar affixed to the doorway of Darryl's bedroom and mustered up enough strength to pull off five chin-ups while asking him if he'd ever awakened with something he'd been given in a dream.

His rapidly blinking eyes darted poisonously in my direction and away just as fast. A minute passed without response. Punching sounds and cheering from the television filled the space between us. Darryl lay sprawled out on his bed, his back toward me. I was about to leave when he paused the television, looked over his shoulder and flipped around to face me, cheeseburger in hand.

"Are you crazy?" Are you on drugs or something? Why would you ask such a ridiculous question, Levi?" He then stuffed half the quarter pounder in his mouth. A glob of ketchup dripped onto his comforter. It almost matched.

"I'm serious. Did you ever wake up with something you'd been given in a dream?" I asked again from where I now sat on the bed beside him.

"I'm serious, too. Have you been eating some of those mushrooms from the neighbor's lawn again?" he asked, ruffling my hair.

Darryl always had an odd sense of humor. For the record, not once have I indulged in mushrooms from the neighbor's garden.

"Look - I just need to let you know that I'll be moving out by morning," I announced.

Darryl laughed himself off the bed with a thud at hearing this.

"Moving out? You kill me. I've got six years on you. I know what it's like to try to make it out there. It's not easy. Why do you think I'm back here in this go-nowhere-hole-of-a-desert-town living with mom and dad?"

Darryl tossed an empty burger box at a dusty surfboard leaning against the wall.

"You have no money. No job. Not to mention – no skills! Where could you possibly go if you want to survive for more than 24 hours?"

Darryl lay snickering on the hardwood floor. He shoved the remaining half of the burger in his mouth and chewed cow-like awaiting my response.

"I'm going to Universe City in another dimension. I burned the invitation – otherwise I'd show it to you."

Darryl stopped chewing and swallowed hard. He looked at me the same way Dr. Oblivia looked at me during our sessions together. His lower jaw dangled.

The room fell silent. When finally he spoke he said, "Oh, yes. Of course. You must be talking about the new Harvard on Mars for fifteen year old schizophrenic high school dropouts. I hear they have a new admission requirement. You have to BURN your acceptance letter and then – they send a magic carpet to pick you up! I'm sure you'll finish magna cum laude."

Darryl turned his back to me, grabbed the remote controller for his television and blasted the volume.

While I was disappointed that he didn't believe me, I understood that what I was asking him to believe was, well, unbelievable.

As I was about to leave his room I paused to stare into the dresser mirror where the reflection of an endless line of Darryl's tunneled through a second mirror on the bedroom wall behind him. My eyes fell upon the image of an eerie tower inked on his back. My body always recoiled with goosebumps whenever I looked at it. Soaking in Darryl's reflections I realized that this may be the last time my eyes would look upon my only brother.

The sound of snoring pierced my sadness. I followed it to the living room. My eyes raked over the scene. There were candy wrappers, a cigarette butt-filled ashtray, an oxygen tank, and a thick leather belt on the table beside the couch where my father lay sleeping. Half a tear slid down my cheek. I wasn't sure if it was a tear of sadness for his illness or relief that I'd never again have to feel the burn of his misplaced anger against my skin.

I picked up a faded photograph from the nearby end table. My nearly unrecognizable, love-intoxicated parents sat embracing in the back seat of a limousine on their wedding day. I couldn't recall the last time I'd seen such warmth between them. My eyes soaked in the image.

"Thanks for everything you two. I know you did the best you thought you could," I whispered, as I kissed the photo of my mother and placed it face down on the table.

Walking down the hallway toward my bedroom I tried hard to hold back the flood of tears. Flopping onto my bed I grabbed a clump of tissue from a nearby box. I brushed Alphia and pulled her close. She whimpered and gazed at me knowingly. Sometimes, I feel like she can read my mind. This was one of those times.

Thus far, this had been the longest night of my life. I looked at the clock. It was one o'clock in the morning. *What if sleep never comes?*

Pulling open a drawer in my nightstand I grabbed a notebook, ripped a sheet of paper from it and wrote a shoddy will leaving all my belongings to my brother. I then wrote a brief note to my parents reassuring them that there was no reason to worry about me for I'd just gone to a better place.

Alphia hopped up on my bed with one of her toys in her mouth. We started to play tug-a-rope but it wasn't much fun. It reminded me of the nightmare I'd had the previous night. Sner wasn't in this one. Instead, enormous beasts looking as though they were half dragon, half dilophasaurus, played tug-a-war with my body. The cruel glare of their fluorescent purple eyes, vacant of even the remotest vegetarian twinkle, sent chills through my body. Their breath smelled of things gone foul. They flapped their gargantuan wings, first the one to my left, then the one to my right. Each flap created a current that violently sucked me back and forth between them. I felt they were doing this deliberately. Not sure how I know this but these beasts are called, clawcons.

I apologized to Alphia for not wanting to play tug-a-sock. She tossed me her saddest expression and I twitched with guilt.

Waiting for *it* to happen was stressful. I crawled out of bed and opened my bedroom window for some fresh air. I couldn't believe my eyes and didn't want to. The shadow of something unearthly large moved across the moonlit lawn and crawled up into the eucalyptus tree less than twenty yards away. Two fluorescent purple eyes pierced the darkness. I slammed the window shut, locked it and drew the curtains at once. My heart raced.

I pinched myself to see if I was in a half-dimension but I couldn't tell. As I stood in front of the window planning my next move a putrid scent blew through the room and wind ruffled curtains – but the window was closed.

Alphia growled. She and I exchanged petrified looks. I jumped onto my bed and bolted beneath the covers. Alphia joined me.

"Did you smell that?" I asked through the darkness. My body quivering beside hers. She barked twice. "And the curtain? Did you see it move?" She barked again.

Then the room shook violently. I could hear my possessions being tossed fiercely around the room. "What's happening?" I gasped.

CHAPTER THERE

IT HAPPENS

We huddled beneath the covers and that's the last thing I remember. I later learned that at precisely 1:11 a.m. Alphia and I fell unconscious and unbeknownst to me a chain of strange occurrences ensued.

Outside the bedroom window appeared a brilliant, spinning purple orb of light. Stretching itself into a laser-like beam it etched the phrase, *SIFTER'S CROSSING,* letter by letter into the glass.

Branches of nearby eucalyptus trees whipped the house. Something howled and purple eyes peered eerily through the window. Breath fogged newly etched glass. Claws carved deep scratches through the etching.

Water from the nearby creek savagely swirled itself into a funnel. Feet first, the funnel sucked me from my bed. And then, as if someone had unzipped the fabric of time and space I was catapulted through an opening that appeared in mid-air above the garage.

All around town people in their night clothes stood soaked and stone-like, their garments stained purple. When finally shock wore off none could recall what had happened. The event would have remained an unsolved mystery if not for a neighbor's security camera.

The phenomenon made a good cover story for the local *Ordin Acres Times*. Within 24 hours the news spread across the country like flu. Television programs were interrupted to let the world know about the strange and unprecedented purple funnel that stunned the town of Ordin Acres, California.

Until this stupefying occasion the mining town with a population of 1,111 had been an historically uneventful place. Dozens of hopeful gold-digging tourists passed through regularly but nothing big enough to make the town map-worthy had happened – until now. The world gossiped about the mysterious fluorescent tornado unaware that I, Levi Levy, was inside it.

I awoke to find myself traveling through a purple funnel at inconceivable speed unable to move, or breathe. My body vibrated to numbness. I hadn't considered the possibility of going to Ceres alone but alone I was rocketing through time and space. I called out to Sner. I heard my voice echo as though I'd said his name a thousand times but he didn't respond.

Psychedelic images flashed around me. I saw my mother sitting in her black leather recliner watching her favorite soap opera, *Days of Other People's Lives*. I saw my father lying on our brown faux fur couch eating a candy bar and my brother watching championship wrestling on television. The images were distorted. They kept changing size, melting, and transitioning into other images. It was entertaining and frightening.

A flash of Alphia sitting at our mahogany spinet waiting for me to play for her brought a tear to my eye. A fistful of emptiness punched me in the stomach as I watched the images fade into the abyss. I called again to Sner without response.

Deafening whistles roared in my ears. The pressure hurt. Soon the whistling turned into music. Orchestral. Then tribal. Then a kind of indescribable music I'd never heard before. An accelerated version of my life in reverse played like a motion picture around me. I saw my house, my school, the local grocery store, and years full of people, places, and things I'd all but forgotten.

The bluish ball I recognized as Earth disappeared into a trail of stars. Noises and images came with nauseating velocity. What sounded like a semi-truck crashing into another semi-truck made every muscle in my body tense. I felt as if all two hundred and six bones in my body would shatter. Beams of light shot past me. I could do nothing but wait. In that waiting I realized that the only thing I had any control over was my thoughts which now raced uncontrollably.

My sense of time was distorted. I couldn't tell if I'd been traveling for minutes, or years. I recalled watching a science fiction movie about a boy who embarked upon a journey through space and ended up an old man when he reached his destination. I couldn't help wondering if I, too, would end up an old man if ever I reached Ceres.

In time fear transformed into reluctant acceptance as I realized that nothing terrible had happened, yet. I also realized that fear is exhausting.

A sound similar to the churning of helicopter propellers brought my journey to an abrupt end with an unanticipated jolt. I lay on the ground unable to feel my body. It took several minutes for the numbness to turn to tingling torture. I wondered how long I'd been traveling. Had I aged?

As I lay there scared, but grateful for ground beneath me, I heard the crunch of approaching footsteps and smelled something foul.

"Who's there?" I moaned, rubbing my eyes but seeing only flashes of blur in the distance. "Who's there? Sner? Is that you?"

CHAPTER FOUR

THE UPROOTED FOREST

An unfamiliar voice sliced the silence. Looking up toward it I saw several heads as though I were looking through a periscope. Disoriented, I rubbed my eyes and the images blended.

Standing before me was a boy wearing a grey baseball hat and matching jumpsuit made of thin, glossy material. He held a black broom-like object at his side. Bristle-like tubes extended from a shiny metallic pole which gave the impression it was motorized.

"Crossovers are a trip, huh?" he asked, extending a hand to help me up. His other hand hurriedly pulled dark sunglasses from his jacket pocket and slid them on.

"By crossover – do you mean what just happened to me?"

"Yeah", said the boy grinning menacingly.

"Then yes. I'd have to say that crossovers are most definitely *a trip*," I said, reluctantly grabbing his outstretched hand.

He pulled me to my feet.

"You're a sifter, right?" he asked, twirling the sleek apparatus between gloved fingers.

"Uh – well – Sner seems to think so," I hesitated. I felt

uncomfortable labeling myself as a sifter being that I didn't yet fully comprehend the word.

"Do you know Sner?" I asked.

"Nope. But I know that sifters are supposed to enter above the crater on the far side of the Uprooted Forest. You came through the doors."

The boy pointed toward a majestic golden arch featuring three large spinning doors at its entrance. Words engraved across the arch read: *Ethereal Revolving Doors.*

"Why – how'd you get in that way?" he asked.

I shrugged as I looked back toward the doors. The golden, pulsating aura surrounding the arches was breathtaking against the double moonlit sky. Those doors reminded me of the revolving doors at department stores except that these had spun much faster. Still, I had no idea *what* they were let alone *why* I'd entered through them. Learning that I'd entered the wrong way gnawed at me.

The boy twirled his sleek device, again.

"What is that thing?" I asked sharply.

"A parasike."

"What does it do?"

"Gets me around," he answered evasively, jabbing its back end into the ground.

"So, I have to get to the crater, huh?" I asked, brushing dirt from my knees.

"Yeah," he answered, emptying gravel from his shabby boots.

"How? How do I get there?" I asked, noticing several slashing scars on his neck. Just as I was about to ask how he got them he caught me staring and turned away at once. He threw a lanky leg over the parasike and was airborne in a flash. I was surprised by the silent and seemingly motorless takeoff. I heard only wisps of wind as a swirling dust cloud enveloped me. I coughed.

The boy paused mid-flight and hovered nearby. He turned toward me and yelled, "Follow the crystal road through the forest. Can't miss it."

Then he disappeared into the night. Seconds later something tumbled through the air landing on the ground beside me.

The initials V.S. were embroidered in gleaming grey thread on the front of the baseball hat. I couldn't help wondering if these were his initials. I realized too late that I hadn't asked his name.

I put the hat on and as I did pieces of the clawcon-filled nightmare I'd had flooded my head in chilling detail. Moonlight reflected off veins of water hundreds of feet below where I flew. Whistling wind and the flapping of my t-shirt pounded my eardrums. A clawcon flew eye to eye with me as if it were challenging me to see which of us could fly faster. I caught its scent and gagged. Steam coiled into the air above its flared nostrils and my insides squirmed. The flock multiplied along with my fear. I quivered in the cold night air anticipating its next move.

"We'll have to tell Orable about this one," the thing bellowed. "He's got no business flying near the tower." Another honked miserably as if in agreement.

Recalling this nightmare felt as real as the nightmare itself except that my memory of the nightmare seemed to extend beyond the nightmare. It was as if I were watching episode two although I'd only experienced episode one.

I ripped the hat from my head and the unpleasantness ceased. I couldn't help wondering if the hat had something to do with this strange phenomenon but I dismissed the thought as absurd. It's just a hat, I reassured myself, securing it to a belt loop on my jeans.

I looked toward the Uprooted Forest. With a stick in one hand and a rock in the other I mustered enough courage to begin the unavoidable journey. I reminded myself that I'd agreed to all this uncertainty when I accepted the invitation. I was here of my own choosing and would, bravely as I could, accept the consequences.

Looking up I realized that not only did the trees appear to be growing upside down but they really *were* growing upside down. Bending over I attempted to see the forest right-side up but the image was still amiss.

Does the crystal road really exist? As I took my first step upon the narrow passageway I pushed aside dirt with my sneaker. This revealed a thick layer of shiny amethyst crystals. Not only did the crystal road exist, but I'd found it. I thought I'd feel relieved but I didn't.

Cool musty air tickled my nose as I entered the cave-like jungle. Moonlight peeked through tangled roots above me scattering slices of light and crooked shadows across the trail. It reminded me of something out of a horror movie and I am *not* a fan of horror movies.

The upside down tree growth made the forest unusually dense. It would have been impossible to walk through if not for the hand-cut, tunnel-like trail. I tried *not* to think about clawcons but like it or not thoughts of clawcons came.

As I struggled through the trail I tried to imagine that I was walking home from school beneath the comforting California sun. This worked. For a few seconds. The warm, familiar feeling faded as I spotted a pitiful scarecrow hanging from a pole off to my left in a small clearing. Dressed in a shiny silver jumper, similar to the one the boy on the parasike wore, it hung sadly. Slivers of light from twin moons reflected off the torn tinfoil outfit dripping glitter on trees. It was a beautiful, horrible sight.

Eyeing the creature up and down I noticed it was missing a leg. I halfheartedly looked around for it then poked it with my stick. As I suspected it didn't complain. I said goodbye to my lifeless friend whom I'd found almost comforting.

As I turned to leave something cracked beneath the weight of my foot. I bent to pick up a bamboo-like rod trimmed with matted white fringe on both sides. It was at least six feet long. My heart sank as I realized that this was the feather of a clawcon.

Without warning a nearby branch shook violently. I heard a growl. A burst of air shot forth from an opening in the foliage. I gagged. It was the familiar, putrid scent of clawcon breath. I ran as fast as I could all the while looking over my shoulder.

Bushes rustled alongside the glistening trail. I screamed for Sner as my sneakers pounded amethyst gravel. My heart raced. Memories of the creature outside my bedroom window flashed unwelcome through my mind. A sudden and very loud noise echoed through the forest. Breathless from the impact I fell to the ground.

CHAPTER FIVE

UNNECESSARIES

It took me a long moment to catch my breath. My eyes raked the surrounding brush from where I lay trembling. Where was the thing that had growled at me?

I grabbing ahold of a nearby branch and stood realizing that I'd been blown off the trail and hurled into a directional sign.

The sign was overgrown with foliage. Was this a coincidence or did someone, or something, deliberately blow me into it? Either way, I didn't want to stick around to find out. I pulled back branches to read the floating in mid-air sign:

THIS WAY

TO THE SIFTER'S CEREMONY

An arrow at the bottom of the sign pointed in the direction of an ominous mass in the distance. Drunk with fear I stepped into the clearing and rushed toward it all the while looking back over my shoulder.

The crater was large enough to hold the water of hundreds of swimming pools and its rim jutted sixty to seventy feet above ground.

Loud plopping sounds erupted from above and bucket-size globules of water dropped like bombs around me. Mud sucked at my sneakers. Craning my neck back I saw, at the top of the crater's rim and all around its edges, bleachers filled with spectators. Flashes of multicolored light whipped through darkness. Bleachers vibrated.

Unrecognizable forms soared in circles above me. An explosion shook the soggy ground sending ripples through puddles. I slipped. Gazing up from where I lay in mud I watched bursts of smoke form the phrase – *WELCOME THOUGHT SIFTERS* – across the sky. Humming and chanting erupted from the bleachers. The night came alive with light as though the sun had mistaken midnight for morning.

Fright subsided and I started to feel intoxicated with excitement. I searched for a way up. The task was beyond laborious. With each step I sank past my ankles into mud. Repeatedly, my sneakers were sucked from my feet. Digging them out again, and again, wasted time. I left them behind.

Numb-toed from the cold I walked around the base of the crater unable to find a way to the top. Trying to climb up the sides was futile. With each step forward I slipped two steps back. It was time to try plan B. I wished I'd had one.

Just then I noticed a purple, transparent, bubble the size of a compact car floating toward me - its flood light blinding. My heart raced. I felt the way I imagined an escaped convict might feel. There was a loud crackling noise, then someone spoke. The voice carried as though sent over a megaphone.

"Hold on – be right there. Duck!" came a female voice with a sort of British-sounding accent.

As the strange vehicle neared I saw the most beautiful girl I'd ever seen sitting inside. I couldn't decide which of them was more awe-inspiring – the vehicle, or the girl.

The craft came to a stop and hovered above mucky ground beside me. The girl passed right through the side of the vehicle. She smiled and I swallowed hard.

"Oh, no! You missed the crater! Doesn't happen often but it does happen" she said, floating toward me. Black licorice-colored hair smelling of honeysuckle blew softly in the breeze. Wind-pressed her shimmering pink dress hugged the curves of her body. I felt the flush travel up my neck. Speechless, I could do nothing but stare.

"Are you okay? Nothing broken I hope," she said, passing her hand over me. "Oh, thank goodness," she said, giving me no time to respond. She grabbed my arm and pulled me toward the bubble. I barely noticed that I, too, was now floating.

"You look a bit in shock. Must've been a dreadful fall," she said, looking up toward the bleachers.

I hadn't heard a word, my eyes affixed to her glistening lips.

"I'm Sarabella," she said, extending her hand.

Holding her hand for a moment I tried desperately to remember my name – as if it really mattered.

"Levi," I stuttered, at last. "I'm Levi".

"He speaks. Bravo, Levi," she said, teasingly. "Good name. Someone in your gene line must have been a great levitator, I'm guessing. Thus the name, Levi?"

My eyes were still too busy absorbing her beauty to hear her. I nodded *yes* nonetheless.

"Hop in. I'll take you back up. I'm assuming this'll be your first time in an auraplane," she said, as an enormous water globule narrowly missed her.

"Yeah – my first," I said, covering my head.

A water bomb the size of a beach ball crashed just inches away. Ten more riddled the auraplane in rapid succession. Mud splattered and my eardrums throbbed painfully as each exploded.

"Duck, Levi! Crater slippage isn't likely to kill you but it can knock you out – or give you a *killer* migraine," she warned, belatedly.

Still holding her hand, and therefore still floating, I searched for a door as we approached the strange vehicle. Sarabella gracefully entered the way she exited. Our hands parted and I sank into mud past my ankles.

"Excuse me, Sarabella, but – is there an easier way to get inside?" I asked, feeling emasculated as I knocked on the outside of the auraplane.

She giggled. "Just get in. It's easy."

"Easy for you. I really think I need a door." I knocked again.

"Well – *why* are you thinking that?" she said, rolling her eyes and tossing her delicate manicured fingernails through the air as if she couldn't be bothered with such inconsequentialities.

Reaching through the vehicle she pulled me inside. Slurping sounds and peeling sensations overtook me as I passed through the door. I felt cold, then hot, then mushy. It was like I'd melted and become solid again. If I hadn't experienced this firsthand I wouldn't have believed such a thing possible.

"There are always doors, Levi. You'll have to learn how to

maneuver dimensions to find them. Things aren't really solid. Everything's just pieces of vibrating light."

Sarabella tossed me a pink towel. She then fastened a seatbelt across her body, then another, and another, and yes, another. She motioned for me to do the same.

"Vibrating light, huh?" I laughed nervously as I studied the web of belts that secured her like a black widow's snack.

Two straps crossed her body vertically, one crossed her chest diagonally and two more crossed over her thighs. Just when I thought there were no more she buckled another across her waist.

I twisted and tangled my own belts all the while maintaining a nonchalant *I'm a guy and I've got this handled* façade. I felt like a complete moron but I buckled the belts. I'm sure I did it all wrong because my body ached and, unfortunately for me, she noticed.

"Hmm. Are you comfortable like that?" she asked, staring at me worriedly.

"I'm fine," I snapped. My voice sharp and higher than usual.

"It's just - you're turning a lovely shade of rigor mortis purple. We could loosen those." She reached toward me.

"Thanks but – I'm good," I lied, intending to loosen a strap but tightening it even more. Gasping in pain unkind thoughts rushed my head.

"Oh my. You're angry," she whispered.

"Can you hear my thoughts?" I asked urgently, hoping she couldn't.

"I can. I can also feel your feelings," she confessed, applying another layer of glistening pink lipstick.

"But – how? We're not in a half-dimension are we?"

"You're not dreaming if that's what you're asking. All dimensions above nine are telepathic. We're in eleven."

I had no idea what she was talking about and hated the fact that she could hear my thoughts.

She waved her hand over the control panel.

"Top'a the crater, please."

The auraplane shot straight up. It landed smoothly on an indigo blue marble deck. If not for the seatbelts I'm convinced I would have blasted through the roof.

Sarabella smiled. She pressed a shiny red button that released the belts. My thirsty veins and arteries stung as blood rushed in. That was an unpleasant ride, I thought.

Sarabella cocked her head curiously and pouted in my general direction. I could only assume she'd heard my complaint.

If the top of the crater looked exciting from the ground it was nothing compared to what it was like being there. Painted bodies danced around bonfires. Silhouettes soared across the night sky. Vibrations caused by overzealous drummers and singers sent ripples across the surface of the crater water.

I couldn't help noticing everyone's attire. So many clashing designs, colors, and symbols annoyed me. Some wore tall hats and tie-dyed robes while others wore knee-high socks, neon short shorts and crocheted ponchos with bells and chimes. The only piece of clothing that looked remotely familiar was a black t-shirt worn by a child with the words: *Son of a Sifter,* printed in reflective gold across the front. I wondered if these were costumes, or if they really dress this way.

"A little of both," answered Sarabella, without my having asked. "Welcome to Ceres, Levi," she said, as she pulled me out of the auraplane the same way she had pulled me in.

A deep, captivating voice sounding as though it had been sent over a loudspeaker filled the air. The crowd fell silent.

Sarabella grabbed my arm and towed me to a front row seat on the bleachers.

"Let's sit here. Our master of ceremonies is about to speak," she said, pointing.

My eyes surveyed the crowd. "Do you mean the tall guy over there with the silver hair?" I asked, pointing.

"Yes, that's him. Elton Hemphelius the III, more commonly known as, Hemp," she answered.

I studied Hemp from the top of his silver pony-tailed head to the bottom of his multicolored, toe-sock wearing, huarache-sandaled feet. He climbed a podium at the center of the deck and perched himself upon it.

"We are gathered here today to welcome a group of high school sophomore thought sifters eager to participate in our universally acclaimed, life-transforming *Selective Thoughts Studies* program," he bellowed.

Wild applause erupted at his words. After a long minute he continued, "Each of you has subliminally requested and consciously accepted our invitation to study here at the *Universe City of Ceres* where we ensure that every sifter be given the opportunity to claim their natural-given right to joy, freedom, and the manifestation of their wildest dreams. Let the dimension surfing begin!"

The crowd roared. Hemp tore off his socks and sandals, jumped down from the podium and did a spectacular backflip into the crater. Streams of sparkling pink water washed across the marble deck. It was a brilliant sight. The temperature sensitive deck transitioned through vibrant shades of blue and green as water washed across it.

The crowd continued to roar as Hemp exited the crater and danced across the deck.

"What have I gotten myself into?"

"Fun, Levi. You've gotten yourself into a lot of fun. You're going to love it here!" said Sarabella.

I could feel my eyebrows roll into a question mark.

A magnificent hum rose from the bleachers. I realized everyone was chanting the word, YES.

Sarabella explained that there's great creative power in words and specifically the word - yes. She said something about how the very mention of the word opens portals. I had no idea what this meant. I was feeling too preoccupied by the strange and unusual happenings around me to ask for an explanation.

From the corner of my eye I watched a chubby older woman, sporting a long red frock, fill a sizeable bottle with water from the crater. As she drank the glittery liquid her face stiffened. She gagged. Right before my eyes she grew younger and thinner.

"But – I don't want to be younger, or thinner," I blurted, without realizing I said it aloud.

"Then don't drink bottles of crater water, stupid. Besides – it only gives you what you *think* you need."

I wasn't sure if I'd heard someone say this, or if I'd thought it. My eyes scoured the faces of those seated on the bleachers for a clue. A cantankerous old man with a patch over his eye and a golden cast on his arm smirked at me

Was that you? I thought.

The man laughed.

Sarabella nudged me.

"He's deaf. In body and mind."

"Oh," I said flatly, unconvinced.

"Let's join the others," said Sarabella, pointing to a stretch of bleachers where about thirty new arrivals sat wrapped in fluffy neon green robes, sipping steaming cups of chai.

Sarabella and I wove our way through the rows with lots of *excuse me's and hello's* until we found an unoccupied spot of bleacher.

Chatter filled the air. I looked the others over. There was nothing odd about them. The only difference between us, as far as I could tell, was that they had robes and I didn't.

"Who – did they – how?", I began incoherently. Luckily my thoughts must be clearer than my words because Sarabella knew what I was asking.

"Yes. They burned their invitations just like you did!" she answered.

I felt a sense of comradery now. I was no longer the lone, paranoid and delusional invitation burner. There were rows upon rows of us.

Sarabella excused herself. A few minutes later she returned with two steaming cups of chai and two oversized vegan, chocolate chip cookies for us. I thanked her and devoured both. They were delicious.

Just then a loud guttural horn sounded.

"They're coming! Sifters are coming. The second batch is starting to cross. You were in the first," said Sarabella.

The sense of comradery I felt began to fade. I hadn't arrived as the others had. I was about to tell her when she shushed me.

Hemp began to read names from a scroll he pulled from the pocket of his pants. The first name called, from batch number two, was Garby Vanderlin.

I scanned the crowd searching for this Garby.

An urgent sound cut through the air. At first it was a small, faraway echo but grew louder. When I noticed the other sifters with their necks bent back looking skyward I, too, looked skyward.

There in the once festive but now darkened sky I saw something, or someone, falling from it. That something splashed mightily into the crater ending the prolonged, bloodcurdling scream.

Everyone cheered.

I put my hands together and clapped silently to blend in.

"What was that?" I asked, blown away by what I thought I saw.

"That's a sifter – Garby Vanderlin. I sink dat is his mame," said Sarabella, her mouth stuffed with cookie.

"Wha — they just fall from the sky like that?" I asked, my neck bent to the point of discomfort.

Sarabella nodded.

That has to hurt. If he was travelling as fast as I was upon entry the fall, at that speed, would kill him, I thought. This reasoning made me wonder how I survived the fall.

"Physics," said Sarabella. "We've made a few atmospheric

adjustments that slow the velocity of entry. Otherwise, yes, the fall could kill. But, death *is* just a doorway."

Shooting her an unpleasant look I tried not to think about how increasingly violated I felt at her knowing my thoughts. And doorway or not, I wasn't interested in dying just yet.

Hemp continued to read names from the scroll and bodies continued to fall from the sky into the crater.

"Penelope Aubry, Edyl Cartel, Kristin Paterson, Cali Berns, Shane Fargone, Dillon Candill…"

My eyes strained to catch a glimpse of them dropping. By the looks on their faces it was apparent not everyone experiences dimension surfing the same way. Some looked elated with wide wondrous eyes and smiles. Others personified fright and shook uncontrollably.

I heard plenty of screaming, whether from joy or fear was difficult to tell. But the one thing they all seemed to have in common, the one small detail I could not ignore, was the fact they were all naked as they exited the crater. I was certain they'd been clothed when they dropped from the sky.

"What happened to their clothes?" I whispered, tucking my shirt into my jeans and tightening up my belt a notch as if this would somehow prevent my clothes from vanishing.

"Crater water dissolves *unnecessaries*," said Sarabella, sipping chai.

I sat speechless for a moment contemplating this.

"So, are you saying clothes are unnecessary?" I asked, stuffing my hands inside the pockets of my jeans.

"The water thinks so. That doesn't mean we all run around naked.

We can choose not to follow the water's advice."

Contemplating the idea that water could speak, or think, was mindboggling. This was a bizarre ritual and I had mixed feelings about it. Part of me thought it would be fun to fall from the sky into the gigantic crater of purple, clothes-dissolving, opinionated water but the rational part of me dreaded the thought. Still, I couldn't help reconsidering when I saw how the soulguards greeted the sifters as they exited the steamy crater.

Dressed in bright orange board shorts, matching hats, and footwear resembling flip flops, the guards quickly wrapped each new arrival in a plush lime-green robe and handed them a gear-filled bag and steaming cup of tea. This was quite different from the welcome I'd received. I reassured myself that although the sifters were naked as they exited the crater, the soulguards were adept at wrapping the robes.

A few minutes later as a soulguard was about to wrap up one particular slight boy, the robe fell from his hands. It was at that moment I changed my mind and decided to avoid all potential humiliation by just viewing the ritual as any other audience member.

Then Hemp read the *List of the Missing*.

"Levi Levy is the only absent sifter. Hmm. What could have happened to this Levi Levy fellow?" he whispered, too close to the microphone, to one of the soulguards.

Again Hemp called my name.

Crouching on the bleachers I hid partially behind Sarabella wishing they'd cross my name off the list. After all, I was already there.

"Has ANYONE seen LEVI LEVY?"

"Levi, he's calling you," snapped Sarabella, tossing her blanket.

She grabbed my hand and waved it high in the air in Hemp's general direction.

"HERE HE IS," she shouted.

Beautiful or not, at that moment I thought of at least ten terrible things I could do to her. I settled for yanking my arm out of her grip. I dashed up the bleachers out of sight. She followed me.

"What's the matter? Don't you want to cleanse yourself like the others? Look at you. You're covered with mud."

This can't be happening. Is this really happening? I thought, as I hid behind a group of wild spectators and yanked the baseball hat from where I'd attached it earlier to my jeans. I put it on, pulled it over my eyes and shook my head vehemently, *NO.* A surge of unpleasant thoughts raided my head at once.

Sarabella slid in beside me. Her eyes darted to the hat.

"Where'd you get that? Tell me immediately!" she said, her hair turning a vibrant shade of red.

You're pretty but way too bossy, I thought, just before I told her about how I acquired it, and the boy to whom it belonged. Despite all that was going on I still couldn't help being preoccupied with her sudden change of hair color.

"Firstly, my hair color is irrelevant. Secondly, I'm not bossy. And, thanks for thinking I'm pretty but please tell me you're joking about the hat. Do you have any idea to whom it belongs?" she asked, her mouth dangling open.

I was about to answer when I heard a bellowing, "Where in the world is LEVI LEVY?"

Sarabella ripped the baseball hat from my head and tossed it onto the bleachers. It fell some twenty feet below.

"Oh dear," she cried, looking back and forth between the direction of Hemp's voice and the hat. She grabbed my arm again and started waving it like crazy.

"HERE. LEVI LEVY IS HERE. HE ENTERED THROUGH THE DOORS," she yelled, as if that explained everything.

I hadn't told her I'd entered through the doors.

"Please stop it," I insisted, in a serious voice, ripping my arm from her grip but it was too late. Hemp's eyes moved swiftly and directly upon me. He made his way through the crowd, stood before me and peered at me over titanium-rimmed eyeglasses.

"Pleasure to meet you, Levi," he said, extending his hand. The bolero sleeve of his white gauze shirt flapped as we shook.

Hemp's hand was twice the size of mine, but for as large and intimidating as it looked I sensed an unmistakable kindness when I stood to grasp it.

"Is it true you came through the doors, boy? Or – did you miss the crater?"

"I came through the doors, but it's not like I planned it," I admitted apologetically, feeling guilty of an unknown crime.

"That's fine, Levi, my lad. Not to worry. It's just..." and he paused as if to find the right words, "...a rare phenomenon." He smiled and pointed toward the water. "You're the last in."

"Do I have to?" I asked. "I mean – is the whole crater thing mandatory?"

Hemp smiled as he slipped his hands inside the pockets of his tie-dyed balloon pants. "Crater cleansing is an important segment of the initiation, Levi. It feels wonderful. I guarantee you won't want to get out once you're in."

Of course I won't. Who wants to parade around naked in front of thousands?

"You won't want to get out because it feels incredible. For your peace of mind please rest assured knowing that we've placed a visual distortion barrier at the exit point. It blurs details." Hemp winked and skipped away.

I felt relieved by this piece of information but frustrated with the whole telepathy thing. Knowing others could hear my thoughts had me feeling vulnerable at best, violated at worst.

Can everyone hear my every thought?

"We're all telepathic to different degrees. Natural laws vary. There are oodles of exceptions," said Sarabella.

"How does that work?" I asked acerbically, watching, dumbfounded, as her hair returned to its original shade.

"Some are better at it than others," she said, twirling a chunk of satiny black licorice-colored hair between her fingers. "Some only hear what you want them to hear while others hear everything. Some have to be physically close while still others can hear across dimensions. It depends on a variety of factors including astrological and karmic connections. That's how you were found," she said, unscrewing lids from two clear bottles labeled *Ginger Mindfire* and handing one of them to me. She returned our empty ceramic teacups to the concession stand.

I pretended to understand the arbitrary laws of thought-snooping.

"There are some thoughts I don't want others to hear," I said, taking a swig of my chilled-to-perfection carbonated drink – with just the right amount of fizz.

"No sense worrying about it. It'll drive you mad. Besides, most telepaths can hear only so many thoughts at once particularly in a crowd. It's hard to know who's thinking what. You'll learn how to direct your thoughts and tune in better in *Selective Thought Studies*. That's why you're here, right?"

This was a very good question, and one I couldn't answer. *Why am I here? I don't even know what Selective Thought Studies is. I was bored with my life and tired of school. I woke up with the invitation. It said to burn it. I did. And, here I am.*

"Right," said Sarabella. "I realize you feel a bit overwhelmed but, no worries, everything will be alright."

I wanted to be mad at her for hearing my thoughts but she was being so reassuring.

As I thought more about telepathy I realized that while it has a downside, it definitely has an upside. Yes, it would be horrible if everyone were to know my every thought but I could think of several occasions when knowing the thoughts of others would come in handy.

As I sat contemplating the pros and cons of telepathy Sarabella's scent wafted across my face. Before I could control myself my mind wandered. *Does she have a boyfriend? Does she like me at all? Do her lips taste like cherries?* Thoughts flooded my head so spontaneously that I didn't have time to process them let alone edit them. No sooner had I realized that my thoughts were not under my control than they did it again.

It would be so embarrassing if she knew I want to kiss her. Oh, please tell me she didn't hear that.

Sarabella burst into laughter.

"What's so funny?" I asked, folding my arms across my chest, feeling mortified. "Did you hear what I was thinking?"

"No. I wasn't tuned in," she giggled. "I was laughing at the game going on over there."

Relieved, I turned to see what she was talking about and saw at least two dozen players flying around the perimeter of the crater yelling at one another. None of them had a ball, racket, or anything as far as I could tell. It was clear to me that I was observing a group of vest-wearing individuals flying recklessly through the air yelling at one another. *This is a game?*

I watched player after player plummet to the mud below. Within a short period of time all were unrecognizable. I studied them trying to understand this peculiar sport. Turning to Sarabella I asked, "And that's funny because – ?"

"It's hilarious for several reasons, Levi. None of which you'd understand at this point."

I pressed her for an explanation. I wanted desperately to understand.

She eyed me skeptically head to toe then sighed dramatically, "Oh – all right. See the vests the players are wearing?"

I nodded.

"They store thought energy. The purpose of the game is to get your opponents to sink to the mud by draining the energy from their vests while keeping your own vest charged."

I leaned forward expectantly waiting to hear more but that's all she offered.

"That's it?" I blurted, tossing my hands in the air.

"That's basically it."

"How do you drain energy from someone's vest? Do you have to pull a plug or something?"

"Nope. No plugs to pull."

"What then?" I asked impatiently.

"You send disempowering, pessimistic thoughts their way and hope they'll overpower their own thoughts. Negative thought energy drains the vests. Positive energy charges them. There are as many factors affecting the vests as there are models of them. Some vests only store the vest wearer's thought energy. Training vests allow the thoughts of others to be stored. Still other vests do other things."

The game intrigued me. I had so many questions I wanted to ask but a voice bellowed startling us both.

"LEVI LEVY, IT'S GETTING LATE. PLEASE REPORT FOR CLEANSING."

The crowd grew restless. Patches of them chanted my name. Others stomped against bleachers. I felt the resulting vibration travel through my body. I imagined that this is what it must feel like to be a celebrity and I must admit it was, unpleasant.

"LEVI TO THE CRATER. LEVI LEVY TO THE CRATER, PLEASE."

"I want to know more about the vests. I was hoping they'd forget about me," I said, as I climbed reluctantly down the bleachers. Maneuvering my way through the crowd I reached the crater and stood at the water's edge.

Hmm. I hope the water doesn't find you unnecessary. Oh, just get it over with!

I examined the faces of those around me unsure if these were my thoughts. In any case, I jumped into the water. I tucked my legs up and did a backflip the same way Hemp had done. Every inch of my body tingled. My clothing dissolved in a sizzling froth.

My original plan was to jump in, swim as fast as I could toward the exit, and accept a robe without anyone catching so much as a flash of my blurred nakedness. But, that's not what happened.

The water was soothing yet invigorating. Calming but thrilling. I opened my eyes underwater. I could have sworn I saw people laughing and talking through the sparkling pink and purple effervescent liquid, but when I reached out to touch them no one was there.

The water felt amazing just like Hemp said it would. It was as though all my troubles dissolved along with my clothing.

"Hey, Mr. Dreamy. Time's up. You've been in there half an hour. Get out now so I can eat dinner," said one of the soulguards who then mumbled, "Why do I have to get the perceptive ones?"

I swam toward the soulguard who stood waiting with an impatient look on his face. I rushed the ladder, exited the crater and thanked him as the robe enveloped me. The whole naked thing was a non-issue.

I loved the way the plush lime-green robe felt – soft, cozy, and the perfect temperature. It dried me instantly. On the left side near the collar silver thread embroidered:

LEVI LEVY – SIFTER

This robe is amazing. It feels like it just came out of the dryer.

"And, so it should. Each robe is ethereally engineered to adjust to the precise normal body temperature of the person wearing it," said the soulguard.

I tossed him a skeptical look. I wanted to be angry with him for eavesdropping in my thoughts but I was too fascinated by the robe.

Hemp waited for me near the bleachers.

I practically floated across the now sapphire blue deck toward him. As I tightened the belt on my robe I looked around at empty bleachers. I'd stayed in the water so long that, in addition to my fingertips being wrinkly, I was the only sifter left at the crater. The others had been paired and shuttled to their assigned cottages. Since I missed the last shuttle Hemp offered me a lift and invited me over for a late night snack. Of course, I accepted.

"I've got to grab a few towels. I'll meet you over there," said Hemp, pointing in the direction of an auraplane awaiting me on the crater's ridge. As I walked toward it I noticed that beside it stood an iridescent, sage-green creature no taller than a doorknob.

"SNER?" I yelled running toward him.

CHAPTER SIX

UNANTICIPATED

I had so many questions I wanted to ask Sner but as I ran toward him a disturbing voice reverberated in my head.

Thanks for nothing.

I scanned the area but saw no one. The voice came again.

You think you can just go off gallivanting across dimensions, build a new life for yourself and leave me in that town-without-a-down. Oh, no you don't. I won't be left behind. Besides — you need me.

My right eye developed a tic as I saw her standing before me. *Is that MY dog, or is someone playing a trick on me? How'd she get here and without an invitation?*

I was happy to see Alphia but hearing her thoughts was unpleasant.

Well, I didn't get here with any help of yours now did I? No. I dangled through eternity in that purple tornado, my paw caught in your stupid sheet. I barked the entire trip. You just ignored me.

Apparently, at this point I fainted. A few minutes later I awoke to Alphia repeatedly pressing her paw against my cheek.

Oh, come on! This can't be THAT traumatic. Don't faint again. We need to get to Hemp's. You're probably suffering from low blood sugar and frankly – I'm famished!

I opened my eyes reluctantly, secretly hoping she'd be gone.

"Our relationship will never be the same. This is incredibly weird. And honestly, you seem a bit bossy. I never noticed that before," I said. As if hearing her thoughts wasn't traumatic enough, I could now hear her speak.

"Bossy? I'm not bossy. I should bite your schnozzle off. You abandoned me. I'm traumatized. Just get up and take me to Hemp's where you can feed me properly."

I picked Alphia up and held her close feeling as though I were cradling the commandant of the Marine Corps in pet form. My attention shifted to Sner.

"Where were you? I thought you were going to cross over with me. I had no idea what I was supposed to do."

"You prematurely funneled. By the time I got to your house you were gone," said Sner, hugging me.

I explained that I'd entered through the doors.

Sner congratulated me.

"But, why? Why didn't I enter the right way – like the others?" I asked.

"It's not a matter of right, or wrong. It's just not typical. You have to know some stuff to come through the doors – alive. Which you obviously did. So – congrats!"

Just then I saw two Sners. I assumed my vertigo had returned. The only problem was that the Sners were different colors. One was sage green, the other lavender. One had braces, the other glasses.

"This is my brother, Mobert," said Sner, tickling Mobert's belly.

Mobert glared venomously at him and grabbed his finger mid-tickle.

I heard knuckles crack.

"Ouch! Be nice. You need to work on your first impression," said Sner.

I thought I heard Mobert growl at me. This reminded me of the growl I'd heard in the Uprooted Forest. Sner took me by the arm and walked me toward Hemp's vehicle while casting stern looks over his shoulder at his brother.

Neon green peace signs gleamed from the vehicle's hood and trunk. The license plate read: HEMP III. Purple flower-power decals and a smattering of stickers covered the bumper. I read a few:

Question the Answers

Be the Change You Wish to See in the Dimensions

The Only Wand You'll Ever Need Is A Better feeling Thought

What You Think is What You Get

Miracles Are Thoughts in Action

Sift & Shift

Chauffeur-like Sner opened the door for me.

"Wait a minute. I thought these things don't have doors," I said, stepping inside.

"Who told you that?" asked Sner, pressing a button that caused the window to open.

"Sarabella. The girl who flew the security auraplane around the crater tonight," I answered, as I ran my fingers over the furry tie-dyed seat covers and matching shag carpet.

"It figures," said Sner flippantly.

I held my breath awaiting his next words hoping to learn more about Sarabella. I liked her, then hated her, and liked her again all within a few hours.

"Sarabella? Well – she…" began Sner.

"She drinks too much crater water," wheezed a creepy voice from behind me.

Goosebumps marched up my forearms. I turned toward the voice. It belonged to Mobert who glared at me from where he sat in a purple skull-decorated auraplane hovering nearby.

"Don't look at Levi like that you'll scare him. Time to go. Buckle up," beckoned Sner.

After several minutes of confused searching I buckled *one* belt. Just as I was about to ask Sner why his vehicle had only one seat belt Mobert's face appeared in the open window beside me.

"Because the psychpire likes to play games," he whispered.

I cringed as Mobert's icy breath violated my ear.

"Badger off, Mobert," snapped Sner, as he pressed a button that closed the window. "Leave the kid alone."

Mobert stared at me through the auraplane window, his glare so sharp I thought the glass might shatter.

Sner apologized for his brother.

"He can be a handful."

Hemp arrived with a stack of towels. He climbed into the auraplane and we were off in a flash.

It was a smooth flight and my mind wandered.

What had Mobert meant when he said Sarabella likes to play games? Is there really such a thing as a psychpire, or is that just a name he calls her? It doesn't matter. I'll probably never see her again. Of course, a small part of me hoped I was wrong.

As we approached Hemp's I strained to see beyond the morsels of land the headlights and dimly lit twin moons grudgingly exposed. I caught glimpses of trees, a pond, and stone arches.

"Don't you guys have street lights?"

"We prefer natural lighting whenever possible," answered Hemp.

As we entered the cottage I felt powerful pockets of air above me. Crashing sounds bounced through the darkness. I crouched and shielded my head with my arms.

"What was *that*?" I asked, startled.

"Something got knocked over," answered Sner.

"No. Not that. I mean the swooshing over my head," I said, my hands flailing through the air.

"That's Rupert. Poor thing went blind after all those experiments," said Sner.

"What is Rupert?" I asked.

"Whatever it is – it reeks. Can't imagine why you'd let anything in the house smelling that nasty," complained Alphia from where she sat safely nestled in my arms.

When I learned that Rupert was a clawcon my only thought was of escape.

"There's a clawcon – in the house?" I panicked and ducked, making sure to keep my head low.

"Turn the lights on before the ghastly creature destroys the place," growled Mobert.

"I'll light a few of my Eterna-burn candles. I invented them last week," said Hemp promotingly. One candle burns a lifetime!"

Crashing sounds continued as Hemp searched for candles.

A powerful puff of air flattened me against the wall with a thud. Alphia was tossed from my arms. Skidding sounds moved across the hardwood floor followed by a single melodramatic yelp.

CHAPTER SEVEN

ORDERED CHAOS

I felt my way around the cool hardwood floor. "Alphia, are you ok?"

"Abandonment followed by physical abuse. Best day of my life."

I followed the sound of her voice.

"Reminds me of the time you took me for a ride in the basket of your bicycle – and hit the curb."

No sooner had she said this than the sound of fingers snapping filled the air causing a roaring fire to blossom in a nearby fire pit. Flames illuminated a piece of cottage. I gasped as I watched an enormous shadow devour an unidentified something.

Hemp lit candles and turned on a lamp that cast a purple glow across the room.

"That's Rupert," said Sner.

My eyes traced the shadow, ceiling to floor, to the point where it was attached to this enormous creature. My heart skipped a beat.

Rupert stood about eight feet tall - with a wingspan even wider -

and claws the size of steak knives. I stared and Rupert stared back through piercing purple eyes quite unlike those I'd seen through my bedroom window the evening of my crossover.

Alphia watched apprehensively from beneath a rocking chair.

"Rupert's white. The ones I saw were black," I said, stuttering.

"You saw clawcons? Where?" asked Hemp urgently, returning from the kitchen with several bottles of chilled *Mindfire*, his bare feet slapping hardwood floor.

"In a dream – more of a nightmare really," I said, watching Rupert swat at something that resembled a fly.

"Where did this dream take place?" asked Hemp, tossing Sner a questioning look.

"It was dark. I was flying over a river. One said something about a tower – mentioned the name, Orable."

"You flew with the island clan," said Mobert darkly, from where he sat swinging on a nest-like couch suspended from ceiling beams.

The room fell silent except for the repetitive squeaking of the swing.

"To see black clawcons one must fly close to the island. Flying in the no-fly zone could be one's final flight," said Mobert darkly.

Sner hid his face behind a bright orange, jewel-fringed pillow.

"What island?" I asked, my eyes moving from Sner, to Mobert, to Hemp.

"Incantation Island. Orable's Island," said Mobert, filling a silver goblet with a thick green concoction. He chugged then slammed the empty goblet down on a wooden chest beside the couch. Dust particles danced through candlelit air. He burped.

"Who is this Orable guy?" I asked.

Again the room fell silent.

Sner squirmed.

"Do you know that clawcons can fly close to a hundred miles an hour?" asked Sner, tossing a fluffy sky blue blanket across both our laps.

"No way," I responded, so intrigued by this trivia that I failed to notice my question hung in the air unanswered. "How fast can the fastest sifter fly?"

Hemp peeked out from the kitchen at hearing this. Mobert lowered his newspaper and glared at me. Sner stopped flossing. All three stared at me as if the question had never been posed.

"Do you mean with, or without an elevest?" asked Hemp.

Putting two and two together I assumed that elevests were the vests sifters wore earlier during the *fly-around-and-yell-at-one-another* game. I was just getting used to the idea that it was possible for one to fly *with* a vest. I hadn't even considered the possibility of being able to fly without one.

"I'd like to know both speeds," I said, but again my question went unanswered.

Rupert chirped and stared at me raising and lowering an eyebrow. For the first time I noticed that Rupert was missing a digit – or whatever a clawcon finger is called. When I pointed this out to the others Sner explained that Rupert had lost it on a rescue mission – something to do with handcuffs. I took a seat on the couch between Mobert and Sner and watched as Sner tore an excessive stretch of floss from a roll he had stashed in his pouch.

"What kind of rescue mission?" I asked, graciously accepting three feet of dental floss from Sner.

"For kids," said Sner woefully.

Rupert approached me and rubbed affectionately against me.

"Rupert likes you," said Hemp, picking up a plaque that was knocked to the floor during our chaotic entrance. The plaque read:

Universal Peace Prize
To: The Honorable Hemp
For: Freeing Laboratory Creatures

"I like you, too," I said, stroking Rupert's head.

Then, without warning, Rupert bolted toward the back porch and flew off into the night.

Alphia and I ran outside.

"What DOES that thing eat?" asked Alphia, blinking rapidly.

"Not you. No need to worry," I said, picking her up and holding her fast against my chest. As I gazed out into the night sky I couldn't help wondering if there were more clawcons like Rupert so I asked Hemp.

"Sadly, there are no others like Rupert of which we are aware," he said, joining us on the porch.

"He must be lonely," I said.

"He's a she," said Sner.

"Oh!" I said, confused.

Sner explained that a group of clawcon thieves from *Dimension 7* learned that Hemp had a clawcon. Being that they only want females for breeding Hemp gave her a male name hoping they wouldn't try to steal her.

"Clawcon thieves? Why would anyone want to steal clawcons?"

"Some dimensions use their feathers for bedding, others consider them food, and still others experiment on them," said Hemp.

All three reasons irritated me and my thoughts wandered to unpleasant places. I nervously glanced at my watch-less wrist.

"Does anybody know what time it is? I lost my watch," I said, stepping back inside.

"It probably dissolved in the crater," said Sner, a piece of dental floss stuck in his braces. As he spoke it blew wildly in the air like ribbon tied to a fan.

Mobert rolled his eyes and tossed Sner a look of disdain.

"You cannot floss with braces. You need a special threader. I tell you this daily."

"Don't interrupt, Mo. Levi wants to know about time and his watch is gone," said Sner, taking scissors to the stuck floss.

I rubbed my wrist. I didn't agree with the water's classification of my watch as an *unnecessary* but it didn't matter, it was gone.

"Ah, yes, the elusive dimension of time where one feels a semblance of order with regards to the events of our lives. If it's order you want, best check the timekeeper," said Hemp, pointing to a cylindrical object on a nearby table.

My eyes raked over the transparent contraption with cylinders pointing in 12 directions, each one covered with lines and arrows, digits and dots; each one gyrating with no discernible pattern. Walking around it I assessed it from several angles.

"This can't be how you tell time. It seems ridiculously

complicated."

Hemp raised an eyebrow.

"It's quite simple," he said, before explaining the mechanism in full, incomprehensible detail.

I didn't get it. Most baffling was the mechanism's ability to keep time and track events for the past, present and future of not one but twelve dimensions, simultaneously.

The idea of tracking twelve dimensions, juggling past and future with the present boggled my mind. Its ability to track future events really intrigued me as I was able to anticipate serious advantages to knowing future events. But Hemp said the future is *malleable*.

"One has the power, through the thoughts they entertain and the resultant feelings those thoughts invoke, to change future events. Being that time is nondimensional we never really know if we're experiencing past, present, or future in any given moment," said Hemp, dusting off the device with a fluffy white cloth. "There's an entire semester dedicated to the *Philosophy and Mechanics of Timekeeping*. It takes years of study to fully understand. Until then – this should suffice."

Hemp handed me a shiny silver pendant. It was a digital clock on a chain. In the background was an iridescent image of Ceres that he explained absorbs light during the day and glows in the dark.

I thanked Hemp but my thoughts grew heavy. I set the alarm on my new digital pendant and asked him what the timekeeper would look like at midnight, in thirteen days.

"That's quite specific, Levi. Why do you ask?" Hemp leaned in with perked ears.

"The night before my crossover I overheard a clawcon say that Orable would be abducting a dozen sifters in two weeks."

Hemp's eyes bore down on Sner who covered his face with a pillow and moaned.

"Sner, did you not monitor Levi's dreams? It's your job to make sure our new arrivals are kept from harm's way. Flying in half-dimensions with clawcons so close to the Island is never a good idea."

Sner was at a loss for words.

Hemp paced between the porch and couch twisting sections of his beard into ropes.

"What *were* you doing while Levi flew in the no-fly zone? Wait. Allow me to guess. You were eating *Coconut Cosmos* while reading *Sensationalism & Propaganda* at the *Don't Believe Everything You Read* newsstand?"

Mobert lowered his copy of the offending newspaper just enough to peek over the top and watch Sner squirm. To everyone's surprise Hemp abruptly changed the subject.

"Do you see that lamp on my desk, Levi?" Hemp pointed to another odd-looking device.

My gaze locked on a glowing orange bulb, the size of a bowling ball, suspended in a purple jelly-like substance, encased in another bulb. It splashed a beautiful purple glow across the cottage walls.

"That's my Espy lamp," said Hemp.

I looked at him and the lamp questioningly.

"I invented it to warn us when Orable enters our dimension."

"Really? About that – why does Orable kidnap sifters?"

"To control thought. To dumb down the more promising up-and-comers." Hemp drummed his fingers on a half-full bottle of *Mindfire*.

"But he can't control thought – can he?" I asked.

"There are many ways to control the thoughts of others – without them knowing, Levi. Thoughts can be siphoned, absorbed, planted and rearranged. You'll learn ways to handle this through your studies here."

"But why? Why does he want to control thought?"

"Power, Levi. He was raised in a strict, fundamentalist home where he had little control over his thoughts. Little control over anything, really. He longs for the power he never had. He thinks that if he can control the thoughts and resultant feelings of Ceres' youth he can eventually control the entire society. Unfortunately – he's right."

I bolted across the room for a closer look at the contraption. It was sheer brilliance as far as I was concerned.

"How does it work?"

Hemp explained.

"Although the lamp is not as simple as the timekeeper, I believe you'll discover – as I did – the fascinating intricacies of ordered chaos. Allow me to highlight the practical application of the ESPY theorem as it pertains to illumination of unambiguous occurrences in the dimension minus one-half. As I'm sure you will agree, its complex brilliance once understood, reveals a simple formula for energy inducement. I was able to harness and forge the energy to create the Espy Lamp. Not so difficult to understand if you consider further recent advances in trans-telepathic treatment as it pertains to the ricochet phenomenon. You see, it really is quite simple," he said, placing his *Mindfire* on the coffee table before heading to the lamp to provide further discourse.

My jaw hung. "Oh, Hemp. You lost me long ago."

"Hmm. Yes – I see. Well – all you really need to know is that when it turns black he's here."

My eyes darted around the room.

"I don't mean *right* here but when the lamp is black Orable is somewhere in our dimension."

"Oh," I said, running my fingers over its warm, glassy surface.

"Does Orable enter the dimension over the crater?"

"No, my boy. The crater portal operates on a secured frequency. But there are portals to other dimensions everywhere and thoughts open or close them."

I digested the new information best I could.

"Black, huh?" I paced in front of the lamp. "Is there a warning alarm? What if I'm asleep? What if we're all asleep?" I paused to chew a thumbnail.

"Now, Levi. You're not to worry. I assure you – the lamp will wake you. Let's enjoy the evening."

Hemp skipped off to the kitchen.

I reluctantly pulled my attention away from the ESPY lamp. My eyes explored the room. It seemed to have a heartbeat of its own. Wiry green vines crawled up wooden walls and twisted themselves around thick ceiling beams. Elderwood flutes and mahogany drums sat inside an old, overstuffed wooden trunk awaiting their muses. My head spun at noticing the unevenness of the hand-carved furniture and bookshelves that strained beneath heavy loads. I took to the books.

"Excuse me, Hemp. What is non-fiction fantasy?"

"My favorite genre, Levi. I created it," he crowed, rushing into the living room, his arms full. "Have a seat and dig in."

Hemp handed me a plate on which a small, leafy, green vegetable floated in sparkling pink water. It grew a good six inches before my eyes. He then placed an enormous pizza, along with a steaming pot of spiced chai, on a glass coffee table in front of the couch. He used the cutting wheel on pizza and offered slices.

"We'll need another fire," said Hemp, snapping his fingers.

I watched in awe as green flames expanded to dance wildly in a second stone pit. "How'd you do that?" I asked.

Hemp pointed to his head. "It's all up here. Directing your thoughts is the key to, well – everything."

"I want to learn how to do that," I said, thinking about all the times I felt as though my thoughts were directing me.

"That's why you're here, my boy. Solarshay will help. It's a game of the mind – but what game isn't? Your first class is in the morning," he said, between bites. "Solarshay manuals and class schedules were handed out on the shuttle you missed this evening. I have a few extra in my study. Be right back."

Hemp excused himself.

I devoured pizza. It was beyond delicious. I tore off chunks and fed them to Alphia. I wanted to know more about clawcons and so I asked.

"They eat children," said Mobert, looking stealthily toward the back porch.

"Oh, stop it. They do not," argued Sner, tossing a longhaired purple pillow at Mobert.

"Yes, but more importantly – do they eat DOGS?" asked Alphia.

Mobert hurled the pillow back at Sner.

Alphia's question went unanswered.

"You've seen the scars on some of those kids. You can't deny the truth," said Sner.

"Scars? What kids?" I asked, as an image of the boy whose hat was now in my possession flashed through my head.

" – and what about DOGS?" begged Alphia.

"Any kids they can get their claws into," said Mobert, yawning.

The room began to rumble. I coughed. I could smell something burning. Everyone followed the scent. Rupert had just landed on the back porch. Sparks spewed from her nostrils. She snorted in Mobert's general direction which caught the newspaper he was reading on fire. Sner grabbed the paper and stomped it out. Mobert growled.

"See – Rupert gets upset when you say she eats children," said Sner mid-stomp.

" – or DOGS?" asked Alphia sternly, tossing him a resentful glare.

"I didn't say Rupert eats children – or dogs. Don't start chaos unless you want some," threatened Mobert.

Hemp returned with my solarshay manual and class schedule.

Rupert and I looked into each other's eyes. It was a touching moment. She gasped and her breath caught a pillow on fire. Hemp seemed thrilled about this. He then explained that not long ago Orable's army had abducted her.

"The chemicals she was forced to ingest caused her to lose both her fire-breathing ability and affected her vision. But, she's improving daily," said Hemp.

"The question is – will she learn to control herself before or after she burns down the village?" asked Mobert, shaking his head condescendingly.

"I recall the two of you being rusty around the edges when you were first set free," said Hemp, as he grabbed the burning pillow and empty dinner plates and fled to the kitchen.

"You guys were experimented on, too?" I asked.

"I don't want to talk about it," said Mobert darkly, paging through a *Darvon's Thought Depot* catalogue.

"He doesn't want to talk about it," whispered Sner, with brotherly sympathy.

I grimaced and nodded understanding.

Hemp got an ice pack and a bucket of carrot juice from the kitchen. He held the pack against Rupert's scorched face. Rupert cooed, inhaled a gallon of the fresh juice, hopped out the door and soared into the night. Flashes of fire painted smoky trails across the double moonlit, star-splattered sky.

After dinner Hemp's jovial demeanor faded with each new question I asked about Orable.

"He wants to monopolize thought, Levi. He believes that if he can weaken and mold the minds of the young, he'll succeed. The best defense against a psychpire is a good offense," said Hemp, handing me a solarshay manual along with a class schedule.

I thanked him. This was the second time I heard the word, psychpire. "What is a psychpire?" I asked.

"A vampire without fangs. Instead of sucking blood they suck optimism. They're everywhere," growled Mobert.

I couldn't help wondering if the process of having one's optimism drained by a psychpire was painful.

"It happens daily. You already know what it feels like, Levi. It comes in the form of opinion, insult, or a well-intended explanation as to why you cannot accomplish the thing of which you dream. It's anything that feels badly coming your way," said Mobert.

Hemp pointed to my class schedule. I felt grateful for the distraction.

"Right. Thank you," I said, turning the paper over and back again. "There are only two classes listed here."

"Ah, yes! We've arranged a few structured classes because we know that's what you're expecting. But, truth is, Levi, beings fail to reach their potential within the confines of conventional models of education. Traditional schools value obedience and memorization. Here at the *Universe City of Ceres* we value joy, expansion and unbridled imagination within the confines of an unlimited universe. Most of your classes will be unrecognizable as such. We disguise learning in the form of life experience. We like to shift the status quo and free the mind. When the mind is free magic happens. Levi, my boy – let joy and the discovery of your limitless potential be your syllabus."

My brain was now on fire with neurotransmitters creating all sorts of new synapses. I never imagined I'd have reason to use the words freedom, joy, and school all in the same sentence. A feeling of gratitude washed over me. I felt lucky at being one of the chosen few enrolled in the *Selective Thought Studies* program. Little did I know that I subconsciously enrolled myself in the program and that it's available to all who seek it.

It was late and Hemp suggested I spend the night. Exhausted, I didn't argue.

"When you tire of reading the manual, place it beneath your pillow. Night school gives one an advantage."

Hemp winked and pulled on a pair of multicolored toe socks. He skated across the hardwood floor to his bedroom. Peeking out from between strings of wooden beads curtaining the doorway he said, "Remember to create tomorrow in your dreams."

I bid Hemp goodnight all the while wondering if it were possible to create tomorrow in my dreams.

I glanced at the cover of my new manual. The title read: *Solarshay: The Sifter's Way, by Maya Solarshay.* Beneath the title was a 3D rendering of Solarius Stadium. The domed structure resembled a football stadium except that it was much larger.

I touched the photograph and as I did the image shifted. I assumed my tired eyes were playing tricks on me so I did it again. Again the image shifted. Each time I touched the photo I was able to see the stadium from a different angle.

Glancing up to share my excitement with Mobert and Sner I noticed they'd fallen asleep. They snored in tandem. I rose from the couch careful not to wake them and padded down the hallway to the guest room. I brushed my teeth and slipped into some climate-controlled pajamas Hemp left for me on the nightstand. I lifted the 100% cotton, ocean blue sheet and burrowed beneath thick, lavender-scented blankets. I can't recall a bed ever feeling quite so comfortable.

Alphia curled up on a pillow and fell fast asleep beside me. I kissed her gently and grabbed the solarshay manual from the nightstand. It was the most fascinating manual I'd ever seen. Beneath the title and above the photograph of the stadium was the slogan: *Have It Your Way, Play Solarshay.* I touched it to see if it would shift and it did, ever so quickly. If only all reading material could be interactive. I opened the manual and read the introduction:

> Solarshay the Sifters Way, is a beginning guide to understanding and utilizing the power of your thoughts. Through an airborne game you will learn to guide your thoughts so that you can fly, or thought propel, as it is called in Ceres. Guiding your thoughts without letting the thoughts of others interfere with your own is the key to success both on and off the field.

Wow. I'm actually going to learn how to fly! Opening the manual to page one I saw a photograph of sifters dressed in glowing bodysuits flying between illuminated planets. I read the following two paragraphs:

> Solarshay is a game of the mind. It is an extremely challenging but very popular semi-contact sport. Beginning solarshay is played by sifters, both male and female, between the ages of 15 and 18. Matches are played in a free-floating, transformable solar system housed within Solarius Stadium. There are other stadiums in other dimensions in which solarshay matches are also played.
>
> There are 11 reduced-in-size replicas of celestial objects in the playing field: Sun, Moon, Mercury, Venus, Mars, Ceres (Dwarf Planet), Jupiter, Saturn, Neptune, Pluto and Uranus. Solarshay matches are played within a domed stadium with a retractable ceiling and seating for 200,000. Chamber gravity is adjusted to increase or decrease the level of difficulty.
>
> Matches are played between three teams of nine. Players fly with the assistance of elevests. Elevests receive, respond to, and store thought energy. Positive thoughts charge elevests and negative thoughts drain them. Flying is often referred to as tpf "thought propelled flight." Players wear, and use throughout play, element-infused storage packs to fuel and conquer planets. The stadium is turfed with air-filled cushioning to minimize potential injury to players.

Reading this material was surreal. I felt as though I were an actor preparing for my starring role in an epic space adventure. My eyes burned trails across the page – and it just kept getting better.

Each team consists of 1 airator, 2 liquifiors, 2 enlighteners, 2 nutrizors, 1 stabilizer, and 1 satiator. Each player provides the planets with a vital life-generating element.
1) The airator oxygenates planets and wears a white element pack.
2) Liquifiors provide water to planets and wear blue element packs.
3) Enlighteners warm planets with sunlight and wear orange element packs.
4) Nutrizors fertilize planets with nutrient-rich plants and wear green element packs.
5) The highly skilled stabilizer roams the solar system searching for players who've been tossed into tailspins and/or are losing altitude. He, or she, helps to charge their vests with uplifting thought energy in emergency situations.
6) The satiator refuels team members' elements and wears a rainbow-colored element pack filled with all four elements contained within vital orbs.

I wanted to read all night, to learn everything I could about this mind-bending game but I'd pushed my body and brain to the limit. My eyelids grew heavier with each word. Stifling a yawn I rifled through the rest of the page. Feeling more excited about being alive than ever I basked in the calming purple glow of the ESPY lamp that peeked through the open bedroom doorway. My final thought - the one that secretly consumed me - was of helping those held captive by Orable. My heart ached for them. I could only imagine how scared they must be. I couldn't help wondering what made Orable so cruel. I didn't believe people were born that way. I took one last look at the ESPY lamp and my eyes fell shut.

CHAPTER EIGHT

SOLARSHAY

Sunbeams trickled through the open bedroom window casting droplets of sunlight across the pillow where I lay sailing in and out of sleep.

Alphia licked my nose twice then ran into the hallway, her nails clicking against hardwood floor. I yawned and tossed the covers back. Wrapped in my climate-controlled robe and slippers I dashed into the hallway with Solarshay manual in hand.

Skidding past Mobert and Sner where they lay asleep on the couch I caught wind of a mouthwatering aroma. My nose led me to the kitchen. There against the refrigerator positioned upside down was Hemp wearing green and white vertically striped pants and a horizontally striped purple t-shirt. I secretly wished I had the courage to dress so creatively.

"Top'a the cosmos to you, Mr. Levy," he said, with a toothy smile, his cheeks rosy.

I nodded. "What are you doing?"

"Yoga," he replied excitedly. "Keep the body flexible and the mind will follow. Vice versa of course."

Hemp flipped upright and his platinum ponytail whipped through the air before me. He handed me a toppling stack of buttered, doused in maple syrup, French toast. I thanked him and headed to the couch squeezing myself between Mobert and Sner.

"I want some, too," said Sner excitedly, rubbing sleep from his eyes.

Mobert rolled over and growled.

While it was the best French toast I'd ever tasted I was unable to relax and enjoy it. Preoccupied with the ESPY lamp I couldn't help wondering how everyone could be so relaxed knowing that at any moment it could turn black.

"Try not to worry. Thoughts are attractive. Whatever we focus on we get more of. Worrying is simply the habit of attracting things unwanted," said Hemp, looking up at me.

It was at this moment that I coined the term – *thought snooper* and decided that Hemp was one of many. Unfortunately, what he'd said about worrying made sense, and this disturbed me.

The fact that I would attract whatever I focus on seemed like an enormous responsibility. I was painfully aware that my thoughts were not under my command. I was now worried that I was worried about worrying.

"LEVI!" barked Hemp, "Surely – you can find better feeling thoughts than those."

"So – you hear my thoughts but – how do you decide which to comment on?" There was a detectable pinch of sarcasm in my words despite my trying to mask it.

"I understand you feel vulnerable. Having someone know your

thoughts feels like an invasion. Telepathy is often more of a liability than an asset. Someday you too shall have to manage your liability." Hemp, stretched into a *Downward Dog*.

Gazing toward Mobert and Sner I couldn't help wondering if they too were telepathic. Mobert had said earlier that he was intuitive and that there was a fine line between *intuitive* and *telepathic*. But this just confused me.

"Can you guys hear my thoughts?" I asked.

Mobert and Sner exchanged curious looks.

I got the impression the two were checking in with one another to see how they should respond.

"Umm – nope – we're nelves. Nelves aren't typically telepathic," said Sner unconvincingly, licking maple syrup from his plate.

The two then scurried out the front door with Sner calling out, "We're going to head to the stadium in fifteen minutes – be ready."

I looked at my wrist to check the time. It was a habit. I then checked my pendant. I tried liking it but I really missed my watch. Looking over at the ESPY lamp I wished I could take it with me everywhere. A brilliant idea burst into my head. If I had a watch that did the same thing as the ESPY lamp I'd always know when Orable's around.

I glanced over at Hemp where he reclined on a pink and purple yoga mat beside an empty breakfast plate. Wanting to experiment with the mysterious phenomenon of telepathy I focused all my thought energy on him. In my mind I asked him if he could make me an ESPY watch. I waited but he didn't respond.

"So – can you?" I blurted, impatiently.

"Can I what?" asked Hemp.

"You know. What I was just thinking. Can you?"

"Sorry – I wasn't paying attention, Levi. I don't know what you're referring to."

"But – I thought you hear everything I think."

"No, my boy. But – I like you to think so." Hemp winked.

"Can you make me an ESPY watch?" I asked desperately.

He jumped up at once.

"What a brilliant idea, Levi! You're a genius," he said, darting to his workbench while mumbling inaudibly.

Hemp tinkered while I gathered plates and took them to the kitchen. As I washed handspun pottery my thoughts wandered to my solarshay manual. I'd read a good bit of it before passing out at 2:00 a.m. I placed it beneath my pillow as Hemp suggested and I'd had the most invigorating dream. I flew at breathtaking speed through a vast and chilly cosmic space. It was an amazing feeling and I wanted to feel that way again.

As I headed toward the guest room I passed Hemp who was busy drafting designs. I slipped into a pair of sharp blue jeans he'd left for me on my nightstand. The label on the pocket read: *Sifter's 11:11*. I loved the way they felt – soft and light.

I caught a shirtless, sideways reflection of myself in the mirror. My typically washboard abs protruded. "Too much French toast," I said aloud, pulling on a t-shirt.

"Time to head to the stadium," called Sner, peeking into the cottage through the front door.

I tucked my class schedule and solarshay manual into my jacket pocket and said goodbye to Hemp.

Sner's auraplane was loaded. In addition to the incredible sound system it had an automatic chai dispenser, shaggy blue carpet, reclining cushioned seats and plush purple pillows. I snapped my seatbelt shut and down went the roof.

Leaning over the side of the auraplane, as we flew ten stories above ground, I saw Ceres for the first time in the light of day. It was nothing like I imagined. I thought it would resemble one of the fantasy worlds I'd seen in a movie, or an impressionistic painting, only not the blurry kind. But, it didn't look like either. It was more beautiful than anything I'd ever seen, or imagined.

Although it was similar to Earth, having sky and land, water and living creatures, it seemed to have something else, perhaps in its DNA, that made it indescribably pleasant. The colors were richer, the trees more vibrant, and the water definitely seemed to have a mind of its own. I suddenly felt as though anything were possible.

"We're flying over the *Fields of Possibility* right now," said Sner. "Can you feel the difference?"

Strangely, I could.

Just then a fluffy yellow star-shaped flower landed on Alphia's nose. She snorted then sneezed. "Pollen, I'm allergic."

I plucked it off.

"I saw that. I saw you roll your eyes," she complained.

"Really? Look around, will you? This place is amazing and all you do – all you've done since you've arrived – is complain."

"If it were so amazing then there wouldn't be pollen in the first place," griped Alphia, indignantly.

We stared tensely at one another for a long moment as the auraplane floated quietly through the air.

To the right in the distance I saw the Uprooted Forest. Traveling through it by foot the previous evening was nothing compared to seeing it from this perspective. The vision of magnificent, twisted roots stretching skyward and leafy branches crawling across the ground in the light of day was awe inspiring. It looked like someone had picked up an entire forest and dropped it upside down. My eyes traced a thick trunk up to a clump of roots where they extended and disappeared into a cloud at least two stories higher than the auraplane.

Three various-sized suns arranged in a triangular position shone brightly across the otherwise clear, coral-streaked sky. Until this moment I had no idea that something other than a beautiful girl could leave me breathless.

As I absorbed the colorful surroundings my thoughts wandered to my family. I was certain they'd never seen such beauty. I promised myself that someday I'd return with photos.

The sentimental moment faded almost painlessly as I dangled my arms over the side of the vehicle pressing my hands against the cool wind. My eyes raked fertile landscape where rolling hills, blue tinted grass and unfamiliar flowers stretched sunward swaying gently in the breeze.

Then I saw it. From the corner of my eye I caught a glimpse of Solarius Stadium. It was a jaw-dropping sight and dwarfed any stadium I'd ever seen. It looked even larger than it had in my dream. The enormous domed structure glistened in the sunlight. My pulse accelerated at the sight of it.

Mobert began the descent. He landed the auraplane on a circular pad in the bustling stadium parking lot. There must have been at least fifty other sifters, about my age, looking around - rather disoriented. I recognized some of their faces from the arrival ceremony. I waved goodbye to Mobert and Sner and stood alone on the field experiencing every possible emotion.

"Holy grasshoppers! I haven't seen a field like this – EVER!" shrieked Alphia, darting across colorful, floral terrain. I watched her disappear into tall blue grass in the distance.

A rather wide boy with red hair and freckles approached me.

"Hey – there are three suns in the sky. Where I come from there's only one and it's much smaller than these. How come we're not burning up?"

The boy stared at me. He leaned forward expectantly as though he assumed I was an expert on the subject. I didn't know the answer. I shrugged and blurted something like, "Maybe the suns here are cooler." It was the first thing that came to mind. My answer threw the boy into a deep state of contemplation as he stared skyward.

"What's your name?" he asked, looking back at me and extending his hand for a robust shake. The bottom two buttons of his flannel shirt were missing and a third about to pop.

"Levi. What's yours?"

"Garby. Garby Vanderlin. So – *you're* Levi!"

Garby planted his hands firmly on his hips. "We're cottage mates. Your name is engraved on the mailbox beside mine. Where were you last night? I thought maybe you drowned in the crater – or broke your neck when you hit the water."

Garby graphically demonstrated a mock casualty.

I shuddered.

"I missed the last shuttle. I ended up staying at Hemp's place."

I remembered Garby from the crater ceremony. His had been the first name called. His splash the most memorable.

"Hemp, huh? You mean the weird guy with the ponytail and striped toe socks?" asked Garby.

"Uhh – yeah – that one," I answered, thinking how much I enjoyed Hemp's weirdness.

"And speaking of socks," began Garby, "I lost a foot during an amusement park ride malfunction when I was five years old. I wear a prosthetic," he added, pointing.

"I'm – I'm so sorry," I said uncomfortably.

"It's not a big deal. I just want you to know. It happened ten years ago. The fake one works almost as good as the real one. Don't treat me any differently than anyone else."

"Oh – ok, I – I won't," I said reassuringly all the while wondering if I could honor my word.

"Hey, I hear we're going to have practice every day," said Garby wriggling his nose as if the thought had a bad odor.

"That's what I heard, too," I said, kicking my sneaker against lavender grass.

"I also heard that all of us new sifters are from Earth. I'm from Pennsylvania. Where are you from?"

"California."

"No way! Lucky you. I've always wanted to go to California. The beaches, the surfing, skateboarding – and can't forget those hot

California girls."

"Yeah. I live a little inland but my friends and I take trips to the beach a lot," I said, reminiscing.

"How about that dimension surfing?" asked Garby, nudging me hard in the side with his elbow.

"Uh – huh." I coughed and rubbed my side. I didn't want to talk about dimension surfing being that I was the only one to have done it incorrectly, or so it seemed.

Garby was preoccupied with something in the sky. He squinted to get a better look. His face twisted with curiosity.

"What is *that*?" he asked, pointing skyward. "Does Ceres have really big birds?"

Garby got my attention with the words – *big birds*. Thoughts of clawcons came in a rush.

"Well, Ceres has clawcons. They're more like a cross between a dragon and dinosaur, than a bird," I offered, extending my arms as wide as possible to demonstrate the vastness of their wingspan.

"No kidding? Clawcons, huh?" Garby scratched an emerging hive on his chest. "Do you think that's one?" he asked, his eyes trailing the erratic flight of whatever was in the sky.

I didn't think it was a clawcon because it didn't seem large enough but I couldn't make out what it was. It was flying too fast for eyes to follow. Unable to see smoke or sparking nostrils I eliminated the possibility of it being Rupert.

"I'm not sure what that is," I said, rubbing the nape of my neck. "But – whatever it is – it's coming our way."

Garby looked around frantically for a place to hide. He ended up crouching behind me. It was an odd sight being that I'm half his width.

With a swoop and whirling sound the mysterious flying creature landed upside down in the middle of an elderberry bush a few feet away from us. The bush shook violently. Berries shot across the field. One hit Garby in the forehead leaving a faint stain as it exploded upon contact.

Garby touched his forehead then looked down at his stained fingertips and panicked.

"I'm bleeding. I'm bleeding! I've been shot!" he screamed.

All eyes turned toward him. I bent to pick up the smashed berry that landed beside his sneaker.

"You're ok. It was just an elderberry, Garby." I squished it between my thumb and index finger duplicating the exact burgundy stain on his fingertips.

"Oh – what a relief!" Garby licked the stain from his finger.

The bush shook. Some huddled around it. Others backed away.

I listened for any indication of growling.

Garby positioned himself awkwardly with his arms extended and hands ready to chop.

Dozens of eyes locked upon the still shaking shrub.

CHAPTER NINE

SIFTERS AND SHIFTERS

The air was thick with anticipation. After much shaking of the shrub out marched a frail woman with silvery hair, chiseled cheekbones and a body looking as though it belonged to someone half her suspected age. She had a naturally commanding presence making her appear much taller than she is.

"Good afternoon class," she said, in a voice over-oozing confidence. Her red tights and matching jacket were muddied from her landing in the elder bush. Garby and I exchanged incredulous looks.

"I think I know why she wears red. This probably wasn't her first shrub-on-collision," said Garby.

"Right," I said, patting him on the back.

We laughed nervously.

All eyes locked upon the woman.

"My name is Maya Solarshay. Welcome to Solarius Stadium named after my great grandfather on my father's side. I'm your coach. Hopefully, one day some of you will play for the most infamous solarshay team dimension-wide – The Ceres Scorpions." She brushed dirt from her tights and pulled twigs from her ponytail.

"Coach? Pff. Can't be. She's too small, too old and looks like she'd break in half if someone bumped her. Plus, she just crashed into a bush," said Garby dumbfounded.

He had a point. An image of my football coach from Ordin Acres High School popped into my head. He was a man with rhinoceros-like legs and the jaw of a pitbull. *That's the way a coach should look.*

My eyes followed her suspiciously as she zigzagged through the crowd examining all head to toe while handing out blank nametags. She instructed us to stick them on our shirts and say our name aloud. No pens required. I followed her instructions and watched in awe as *Levi Levy* appeared on the tag in sparkling red ink. *I don't think I'll ever tire of these unearthly marvels,* I thought.

With arms folded behind her back and her chest pushed forward peacock-like she marched to the front of the field asking that everyone turn to face her.

"The first thing you will all need is a duffel bag." She pointed to a pile of large sports bags off to her right. "Grab one and we shall get started."

There was a stampede toward the bags: red, black, and silver. I grabbed a red one and looked inside. It was empty. I zipped it and placed it on the ground beside me.

"Hope you all had a light breakfast, particularly those prone to motion sickness." She jogged in place, her knees clicking.

I wish I would have known this prior to stuffing myself at breakfast.

Maya shook out her legs and did jumping jacks at a rapid pace.

"Solarshay is a game of the mind," she said. "How well you control your thoughts will determine how well you play the game.

Short, tall, large, small, handicapped, young, old, genderful, or genderless, white, black – and every shade in between – makes no difference. You each possess the same potential."

Garby yelled, "Hoo ha," while punching at air with a fist.

It was odd but I supported him with a strained, "Yeah," while also punching awkwardly at air. The others gawked at us but I didn't mind for I was bonding with my new friend.

Maya yanked a bundle of pamphlets from her duffel bag. She gave a stack of them to a cute blonde standing beside Garby and asked her to pass them along one way while she went the other.

The slogan: *Have it Your Way, Play Solarshay,* was printed on the front of the pamphlets. It was the same slogan as on the front of my manual. I touched the cover to see if new words would scroll in place of the current ones like they had on my manual last evening but was disappointed when nothing happened.

"Your success is determined by your thoughts," said Maya handing Garby a pamphlet. "Thoughts determine feelings. Feelings determine outcomes."

At this point many appeared doubtful, perhaps even bored, obvious by scattered yawns and guffaws. Mostly everyone was busy stuffing pamphlets into pockets. A few read them with what appeared to be genuine interest.

"You all possess greater potential than you realize," said Maya, handing a pamphlet to a blue-eyed girl with long chocolate-tinted hair, tanned skin and a violet flower tucked behind her right ear. Her name tag read: *Penelope Aubry.*

My heart beat faster as I looked at her. I could have spent the entire afternoon staring but Maya's voice distracted me.

"The mind can be utilized in many ways. Isn't that so, Mr. Damos?" she boomed, handing a pamphlet to a squinty-eyed boy with large nostrils and jagged purple hair. I assumed she knew him because she knew his name without his wearing a nametag.

Darvon Damos, Jr. didn't answer. He shot Maya a menacing look similar to the way a rattlesnake looks at a mouse before the pounce.

Maya wove her way across the field eyeing each of us from head to toe. She stopped abruptly beside me. My heart sank.

"What's your name?" she asked, plucking a blade of blue grass from my shoulder.

"Levi," I said softly, pointing to my nametag.

"So – *you're* Levi. The same Levi who entered through the doors last evening instead of over the crater like the others?" She leaned into me awaiting a response.

"Yes. I'm pretty sure that was me," I said, scratching my head and feeling like an idiot.

Maya circled me slowly. She looked puzzled as though she were trying to solve a very complicated mathematical equation. I was unable to move any body part but for my eyes which followed her as far as they could see as she circled me.

"How?" she whispered desperately, leaning into me again.

"You know – I really have no idea." I shrugged and stuffed my hands into the pockets of my jeans. I wasn't sure *what* I'd done let alone *how* I'd done it. I hoped she would move on and interrogate someone else.

"Interesting," she whispered. "One must have powerful focus to shift vibrational currents as you did." She walked away mumbling. And, while I don't think she intended for me to hear, I heard her say, "Oblivious."

Oblivious? I've been called worse. Is that what I did? I obliviously shifted vibrational currents? I thought I was a sifter, not a shifter. Why does it matter that I came through the stupid doors?

I must have been thinking aloud because Maya turned toward me at once. She peered at me with probing eyes. Although her lips didn't move I heard her say, "Careful young sifter. Every thought counts. Thoughts are the paintbrushes – your life the canvas. The doors are not stupid. Think well of them lest they take you places you dare not want to go. And for the record – there are *sifters* and there are *shifters* just as there are beginners and professionals."

Goosebumps marched up my spine. The icy chill made me quiver. I studied the faces of those around me searching for a sign that someone else had heard this but found no indication that anyone had.

Finally, she moved on and the overwhelming dread passed.

"Do we have any seasoned sifters here today? Anyone who can fly? Please raise your hand if you can fly," yelled Maya across the field while shooting questioning looks at me.

I shot questioning looks at those around me but saw no hands raised.

"Really?" she asked, while looking only at me. "Hmm. Well, it appears that we're all on equal ground. That would of course include you, Mr. Damos," she cracked, a pinch of disgust in her voice.

"I didn't want to waste energy raising my hand. I can fly circles around anyone here. Even *you*," cracked Darvon, staring at her challengingly.

Maya laughed gutterally as she circled him.

"You always have had a vivid imagination, Mr. Damos. Too bad you use it to your detriment," she said caustically.

A small indignant grunt escaped Darvon's crooked mouth.

Maya moved on and circled a slight boy beside him.

This was the boy unfortunate enough to have had his robe dropped by a soulguard the previous night as he exited the crater.

"Edyl Cartuff," she said, bending to read his name tag.

There on the grass beside Edyl sat his duffel bag.

Maya unzipped it and pulled out an interesting vest.

Edyl was floored by this.

"Hey – I looked *twice*. That wasn't in there," he said, reaching into the bag and shaking it upside down a few times.

Maya winked and instructed him to put it on. She walked among the others while Edyl suited up.

"The main thing we shall focus on today is developing our ability to thought propel" she said, stretching her arms above her head.

A look of raw panic sucked the color from the faces of those scattered across the field. Now that I knew what thought propelling was I wanted to know how it works.

"I'll explain thought propelling momentarily," she said, looking back at me from the corner of her left eye.

I wanted to scream or punch something. If only I could stop thinking entirely. I felt violated and I'd never been more aware of the ungoverned activity going on between my ears.

"Each of you shall find a vest in your duffel bag. Please put it on," said Maya, as her hands unsuccessfully searched her lean frame for hips to rest upon. Mumbles and grumbles filled the air. Most complained that they hadn't received a vest.

"I didn't get one. My bag is empty," grumbled Garby, a sense of urgency in his voice.

"Me neither," came several frustrated calls from the group.

"You all have vests in your bags. Please look again," she barked impatiently, her nose twitching.

I had already looked inside my empty bag twice but followed her instructions nonetheless. Unzipping the bag I found – much to my amazement – a perfectly folded, sharp looking black vest with the word *SIFTER* on the front and the phrase *THOUGHTS TO DIE FOR* on the back. Both were embroidered with red metallic thread.

Mixed reactions fell across the faces of my classmates. Some gasped in disbelief while others turned their bags over and inside out trying to figure out how the vests could have gotten inside.

I felt like I was discovering ancient secrets that contradict most of what I'd learned about life. The strange and unusual phenomena I'd witnessed since I received the invitation pointed to the fact that reality shifts and so many of the things I once considered impossible - aren't. This realization was exciting but frightening. It shook the foundation of my belief system and placed a lot of responsibility on, well - me.

I put my vest on. First the right arm, then the left. It felt like a symbolic ritual. An initiation into a new phase of my life - like a first kiss, a first car, or leaving the security of home. I knew I was venturing into unknown territory that would leave me forever changed, for better or worse, and that the outcome would depend entirely on me. I could either panic, or embrace it. I was pretty sure I'd do both.

"These are your training elevests," said Maya. "Being rookies you will need them. As your ability to direct thought advances they'll be of no use to you. By the way, these vests were worn by some of the most renowned solarshayers dimension-wide. They all started here just like you."

Many exchanged hopeful looks at hearing this.

"Simply put – thought propelling is the art of finding a better feeling thought."

Maya explained how the vests work. Even though I'd read about them the previous evening and learned about them from Sarabella I still didn't fully understand them. It seemed unfathomable that a simple vest could store the energy of my thoughts and use that energy to propel me through the air at phenomenal speed. At the same time, I'd seen them work and couldn't wait to experience one.

My hands grew cold and clammy. If my ability to control my thoughts was the foundation of solarshay, and generally my survival, I knew I was in big trouble.

An unexpected flash of optimism carried me away for a heroic moment. I visualized myself flying masterfully, zipping past pessimists. I even imagined myself soaring beside Rupert on a rescue mission. I basked in this sense of accomplishment until an annoying voice interrupted my visualization.

"It is possible that outside thoughts can – if felt with great conviction – charge or drain your vest, with or without your consent," said Maya.

"She must be joking," whispered Garby, trying to zip his vest but finding it at least two sizes too small.

"I am not joking Mr...." Maya paused to read Garby's nametag. "Vanderlin." She positioned herself directly in front of him. "Why do you find this so difficult to believe?"

"I – I just don't see how it can work," said Garby shrugging. "It's just a vest," he laughed agitatedly.

I was anxious to hear her response for I agreed – it was just a vest.

"Just a vest? *Just a vest!*" she repeated dramatically, as she circled Garby with a critical glare in her eyes.

"A *thought*, Mr. Vanderlin, is a spark of energy. A *spark of energy* ignites an entire chain of quantum events. And this..." she said, pulling the much-too-small-for-him vest right off his back and holding it high in the air for all to see, "...is not *just* a vest. This is a highly organized quantum energy holding tank."

Silence fell across the field followed by heavy whispering.

"What does that mean? A whole chain of quantum events?" asked the pretty girl with the green eyes and long chocolate hair standing next to me. Again, my heart beat faster as my eyes fell upon her.

"Excellent question, Ms. Aubry. Penelope Aubry," said Maya, leaning in to read her nametag. "Is anyone here familiar with quantum mechanics?"

No one responded.

"I can't hear you," she said, looking as though she wanted to pick someone up and shake an answer from them. Some nodded their heads *no* while others shrugged.

"Right then. Research this later. Tell me next session, twenty words or less, based on your understanding of quantum mechanics –

or any mechanics of your choosing – how this vest works."

Moans rippled across the field. Disapproving looks darted at Penelope from all directions.

"Homework? Who would have thought there'd be homework in the 11th Dimension?" whispered Garby, shaking his head in frustration.

Maya glared at him and spit out a loud, "Shh."

"While it is interesting to know *how* something works, it is more useful to know that it *does* work," said Maya, slipping on a vest. "If I can fly, you can fly."

"Why are you wearing a vest? I saw you fly without one," said Garby.

"Excellent point, Vanderlin. I want to be on the same playing field as all of you. I need to see if anyone here can affect my vest with their thoughts."

Garby leaned toward me and whispered, "First off, she's crazy. Secondly, I can't fly. I'm too…large." Garby sucked in his belly in a final desperate attempt to zip his vest. "Thirdly – did I already say she's crazy?"

"Pluck it Vanderlin! Negative thoughts are like weeds. They strangle the positive ones and make it difficult to get up in the morning – let alone fly across that river," scorned Maya, before dropping to the ground for a set of twenty single-handed push ups.

"I'm not being negative. I'm being realistic. Plus, I whispered that. How did she hear me?"

"Telepathy," I whispered back.

"What's telepaley?" asked Garby, mispronouncing the word.

"I'll tell you later," I answered, not wanting Maya to hear us speak, or think.

"As for negative and realistic – the two are often one in the same, Mr. Vanderlin," said Maya, pointing in the direction from which pounding waterfalls could be heard.

"To create a new reality one must act as if the current one does not exist."

Maya followed this statement up with twenty more single-handed push-ups – this time with her left hand. She jumped up, stretched and added, "Over there is the Thinking River. It is a wild, raging river believed to hold universal secrets. Many have had mind-altering experiences while submerged. Under certain circumstances, one can hear every great thought *ever* thought. It is a conductor of raw, flowing consciousness. The crater is filled with this water, but it's filtered else it would *overwhelm* the senses."

"Does *anyone* have *any* idea what she's talking about?" spit Garby blinking rapidly and tossing his hands in the air.

Maya flew toward the river and motioned for everyone to follow.

Garby froze in his tracks, his eyes bulging.

"Seriously? Seriously. Fly across a river? Wha – right now? Is she trying to kill us all the very first day of class?"

CHAPTER TEN

TO FLY OR NOT TO FLY

The entire class, with a heavy hum of chatter, followed Maya to the river. The sweet lilasuckle breeze and melodic hum of waterfalls diminished as I glanced at my wrist. I desperately wanted a new watch and impatiently waited for Hemp to make me an ESPY watch.

Not for the first time my thoughts drifted to Orable. I reminded myself to find better feeling thoughts but it wasn't as easy as it seemed it should be.

Finally, we reached the river where Maya jogged in place, her ponytail bouncing as she spoke.

"Since you are all beginners you will be able to take advantage of the fact that my thoughts will help charge your vests so you can fly."

I felt excited, but doubtful. For as long as I could remember, I wished I could fly but looking at the river and boulders over which it rushed made my breathing faster, my head lighter, and my doubt stronger.

"If you are not in control of your thoughts, others are controlling them for you. It's that simple. Now – who here does not believe they can fly?" she asked impatiently.

Everyone raised their hand. Garby raised both hands.

"Wonderful. I have a group of optimists this year." Maya shook her head disappointedly. "You have all seen me fly thus logic would have it that flying is possible. Agreed?" She paced in front of us.

"She crashed into a fricking bush," whispered Garby. "Am I the only one who noticed?"

"I can't hear you. Do you all agree that flying is possible?" she repeated.

The faces of those around me turned doubtful. Some of us shrugged. Others shook their heads and mumbled. Maya's gaze fell hard upon someone in my general vicinity. I desperately hoped it wasn't me.

"Yes – *you!*" she said, pointing at me. "Come here, please."

Oh, *no*. Not again. My heart skipped. I walked toward her feeling as though someone had a blow dryer aimed at my cheeks.

"Do you mind if I use you to demonstrate the power of belief?" asked Maya.

"Me?" I asked, wondering why, out of all the skeptics surrounding her, she'd chosen me. I wanted to say that I did mind and was trying to muster the courage to do so but before I was able to say anything she cut me off.

"Good then," she said, standing before me, resting her hands heavily upon my shoulders.

The pressure of her hands caused me to have a flashback to the time Dr. Oblivia placed her hands on my shoulders as she told me the invitation *couldn't be real* and that other worlds *simply don't exist.*

Boy was she wrong.

As if I wasn't nervous enough about flying I could now feel the scorching glare of dozens of eyes upon me.

What will she ask of me? What will the others expect of me? Will I end up looking like a fool?

"Today you will fly," she said convincingly.

I swallowed hard, unconvinced. Just looking at that raging river made me feel as if my body were malfunctioning. Flying across a pond or even a swimming pool seemed far more reasonable than this. I wanted to suggest this but dared not. It was obvious that danger is to her what blood is to the vampire.

"Put your vest on. Snap these together," she demanded, pointing to three sparkling silver buckles.

I ran my fingers through my hair and tucked what I could behind my ears. If I was going to die, or worse, embarrass myself, I at least wanted to see it.

Buckles clicked as I snapped them together. Tugging hard on them caused me to lose my balance. I caught myself just before I fell. Salty beads of perspiration dripped from my forehead into my eyes. This burned. As I rubbed them Maya raised her arm. Instinctively, I ducked. Much to my surprise she wiped my forehead with her sleeve. I couldn't help feeling suspicious of this too-kind gesture.

"Levi – do you believe you can fly?" she asked, standing so close to me I swear I heard her blink.

I really wanted to believe I could. I'd flown in my dreams, but all of my attempts during my waking hours failed miserably. I'd grown up believing it wasn't possible so I had no reason to believe I could now.

"Do I believe I can fly?" I repeated, my throat tight with anxiety.

An hour ago I felt as if anything were possible. Where had that feeling gone? Somewhere inside me was a small, hopeful child jumping up and down saying - *Yes, I can fly. I know I can.* Somewhere else inside me was an older version of myself insisting – *No, silly. Of course you can't.* My thoughts ping-ponged between the two and unfortunatley for me, the older one was winning.

"Do you believe you can fly?" asked Maya, tapping her foot on soggy blue grass, arms folded across her puffed chest.

She insisted on having an answer. I had to say *something.*

"Maybe," I said, in a hurried, insecure voice.

"Maybe?" howled Maya, as though I'd just insulted her. "*Maybe!*" she repeated ferociously, trickling into a sadistic sort of laughter. She circled me again and as she did a vision of clawcons circling me in my nightmare danced unpleasantly through my head. She planted herself firmly before me.

"Levi, my dear boy. There is no *maybe.* You *choose* to fly – or you *choose* not to fly."

In this instant it didn't seem to me as though I had an option to *choose* not to fly. My head started to ache from the pressure I now felt.

"Well..." I said, fidgeting with the straps on my vest, "...I've never flown before. I don't know if it's possible for me."

"Whatever you believe possible is possible," she snapped, as she marched toward her duffel bag.

While she was away a sinister voice errupted from somewhere behind me.

"Only fly in your dreams – Earth boy?"

I started to turn to see who'd said this but thought it best to ignore the comment. The voice came again.

"No one flies where you come from. They build metal contraptions – load them with fossil fuel – send them up with roaring engines. What a *joke*."

Curiosity won. I turned toward the hostile voice.

Darvon Damos, Jr. stared challengingly at me. His purple spiky hair stood firm against the wind. This was the first time I'd taken a good look at him. Thick anger oozed from his aloof eyes triggering a strange sort of nausea deep within me. I shuddered.

"Mr. Damos," called Maya abruptly, as she made her way back toward the group. "Having had the good fortune of growing up in this dimension qualifies you as neither expert, nor bully. If you intend to get any playing time I suggest you focus more on your own attitude and beliefs rather than the life cirumstances of others." She bent to whisper in his ear, "You can repeat this class once. This is your last shot."

I turned to take another look at Darvon. I hadn't heard what Maya said to him but somehow he looked smaller than a moment ago.

"Some say solarshy is *just a game* and so it is – as is *life*. To play any game well one must first understand *how* it works. Thoughts are energy and energy creates matter. *Believing* you can do something stirs the quantum particles that bring that experience into your reality. Thus, my philosophy – *don't try, just know*. It's important for you to feel a sample of the exuberance of flight. It will motivate you, I hope, to train hard. Now, Levi. I believe you can fly. I'll charge your vest with my thoughts until you are able to charge it with your own."

I wanted to believe her. I really did.

Maya stood front center. She leaned forward and with her arms outstretched tilted her head skyward.

"To thought propel – or fly as you call it – you will need to master this basic position."

Hearing her in this moment activated memories of the voice that had taught me to fly in my dreams. *Was the voice hers?*

Maya demonstrated the position several times until the group had it memorized. She then asked that everyone choose three happy thoughts and focus on them. Walking among us she adjusted stances, straightened arms and tilted necks.

"If you are unable to find happy thoughts, sing your favorite song instead. It will help to block out the *random and irrelevant* dancing through your head," she said. "But please be aware that this process is not just about thoughts. It is about the feelings resulting from them. Simply – that which you focus on you attract more of. Better feeling thoughts attract better feeling experiences."

"Why is flying so important?" asked Garby, moaning.

"Good question, Mr. Vanderlin," she said, fidgeting with the belt on Penelope's vest. "In addition to the pure joy you'll feel at having mastered the skill of thought propelled flight – your survival depends on it."

Everyone stopped talking at once. Smiles turned to frowns. Garby thought he heard a trumpet play the *Dead March* from the fields beyond the river. I heard only the faint grinding of my teeth.

Maya continued, "Life is not always a picnic no matter your circumstance – or dimension. The quality of your life is determined by your intention. The problem is – there are outside forces and lower-vibrational entities surrounding you daily that are in alignment with darker philosophies than your own – and they are affecting you. The thoughts of one affect all. The intentions of one affect all. What one focuses on increases – regardless of its vibrational intention. If you fail to master your thoughts you will feel things and have experiences that are not – *intended*. An experienced manifestarian is able to create poverty as effortlessly as wealth, health as swiftly as illness, and peace as easily as war – for oneself, and for others. Orable is a manifestarian of the lowest order of intention. He collects young sifters the way an investor collects stocks. Collective thought energy – also referred to as the collective consciousness – is more powerful, more influential, than individual energy. He uses this to his advantage. That's why he is ever increasing his army of Virusian Soldiers. He indoctrinates them with disempowering dogma. Any one of you could be his next unwilling recruit. Please know that you are not victims. Through mastering the art of thought propelled flight you can reclaim the powers that are your birthright – and break this spell of ignorance for yourself and future generations."

Everyone's eyes swept the somber faces of those around them.

"Why'd she have to tell us this now – when we're trying not to drown in the river?" moaned Garby, having given up on fastening his miniature vest.

I knew what the others didn't. Orable's next attack was just twelve days away. For the first time since I'd arrived I seriously considered the merits of returning to Earth. But, recalling the drollness of school, the seemingly senseless stacks of homework, and my less-than-pleasant home life, I quickly opted to stay.

Maya resumed coaching more easily than we students resumed learning.

"Arms out – neck back – run – fly," she repeated, as she demonstrated a stellar take-off. She was airborne in seconds having made the entire thing look effortless.

We were given time to practice before attempting to cross the river. The realization that survival depends upon one's ability to direct their thoughts was difficult for all to hear. The good news is that Maya's speech seemed to work because everyone was now exponentially more determined than before.

Maya landed with a thud, kicking up dirt and small stones.

"Empowering thoughts – find them," she yelled. "Favorite songs – sing them."

It was apparent that we were all seriously concentrating. Trying to conjure up our most pleasant thoughts. A few minutes passed when suddenly bodies randomly and erratically blasted into the air like rampant human cannon balls.

At one point Garby laughed so hard he darted skyward a good twelve feet then dropped to the ground moaning. Penelope propelled thirty feet into the air. She looked like a pro, right up to the bitter crash.

Maya gave some last minute pointers. Eventually, everyone was (to some degree) flying, laughing, and rolling in the wind. That is, everyone except me.

"Are – we – *ready?*" asked Maya, her voice booming with enthusiasm.

"Of course not!" shrieked Garby.

Garby couldn't believe she'd allow us to do this being that we were all so ill-prepared.

"I can't swim. How deep is it?" he asked, attempting to practice his flight position but unable to bend his neck back. "My neck is inflexible – my vest too small", he panicked. He practically begged Maya for a larger vest. She said she'd given him the largest available and told him he needed to slim down.

"Right then," said Garby, blinking furiously. "I'll just drop thrity pounds here in the next, oh, say – five minutes!"

"I do like your optimism, Mr. Vanderlin, but believable goals are key to manifestation. Thirty pounds in five minutes probably *isn't* something you believe possible. Best to revise that. Additionally, excess weight is indicative of a toxic thought pattern. Toxic thoughts often get stored energetically within the body's magnetic field. Thought-cleansing is most effective for weight loss," she said, walking away.

Garby clenched his fist in frustration.

"Toxic thoughts, huh? And, to think that all this time I was foolish enough to believe I'd gained weight from overeating – and not exercising."

Maya gazed over her shoulder at him and exhaled noisily.

"Be sure to hold onto your vest while airborne. You'll be fine. Arms out – neck back – run – fly!" she said, tossing Garby a strained by inspiring look.

"Balance your weight – shift – balance!" she screamed across the field then gave a tall boy standing beside me a hearty shove with her foot.

"Why'd you do that?" he asked, shocked from where he lay on the grass, the wind knocked out of him.

"Always be prepared for the unexpected," she said, doing it again to a girl just in front of him.

I couldn't believe she just kicked over two of my classmates.

She's a *psycho*," said Garby, beneath his breath. "Now I know why they had us sign that waiver before class."

Reactions varied but all watched Maya with apprehensive eyes as if they might be next.

"Seasoned sifters cannot be thrown off balance. Seasoned sifters would not *succumb* to my kick. My kick represents negative thoughts coming your way. Sifters *do not allow* negative thoughts to disrupt their emotional, or physical, balance. I recommend you all find time to get to the wind chamber at least once a week," she said, readjusting my back so it was slightly arched.

I widened my stance anticipating the possibility of a swift kick. *What's the wind chamber?* I thought.

"The wind chamber," began Maya, "is a tool designed to support one's ability to fly."

She's crawling through my head space, stealing my thoughts. There must be something illegal about this.

"Someday you'll be able to do it, too," she whispered.

I hummed my favorite song hoping it would mask the thoughts I was thinking about her.

"Remember – it takes at least three better feeling thoughts to replace the energy drain from one negative, so – put on your happy!" she said, before assigning everyone a position on the grass.

"*Put – on – your happy?*" mouthed Garby. "Could she be any *more* annoying?"

Maya arranged several small groups in "V" patterns across the field and announced that she would escort one group at a time across the river.

The first group was airborne in a flash. All had thought propelled successfully across the river, and back. It wasn't a pretty sight but everyone made it there and back safely.

Up went the second group. They too were awkwardly successful.

Finally, our group would have a go at it. My heart raced.

"V formation," yelled Maya.

"Arms out – neck back – run – fly," I said to myself. The empowering thought I clung to, the one that pushed all others from my mind, was a vision of myself helping to free all those held captive by Orable. I imagined how good they'd feel once they were free. I imagined how good I'd feel as they thanked me. Then, although I could barely believe it, I was flying. It was an incredible feeling.

I felt dips in my flight especially when my thoughts became doubtful. It was at those moments I felt Maya's thoughts intercept my own and yank me up the way a life line pulls a drowning diver from the deepest depths. Knowing that I could fly and that Maya's thoughts could override my doubt gave me a surge of confidence. No longer believing I would die, spine smashed on sharp edges of the boulders below, I relaxed and enjoyed the breathtaking experience. When I looked down at the raging river I felt incredible, whereas moments ago I felt petrified. I looked around at the faces of those flying nearby. These were some of the happiest faces I'd ever seen.

"I'm flying," yelled Garby. A smile stretched his cheeks to

capacity. "I can fly. I'm a flyer."

"You are a *sifter*," yelled Maya encouragingly, through a strained smile, as she whizzed past him.

"Yeah," I yelled to Garby.

"Hoo ha," yelled Garby, as he punched at air with his fist.

I laughed myself into a somersault. This startled me but I liked it and so I did it again.

Garby yelled something but I couldn't make out what he'd said. His voice faded as he spoke and wind whistled in my ears.

"What's that Garb?" I yelled, still rolling through the air. "What did you say?" I steadied myself. When Garby failed to answer, I turned to look for him but he wasn't where he was supposed to be. I checked formation to see if maybe he changed positions but still couldn't locate him. Worry flooded my head and I lost elevation. I searched formation again to see if he was in a blind spot. Just then a thought popped into my head urging me to look down and as I did I saw a big blob. I soon realized it was Garby plummeting toward the river. Without hesitation I dropped out of formation. Diving toward him at an absurd speed I felt as if my skin were being torn from my face. The feeling was reminiscent of how I'd felt during my crossover.

Focusing, I thought only of reaching Garby before he hit land or the boulder-laden river. Faster and faster I fell. The gap between us narrowed. I knew I had to fall, or fly, at least twice as fast as Garby if there was any hope of my reaching him in time. My rational mind reminded me both are impossible. As the gap between us narrowed I could hear his screams. His body tumbled through the air. He kicked and desperately tried to grab currents of wind that whipped around him.

"Garby! Happy thoughts – find them!" I yelled, in a commanding voice I was unaware I had. But it seemed he hadn't heard me because he just kept falling.

"Fast cars – hot girls – money – your mom!" I yelled, in one last desperate attempt to get Garby thinking the kind of thoughts that could save his life.

Finally within reach, I grabbed his arm with one hand and pinched his cheek with the other.

"Happy thoughts – FIND THEM NOW!" I screamed. My words echoed across the canyons. I watched the ground grow nearer, the boulders bigger. I begged Garby to focus his thoughts but Garby said he was so scared he could think of nothing other than how, in a few seconds, his life would be over.

CHAPTER ELEVEN

A MATTER OF LIFE AND VEST

I worried that Garby's thoughts would drain my vest but I couldn't waste even a second more thinking that way. Still, my thoughts drifted to *useless* places again and again.

Why wasn't Maya helping us? Had anyone even noticed we'd gone missing?

Instead of allowing my thoughts to roam aimlessly, in an instant, I made a life-determining decision. I changed my mind. I reached for a better feeling thought. I chose to believe that it didn't matter what Garby was thinking and that I could save him regardless. I envisioned a soft, safe landing and infused my vest with the most empowering thoughts I could muster. I imagined how good I'd feel when at last we were on land laughing about the absurdity of it all.

There was a colossal splash as we went under. Time stood still as if the very heart of all living things paused in hope. It seemed as though the river stopped flowing. An odd sort of silence fell over the land like someone had flipped a switch and made it so.

Downstream our bodies lay on sand. Crying cut through the silence. The sobs belonged to Garby. He cried, then laughed, then cried some more. He turned to the side and water poured from the pocket of his flannel shirt. He looked at me and sat up at once.

"You dead?" he barked, horrified. He shook me and tried to remember how to administer CPR. A long moment passed. I heard him but I couldn't respond. I felt suspended somewhere in time and space, conscious, but unable to move or speak.

Garby shook my limp body again. He choked up. A tear rolled down his bruised cheek. "HOLY SHIT – you're DEAD aren't you – and it's all my fault." Garby wiped mud from the corners of my eyes. He repositioned my head and was about to blow air into my lifeless lungs when finally I opened one of my eyes and responded, "I don't know, are you?"

We broke out into mad laughter.

Garby squeezed and thanked me repeatedly. Salty streams of tears trailed down his face. As shock wore off I tried to process what had just happened. My eyes scanned the sky for Maya and the others but saw no one.

Why hadn't Maya helped us? Was she too busy helping others that she hadn't noticed we'd gone missing? Did she see me go after Garby and decide to let me be the pretend hero while it was her thoughts that saved us? She must have helped. There's no way I could have done this.

Together we reviewed the jaw-dropping adventure.

"Remember when I grabbed you and shook you?"

"I remember you pinched me – so hard. There must be a chunk of my face missing," said Garby, his stubby fingers now tracing his pale cheeks.

Distant voices cut through our conversation. From across the river Maya and the others waved. Garby and I stood and leaned against each other, our opposite arms crossed over one another's shoulders.

"Foot good?" I asked.

Garby nodded. "I've got an awesome prosthetic."

We made our way across a shallow, rocky part of the river basin to join the others.

"What are you doing going off gallivanting on your own?" yelled Maya, as she plodded toward us through rapidly moving, knee-deep water. "You'll never learn to thought propel if you don't practice. Off picking flowers?" she asked sarcastically, plucking a small red flower from my hair. "And why are your clothes wet?"

Garby and I exchanged exasperated looks. This wasn't the kind of welcome we'd expected. *Is it possible she has no idea what just happened?*

Maya droned on about how dangerous leaving formation during training could be. She left no time for either of us to explain. After several minutes of listening to her rant I edged a few words in.

"We didn't mean to – Garby's vest fell of – I went to help him." My words were swift as bullets. I thanked Maya for helping me rescue Garby but she just stared blankly at me.

"Sarcasm is never helpful. Whatever transpired here between the two of you had absolutely nothing to do with me. I only now realize you both went missing."

Garby and I exchanged stunned looks. In unison our eyes shot skyward, back toward one another, and then back to the sky.

"But – I…" I said, pointing above us.

"Yes, Levi. What is it you are trying to say?" she asked impatiently.

"Nothing," I said, replaying the incident in my mind. My body quivered as if drunk from too many shots of adrenaline.

"Where's your vest? If you took it off and left it on the other side of the river you must go back and get it immediately. We wouldn't want your stored thoughts falling into the wrong hands."

I thought she was talking to Garby but she asked a second time while tugging on my t-shirt. I looked down at my vestless chest. I could find no words to express the shock I felt. *What happened to my vest? How did I fly without one?*

"The two of you plummeted well over two hundred feet, two vests lost and you live to tell of it? There are champion solarshayers who couldn't have pulled that one off. Do it again and I'll toss you both out of this class – permanently. Understood?"

Garby and I nodded our agreement still not understanding what had just transpired.

Maya tugged on my t-shirt and smelled it.

"Never mind about going back to look for the vests. It appears they disintegrated." She then yelled to Sarabella, "Scan them, please!"

Sarabella ran her hands over every inch of our bodies without touching us.

"Heart rates accelerated on both. Cholesterol high on this one," she said, pointing to Garby.

"Another good reason for thought-cleansing," said Maya sharply, as she herded the others onward.

"She – I just – *oh* - this is going to be *very* difficult," said Garby, grinding his teeth. He looked toward me. I was in a haze and staring skyward.

"Did you see her?" he asked, as we walked back toward the stadium.

"How could I not. She was standing there yelling – spitting in my face."

"No – not Maya. I mean the little girl in the pink dress with the grey face."

I looked at Garby as though he just spoke in a foreign language.

"No, Garby. I didn't see a little girl in a grey dress with a pink face."

"No! I said pink dress and grey face – not grey dress and pink face."

"I didn't see a little girl with any dress – or face, Garby."

"You mean the one you saw didn't have a dress – or face?"

"What are you talking about? I didn't see a little girl!" I snapped.

Feeling exasperated I wrung river water from my shirt.

"Am I dead?" asked Garby gravely, panic cutting through his voice. He slapped himself then moaned in pain.

"No, Garby. You're not dead.

"But, I saw right through her. She was flying – floating over the water just before we went under."

"Maya?" I asked.

"No! The little girl!"

"Maybe you hallucinated – it was traumatic."

"Do you want to go home?" asked Garby, looking panicked.

"I don't want to think about it right now. I'm freezing, hungry and getting a rash from these wet jeans."

"What better time to think about it?" he shouted.

I pointed ahead to where Maya stood waiting for us as the others walked past her.

"I imagine that ordeal was – unnerving," she said, seemingly having a sudden change of heart. "Let's get you both into some dry clothes."

"Not quite the heartless predator I thought she was," whispered Garby in my ear.

Maya glared at him while blinking indignantly.

"You'll find some new jeans and t-shirts in the closet in the men's room. After you change you're free to go home. Get some sleep and be back here tomorrow by noon. Prepare yourselves for a *demanding* day."

She jogged ahead of us toward the stadium.

"Demanding? Uh – it can't get any more demanding than today – can it?"

"Oh – my dear boys. Today was a *piece of cake*. I believe that's the way it's expressed on Earth," said Maya, winking.

Garby and I exchanged looks of terror. My heart sank.

CHAPTER TWELVE

THE UNWANTED

W hen we arrived at the stadium the following day Maya stood at the entrance asking that everyone form a line. She spoke as she walked among us.

"You are about to enter the most sought-after state of the art stadium in all of the dimensions. Here you shall learn ancient secrets pertaining to the mechanics of life through a fun – but potentially *deadly* sport."

This was one of the best moments of my life. The dread I'd felt yesterday had vanished. I felt alive like never before - hungry to learn whatever it was this strange sport had to teach me. Sure I was traumatized from the events of the previous day but I put it in perspective, found the good in it, and moved forward.

"It's important that you clear your mind of all unwanted thoughts and leave them here," said Maya, as she pointed to a large grey trash bin beside the entrance labeled: *Bin of Bane.*

A voice from somewhere toward the back of the line yelled, "How do we know which thoughts are unwanted?"

"Unwanted thoughts make you feel less than wonderful," she said, kicking the trash can. "Unwanted thoughts limit your potential." She kicked the can again.

"I'll have to empty my entire head," said Garby, rubbing his temples.

Maya tossed the strap of her duffel bag over her shoulder and opened the stadium door.

"All you've ever dreamed of awaits you in here," she said, pointing inside the stadium.

We all stood before the bin concentrating on leaving unwanted thoughts behind. Some of us pretended to remove thoughts with our hands by brushing them off into the bin. Others pretended to throw up, purging hard-to-digest thoughts. Still others shook their heads over the bin and screamed, "Unwanted thoughts be gone!"

Maya said she was impressed by the creative ways we cleared our minds.

Once inside we followed her through a maze of passageways. Soft, lavender turf squished beneath my feet. I sensed a presence. I could almost hear residual cheering from tournaments past. A rare excitement coursed through my veins.

The turf ended where the air-cushioned floor began. I stared in awe at the free-floating solar system where dozens of illuminated planets defied gravity. Objects whizzed through the cool dark space between them. My eardrums vibrated as they passed. The others looked on, their jaws dangling.

A small square object roared through the chamber leaving wakes of thunder. Some of us gasped; others ducked as it whizzed by at seemingly warp speed. I had been the closest to it and as it passed I felt worse than horrible. Within a period of fifteen seconds I thought of at least fifteen seemingly good reasons why I was incapable of playing this game.

"Was that a comet?" asked Garby, a bead of perspiration dripping from his forehead.

Maya explained that the small swirling silver box was not a comet but rather a *cosmic qualm*, the effects of which cause one to experience seemingly insurmountable self-doubt. The results are short-lived but difficult to recover from during play.

"This sport seems dangerous," said Garby, walking as far away from the playing field as he could.

"Dangerous for *you*," said Darvon Damon, Jr. with a pinch of threat in his voice, "*Fun* for me."

Darvon laughed condescendingly then walked into a pole.

I feel a tad guilty admitting the satisfaction that washed over me as I observed this unfortunate incident. Just a tad.

Soon the lunch auraplane arrived with what were clearly Ceresian delicacies disguised in Earth-themed packaging. There were healthier versions of popular snacks and they all had optimistic names. I learned that this was an attempt by the *Department of Dimensional Transference* to make everyone feel at home. I'm not so sure it accomplished this but it was definitely a nice touch.

Daydream Drops by Blisskist were my favorite – pyramid shaped chunks of organic, dark chocolate, with creamy coconut centers, wrapped in colorful foil. The instructions on the label read:

Eat one or two before bedtime.

Focus only on the things you want and your dreams will send you clues as to how to manifest them.

I grabbed several bags of these.

For the next thirty minutes everyone sat on the bleachers snacking, daydreaming, comparing class schedules and getting to know one another. When lunch was over Maya herded us off to a section of bleachers and resumed teaching.

"I shall assume you all have your manuals. Yes?"

Everyone nodded.

"Your assignment was to explain – in twenty words or less – how elevests work?" she said, picking foliage from her wind tousled hair.

Edyl Cartuff stood up with notebook in hand.

"They don't. They can't work. Science – physics – even my imagination says it's impossible."

Maya nodded. No, actually, her head bobbed up and down like one of those silly dogs my great grandfather used to put on the dashboard of his 1969 Toronado.

"Excellent, Edyl. While it's true that science, physics – and your imagination – do not undertand the functioning of these vests – you've experienced them firsthand and know they work."

Garby and I exchanged confused looks.

"Well – they *probably* work when they don't fall off or disintegrate." I whispered. Garby agreed.

"Just because we don't understand *how* something works does not negate the fact that something *does* work," said Maya approaching the chalkboard beside the bleachers and picking up a chunk of lime-green chalk.

"These vests funtion within a territory that when activated by thought morphs intention into experience. This territory is called the morphocognic field. Simply put, it is a territory where what you think is what you get." She wrote on the chalkboard:

What you think is what you get.

She paced before us.

"The M-Field, or morphocognic field exists everywhere in every moment. Through the game of solarshay you can learn to master this field."

She held a book in front of her and smiled.

"This is my book – *Mastering the M-Field Through Solarshay*. You can purchase it online, in *Darvon's Thought Depot*, at every corner coffee shop, the *Enchanted Cupcake* – and the list goes on. It's an extra-dimensional bestseller. I have complimentary, autographed copies for each of you."

"That's generous," said Garby, in an effort to find something he liked about her. He slipped a handfull of *Om & Om's* into his mouth.

Om & Om's are gummy fruit circles dipped in dark chocolate. The label on the bag reads: *A Sweet Meditative Treat manufactured by Solarshay, Co. Inc. – Healthy Foods for Thought Division.*

Garby shared some with me. I read the instructions:

> *Indulge in these pleasant gummy treats whenever you feel*
> *the need to relax. Om & Om's clear unpleasant thoughts.*

Garby stuffed another handful in his mouth and chewed ravenously as a chattering Maya paced in front of him.

"Wow – these things kind'a work!" said Garby, surprised at how, for the first time, he found Maya *almost* not annoying.

"Solarshay, like life, is a game where every thought counts. One thought can hurtle you toward your planetary destination or toss you across the bleachers. The choice is always yours," boomed Maya.

Garby and I exchanged anxious looks. Our eyes scrutinized row after row of silver metallic bleachers.

"They're not padded," cried Garby, opening a second bag of *Om & Om's.*

From the corner of my eye I saw Penelope chew part of a purple thumbnail clear off.

Sarabella yawned.

"Please do not miss the point of this game. Its purpose is not the mastering of flight. Its purpose is the mastering of thought and the subsequent feeling which ultimately results in the mastering of flight. A mastered mind is a joyful mind," she said, stretching her arms to capacity while swirling across the floor.

Everyone's eyes twinkled with newfound hope.

Maya dragged a large wooden trunk from behind the bleachers.

"Today we shall learn the basics of solarshay," she said, with one foot propped upon the trunk. "This is our playing chamber." She pointed all around. "It will change your lives. You shall learn to replace illness with health, poverty with financial freedom, dead ends with the opportunities you've always wanted – and more."

Eyes brightened. Postures improved.

Although I was skeptical of her promises, I believed that what she was offering was possible. Not easily attainable – but possible.

Strutting about in a shiny silver jumpsuit, like a model on a catwalk, she continued, "When the playing field is activated it gets quite cold in here. This is your climate-controlled uniform," she said, pivoting awkwardly to the right. "It operates like the robes you received upon arrival."

Chatter erupted from the bleachers.

"It looks like a – a costume – from an epic space opera," I blurted.

Maya looked agitated from where she stood with several more of these silver uniforms draped over her arm. She stuffed two fingers in her mouth and let out an ear-shattering whistle.

"I am divulging words of wisdom. You – like sponges – are absorbing," she bellowed. All chatter ceased.

She pulled more of these costumes from the trunk and made her way to the bleachers. While handing them out she instructed everyone to put one on. We all dashed to the restrooms to change.

Several minutes later out marched an army of shiny silver sifters. Light from the planets reflected off our uniforms and scattered tiny rainbows over the floor, walls, and ceiling. We looked like a force to be reckoned with. I couldn't help hoping that, one day soon, our skill would complement our presentation.

"The object of the game is to provide as many planets as possible with the four elements of water, sunlight, nutrients, and air," began Maya, counting on her fingers as she spoke. "The team which stimulates life on the most planets before time runs out wins."

"It looks confusing. How will we know if a planet got all four elements," shouted an anxious voice from the bleachers.

"Good question – whoever you are," she said, digging through the trunk. "Planets illuminate when a team successfully delivers all four elements. Once lit, the planet becomes that team's responsibility." She then instructed us to open our duffel bags and put on our dimension goggles.

"Dimension goggles protect the eyes, improve vision on the playing field, and help one to avoid bumping into players from other dimensions."

Gasps and doubtful laughter filled the air. I thought she was joking.

"Bumping into players from other dimensions can occur as a result of dimension shifting. Occasionally, dimensions overlap. This happens for a variety of reasons. It's sort of like an emotional earthquake. All of a sudden you're in *two* – *two* places at once. It doesn't happen often but it does happen. The Burden brothers were killed during playoffs last season due to such shifts – but do not let this piece of information disturb you. I'm required by Ceresian law to share this fact with you but I ask that you categorize it as a non-possibility in your reality."

"Wha – we can bump into players in other dimensions? That's crazy," I said, putting on goggles. Garby gasped. I looked over at him. He looked different. Terror had distorted his face.

"Being that we are visual creatures this would be a good time for a demonstration," yelled Maya.

No sooner had she said this than something darted, in a blur, across the lavender turf and was airborne in a flash. As it wove through the playing field I got a better look at it. Whoever it was wore a silver uniform and mask. Zooming through the playing field this sifter dodged the cosmic qualm and illuminated twelve planets in less than three minutes. Astonished, we all sat on the edge of our seats.

Then suddenly the demonstrator was violently yanked toward a planet and stuck to it like a magnet.

"As you can see our demonstrator has been captured by a lechuck. A lechuck is a planet with a strong gravitational pull. Come too close and you'll be detained until the quarter is over. This has cost many a team the game. This phenomenon is called the UI lock, short for – universal immobility."

Maya walked toward a rubber-padded wall and grasped a large protruding lever. She pulled the lever down. There was a lot of loud clicking as the lights went out followed by a chorus of *oohs* and *ahhs*.

"Your gear, the solar bodies, bleachers, walls, and floor glow in the dark," she said, pointing to the wall where at least fifty fluorescent green, red, orange, blue and rainbow-colored element packs hung from rubber hooks. She turned the lights back on and called everyone to the bleachers beside her.

"There are fifty-four of you here today – nine players per team. That means we must form six teams," she said, doing the math on the chalkboard.

A small voice echoed through the chamber.

"Hey – what about me?"

All eyes turned to the tiny, faraway demonstrator.

Maya flushed with embarassment at having forgotten to release the UI lock. She hurried to a control panel and flipped a switch. The demonstrator plummeted a good ten feet before leveling off and heading our way. Our faces dripped with curiosity. Who was it behind that silvery mask?

We watched as the think facial covering was removed. At first all I could see was incredibly bright green hair.

"Sarabella?" I gasped, as she walked past me on her way to a vending machine where she chugged a Boggleberry *Mindfire*.

"I'da never believed it if I hadn't seen it." said Garby. "That girl can fly like a…" he paused, unable to think of a good comparison.

"Like a clawcon!" I said.

"Really? I've never seen one."

"Trust me. She can fly like one."

"Is that a good thing?" asked Garby.

"Uh – yeah. Definitely a good thing."

"Why is her hair so – *green*?" whispered Garby.

" I don't know. It's the strangest thing. I saw it turn red the night I arrived." Garby shuddered.

Maya held a rainbow-colored pack high in the air and announced that it was time to assign team positions. She explained that assignments would be based on her intuitive understanding of our potential, along with inclinations gleaned from our astrological chart which few of us understood.

"This is worn by the team satiator. The satiator – as you know from reading your manuals – refuels team members' elements," she said, pointing to a large copper ring jutting out from the top of the pack. "This…" she said, taking hold of it, "…is a ring shield. The satiator must do everything possible to avoid letting opponents pull it from his, or her, pack. Losing the ring shield renders a satiator immobile and basically – useless. This means team members can no longer be refueled. Depending on when this happens during play will determine whether or not your team can survive. Garby Vanderlin – this is yours."

"Wha – I'm the satiator? The whole team depends on me? Is she *nuts*?" whispered Garby rather loudly.

"She must think you can handle it or she wouldn't assign you the position," I said reassuringly, nudging him forward. "Go get it!"

"Really? Right! Ok, then. I'm the satiator," he said, bobbing his head cockily as he walked toward her. He accepted the element pack and slid it on. It was a perfect fit.

"I think I've lost a few pounds," said Garby, proudly.

Maya shook her head, *no*. "It's an extra, extra large. That's just until your thought-cleansing kicks in," she said, encouragingly.

Deflated, Garby looked back at her trying hard not to hate her.

Maya continued to assign element packs.

Penelope would be an airator and was given a white element pack. Edyl would be a liquifior and was given a blue element pack. The rest of the team were unfamiliar to me. A boy named Shane Fargone would be a second liquifior and he was given a blue element pack. Kristin Paterson and Cali Berns would be nutrizors and were given green element packs. Dillon Candill and Darvon Damos, Jr. would be enlighteners and were given orange element packs.

Darvon was not at all happy about this and he let everyone know it. Maya told him to direct his thoughts and accept his assignment appreciatively. He grumbled.

All the element packs for that team were gone and disappointment set in. This meant Garby and I wouldn't be on the same team which was a disheartening thought. But, it also meant that I wouldn't be on the same team as Darvon and this was a wonderful thought.

I was sure that only moments ago Maya had said there are nine players per team. I counted those already given vests and element packs. There were eight.

I grabbed my manual. There was one other position which I'd forgotten about that didn't require wearing an element pack.

"Levi Levy," yelled Maya, "*You* are the team stabilizer."

Garby punched at air and yelled, "hoo ha."

"I'm the team stabilizer? Really?"

I couldn't recall exactly what the stabilizer does but I knew it was an important position.

Darvon Damos, Jr. threw a hissy fit as I accepted the vest.

"What the – I should be the stabilizer – me – I was the stabilizer last year!" said Darvon, his voice dripping of rage.

Last year? That could only mean one thing as far as I was concerned. Darvon is repeating the class.

It was apparent that Darvon regretted his slip of the tongue. Now, everyone knew his secret and he seethed.

Maya ignored him. She assigned the other positions and instructed teams to choose team names. After several chatter-filled moments the stabilizers spoke on behalf of their teams.

We decided to call ourselves, *The Levitators.* Some of the other teams chose names like: *The Optimistics, The High Riders, and Minds of Steel.*

When I had a moment I paged through my manual searching for

player definitions. I found stabilizer and read this:

> The highly skilled stabilizer roams the solar system searching for players who've been tossed into tailspins and/or are losing altitude. He, or she, helps charge their vests with uplifting thought energy in urgent situations.

I felt horribly burdened after I'd read this. I didn't want to be in a position with this much responsibility. I buried my head in my hands.

"I don't expect you all to remember everything we've talked about today," announced Maya. "It will get easier to understand the more you play and easier to play the more aware you become of your thoughts. The most important thing to remember is that your thoughts are what make you propel slowly, or quickly, through the M-Field. I *cannot* emphasize this point enough. Choose your thoughts wisely. They mean the difference between victory and defeat, and in rare instances – life and death."

Garby gulped.

I want to say that my stomach had butterflies but it felt more like bees.

All six teams were ready to go with uniforms, training vests, element packs, masks and dimension goggles. Maya assigned us to sections of the stadium marked off by lines painted on the air-cushioned floor beneath the flying field.

"Stay within your assigned sections. Today you are wearing vest #2. These vests are pre-charged and will keep you airborn regardless of your own thoughts for about an hour. Up, up and away then!" she hollered.

Off we all went soaring through small segments of the playing field. While our uniforms appeared silver off the field, on the field they changed color making it obvious there were six different teams. Uniforms on our team turned red.

I couldn't understand why Maya had placed arch enemies on the same team. After some consideration I realized it would have been far worse had Darvon and I been placed on opposing teams.

Maya flew through the playing field with a wireless loud speaker worn in the form of an earring.

"Stabilizers! Your teams depend heavily upon you. Do not let them down. No pun intended," she laughed, as she flew from one team to the next. After we all had a taste of a small section of the playing field Maya instructed us to explore it in its entirety.

"Please familiarize yourselves with the locations of the planets and the distance between them – although both shift during play. The field, like life, is ever-changing."

For seemingly no reason Darvon Damos was tossed into a tailspin. Seeing this gave me the distinct impression that he'd been sucked into the funnel of a tornado and spit out with enormous force.

Maya blew a whistle at seeing this. We all stopped dead in our tracks and hovered.

Maya announced, "Yes – well – I forgot to mention – bluyoles. As you can see, Mr. Damos encountered one," she said, hovering a few feet away from where he lay flattened on the cushion, the wind knocked out of him.

Pointing randomly at spots of nothingness across the playing field she continued, "There are invisible pockets called bluyoles here and there. They suck you in, spin you silly, and spit you out. The effect is quite similar to *uncontrollable* emotion. It takes quick thinking to recover. Most beginners end up like Mr. Damos here," she said, shaking her head disappointedly.

Darvon fumed at her words. He slurred, "I'm no beginner," then passed out.

"Invisible pockets?" I reached out to feel the air in front of where I hovered.

"In time you'll be able to sense bluyoles and avoid most of them. They move around the field in no particular pattern. They have a vibrational frequency that seasoned-sifters are able to detect. The air is a bit heavier and colder around them. You may feel an initial tugging as you approach one."

Maya called to me. She nodded her head in the direction of where Darvon Damos lay unconscious on the air cushion below.

"Mr. Levy – you *are* your team's stabilizer. Please assist."

"Oh – right!" I said, flying awkwardly toward him.

I didn't yet know how to stop and ended up crashing into the cushion beside him. First I checked to see if he was breathing. I was both relieved and disappointed to find that he was. *Now what?* Try to be nice, I told myself. I proceeded to give Darvon a pep talk and he allowed me to – but only because he was unconscious. I didn't really know what to do and the fact that he was such a cruel individual made it difficult for me to want to help him.

Sarabella flew in and scanned him.

"Several old injuries – healed bones – nothing current – at least nothing *physical*," she reported.

When Darvon awakened and saw me sitting there at his side he flipped out.

"Get away from me. Don't EVER send a thought my way or you'll be sorry."

I backed off.

Darvon stood up and limped away. He was back in the air flying sloppily in no time.

"Ok, good – that went well," I mumbled facetiously.

Maya took a deep breath and exhaled hard as if relieved and exasperated simultaneously.

"Well – that's it for today. I hope you all enjoyed your second day of class. Tomorrow we'll have practice matches against one another. You'll wear vest # 3. Keep in mind that each subsequent vest relies more and more upon your own thoughts. There are thirty pre-charged training vests in all. At the end of the thirty days you'll be expected to charge your vests with your own thought energy."

After Maya assigned homework, she handed out journals and instructed us to document *every* thought that popped into our head. She admitted that this was a nearly impossible task for new sifters, but she made it very clear that being aware of our thoughts is the key to becoming a successful sifter.

In addition to keeping track of our thoughts we were asked to replace every thought that made us feel less than wonderful with a better feeling one, and write it beside the original.

"Blah – blah – blah," mocked Garby, waving and smiling as she took off over the stadium and flew out of sight. "Geez – can she talk."

Garby looked over at me. I was visibly upset.

"Hey – you're a stabilizer, dude," he said, about to punch at air.

I grabbed his arm and stifled an impending, "Hoo ha."

"I can't do this, Garby. I can't be the stabilizer. I don't know what I'm doing. I don't know what happened yesterday but it couldn't have been me who saved you. I'm sure of it," I said, holding my head in my hands."

"You're being too hard on yourself – don't you think?" he asked, taking a seat beside me on the bleachers. "When I was assigned satiator you said that Maya wouldn't have put me in the position if she didn't think I could handle it. Well – same goes for you. Just find a better feeling thought, bro" he said, winking.

I stared out into the colossal playing field. The cosmic qualm whizzed by. I ripped off a sneaker and threw it with all my might.

"You have no business in my head. Get out!" I yelled, as my sneaker rocketed toward the qualm. Surprisingly, it was a direct hit. The qualm gurgled and plummeted to the chamber floor.

I could feel the blood drain from my face.

"You don't think I broke it – do you?" I asked worriedly.

"I hope so!" cried Garby and we burst into laughter.

CHAPTER THIRTEEN

GAMES IN THE SKY

Mobert and Sner were waiting in the parking lot to escort sifters to the welcoming party at the *Downstream Diner*.

"Tell me about your day!" said Sner excitedly as he grabbed my duffel bag, tossed it into the auraplane and helped me inside.

I stared at him feeling like a sponge at saturation point.

"It was definitely – a day like no other. I've been assigned the position of team stabilizer," I blurted, as if it were a death sentence.

"Yes! That's an important position," cheered Sner, raising his pawish hand for a high-five.

I declined.

"What's wrong?", he asked sympathetically.

"I'm still in shock – overwhelmed really," I confessed, slouching into a seat.

"Right – and who wouldn't be," said Sner supportively, taking a seat beside me. "You know, Maya wouldn't have assigned you the position if she didn't think you could handle it."

"Right," I said, as my eyes met Garby's.

"That's what I told him," said Garby, stuffing his duffel bag beneath a seat.

"And what position are you playing, Garby?" asked Sner.

"I'm the satiator," he said proudly.

"Wow! Two big positions. How exciting!" Sner beamed.

He and Garby shared a high-five.

"Did you guys see the cosmic qualm?"

Garby and I exchanged mischievous smiles.

"Umm – yes we did, actually," I said, stifling a laugh.

"That thing's a pisser," said Sner.

Garby and I nodded our agreement.

"Well – it's time to relax and have some fun. The *Downstream Diner* party is one of my favorite events of the year – second only to the Sifter's Ball," said Sner, standing on the seat and dancing in a circle. He jumped down and offered rides to passersby.

Penelope waved and headed toward us.

My heart beat a little faster at seeing her.

"Why did you bring that gargantuan spool of dental floss, Sner? Mobert pointed to a spool the size of a toaster. "It takes up an entire seat."

"We're going to a party. Who knows *what* will end up between my teeth. I don't give you a hard time about your idiosyncratic habits."

"It's such – excess. You could just take a few feet," growled Mobert.

Sner waved a disconcerting hand at Mobert as he welcomed Penelope aboard. "What position are you playing young lady?

"I'm an airator," she said, smiling.

"Good one! You're the breath of life!" said Sner ecstatically.

The sound of Mobert's talons drumming on the dashboard filled the space between their words.

"Sner – please place your *superfluous* spool beneath the seats."

"Ok – ok, already!" snapped Sner, ignoring the request.

I called for Alphia. From the corner of my eye I caught a glimpse of her running toward the auraplane. She hopped inside and immediately began to complain.

"And what position are you playing?" asked Sner jokingly.

"She's the annoyer," I kidded, as I picked her up and kissed her.

Alphia yanked herself from my arms. She stood before me on the seat and proceeded to yell at me.

"You didn't call for me once today! I waited – and waited. But *no*, you were too busy. This is the second day you did this. Is this going to be a pattern? I didn't say anything yesterday when you and Garby went off to play games in the sky with that freaky girl with the grey face and pink dress. I couldn't catch grasshoppers because of her. She played that *horrible* death song on her *tinny* trumpet and scared them all away. She really shouldn't be allowed to have that thing. It is *unbearably* out of tune. Didn't anyone suggest she take lessons? And, don't her parents feed her? She looks like she got up on the wrong side of the coffin."

Garby and I locked eyes, thunderstruck. It was at this moment he and I realized he hadn't hallucinated the day before.

Just as I was about to ask Alphia about the girl Sarabella popped her head inside the auraplane window.

"Here," she said, handing me the baseball hat that had fallen beneath the bleachers at the crater ceremony. "I crawled under and got it for you but – we need to talk about this. Do you have room for one more?"

I tugged on the hat but Sarabella wouldn't release it. I stared at her as though she were a puzzle with a few pieces missing. I then looked questioningly at Sner.

"Does she have to be with us ALL the time?" I whispered.

Sner whispered back, "Hemp assigns an upperclassman to every three or four new sifters. You know – to show you the ropes, keep you out of trouble. You got Sarabella."

I wanted to tell her we didn't have room for her but Garby must have sensed this because he elbowed me hard.

"Tell her yes already. Open the door!"

"Oh my – look over there!" said Mobert, pointing.

When everyone turned around Mobert grabbed Sner's roll of floss and tossed it out the window.

"Hey – there's an empty seat right here," said Garby, beaming. He reached across my lap and opened the door for her.

"Where's my floss?" asked Sner, as Sarabella sat where the spool had been just moments ago.

" I – I put it – in the trunk," lied Mobert.

"Oh – thank you," said Sner. "Hey – wait a minute – we don't have a trunk."

As the auraplane took off Sner watched his spool of dental floss unravel across the field some thirty feet below. "Wha – I can't believe you did that!" he griped, tossing Mobert an incredulous look.

Most of the trip was spent reviewing the occurrences of the day. Penelope filled several pages in her journal.

"There must be a lot more going on in there than in here," said

Garby, pointing first to her head and then to his own.

Penelope reminded Garby that a less cluttered mind was not only a good thing but it was, after all, the whole point of journaling.

I wanted to talk to Penelope. I just didn't know what to say and I didn't want to say something I'd regret. So, I just secretly admired her from a distance.

As we were about to land in the parking lot I asked Sner how the diner got its name.

"Who'd want to swim upstream when they can float downstream? It's an analogy – for life," said Sner ecstatically, skipping toward the peculiar diner.

CHAPTER FOURTEEN

THE DOWNSTREAM DINER

The parking lot at the *Downstream Diner* was filled with brightly colored auraplanes parked on individual landing pads. As I walked by one of them I realized it belonged to Hemp.

"Hemp's here," I yelled to the others while pushing against the circular wooden front door of the diner. It was heavy and creaked as it opened. Inside was a small, empty room. Cool, musty air made my nose wrinkle. I sneezed. My excitement wilted like gerbera daisies in a short vase. *What kind of diner is this?*

"This is the diner of all diners. You're going to love it!" said Hemp, gliding into the vacant room.

Garby, Penelope and I exchanged looks that suggested Hemp must be crazy.

"This is the clearing room – similar to the bin of bane," said Hemp, bending to lift a large circular panel from the floor. "Leave all troubling thoughts behind – and be sure to powder your hands."

Hemp rubbed the palms of his hands over a large white stone. He clapped and a chalky cloud drifted across the empty room.

Alphia coughed.

Hemp extended his arms like a human guard rail and asked that everyone step back. He chanted, *"Quiscere faciam polus. Quiscere faciam polus. Quiscere faciam polus."*

Boisterous voices erupted from deep within the hole and a thick copper pole shot up through the opening.

Penelope jumped back. She landed in my arms. I'd never seen her up so close. I could feel her breath against my cheek. She smelled of honeysuckle and was even more beautiful than I'd realized. As I held her I felt an electric current travel between us and lost my breath.

Penelope's cheeks flushed.

"You ok?" I asked, as an unfamiliar warmth blossomed in my chest.

"F – fine. Thanks for catching me," she said airily, stepping aside.

I didn't want to let go.

Hemp's voice pierced the pleasantness. I figured I'd missed a part of what he'd said because what he was saying made little sense to me. It seemed he was giving us a lesson in pole sliding. With chalky palms he grasped the pole and wrapped his legs firmly around it.

"When the light over there turns green it's safe for the next one to slide!" he said, pointing to a small flickering red light.

"I'll get us a table. Yee-haw," he yelled, his hurache sandals screeching against the shiny pole as he faded out of sight.

Looking down the hole into the dismal abyss caused me to lose my appetite, along with my nerve. I couldn't help hoping that someone would volunteer to go next so I wouldn't have to.

The light turned green. I held my breath.

"I guess I'll go next," said Penelope, straightening her jeans and blouse.

I was relieved but felt a bit immasculated in that she had more courage than I.

Penelope chalked her hands, took hold of the pole and slid down in a dignified manner.

I pushed aside my reservations and rationalized – if Penelope can do it, so can I.

While waiting for the light to turn green I chalked my hands. With one hand wrapped around the pole and the other wrapped around a nagging Alphia I followed Penelope into the abyss.

"Two hands please. Both hands on the pole. And, WHERE are we going? This doesn't look like any restaurant I've ever been to. When's the last time you heard of anyone sliding down a *pole* to dinner? This seems like some sort of trap – and we're just willingly sliding into captivity under the promise of a little bacon. At least I assume there will be bacon. I mean, if it's a *real* restaurant there will undoubtedly be bacon. Additionally, you know I don't like holes, especially deep ones. Things that eat other things like deep holes. Snakes and rats like deep holes. Dogs are practical. We dig shallow holes in which to bury stolen goods. This makes them accessible when we…"

"Will you *please* be quiet," I snapped, using both my hands on the pole to appease her. "Everything will be alright."

Deep inside the hole where only I could hear her, she continued to complain. Tightening her grip around my neck she dug her claws into my skin. It hurt and I felt a headache coming on.

"And – be careful with that white stuff – it's all over me – I look like a middle-class poodle."

The drop was a long one. I felt the way I imagined a chipmunk might feel retreating to its burrow for the long winter months. Down, down we went. There was nothing but dirt interwoven with the roots of whatever it was that grew in this lightless void. Despite the chalk my hands chaffed from the friction and my neck bled thanks to Alphia's claws.

Finally, darkness transitioned into a warm, burnt orange glow from the light of at least a hundred vanilla-scented candles scattered about. My mood lightened with the candlelight. The first thing I saw was a sign on the wall that read: Level Three.

As I slid swiftly through Level Three I caught glimpses of sifters dancing to the ethereal music of a band whose members resembled Mobert and Sner.

Sliding through Level Two I saw customers dining, their plates stacked with fine fare. I watched fancy drinks in tangerine-colored glasses, decorated with umbrellas and speared fruit, float from bar to tables. Silky okra-tinted curtains draped sloppily plastered walls. Orange candles hung from ceiling beams and splashed warm light over the patrons.

As I slid through Level One I eyed a large dance floor and shelves upon shelves of trophies behind a bar. Most were silver casts of sifters. A separate cabinet housed framed team photographs.

We soon landed on the crystal gravel floor with a thump.

"Finally – solid ground," snapped Alphia, jumping from my arms. She shook herself vigorously and disappeared into a cloud of complaining chalky dust.

I absorbed the colorful surroundings. Hand-painted, uplifting phrases decorated walls, tables and chairs. Some were carved into the woodwork, some etched in circles around doorknobs, and painted across the ceiling. I paused to read a few:

Thoughts become things.

I create my reality through the thoughts I choose to think.

I can do, be, and have, anything I imagine.

The only wand I'll ever need is a better feeling thought.

Be the change you wish to see in the dimensions.

I couldn't help noticing how good I felt in this place. My eyes scanned the room. Framed portraits hung against thick wooden columns. Hand-carved, life-size statues of those in the portraits were strategically placed between tables. A life-size statue of a woman holding a blank canvas, paint palette and brush sat on the counter behind the juice bar. Engraved on a small silver tag attached to the canvas was the phrase:

Your life is a canvas; your thoughts a brush.

Alphia barked relentlessly at her.

In the center of the room was a statue of Solarius Solarshay. I learned that he was Maya's great grandfather. He was a short, wide man with bowed legs and a high forehead. The statue was carved in detail down to the scratches across the lenses of his dimension goggles.

I turned to see that Garby had arrived. He grumbled about his hands being chaffed from the pole slide then grabbed my arm.

"Look! Look – she's sliding down now!" he gasped, as he watched Sarabella with hungry eyes.

I freed my arm from his grip. "What's come over you?" I asked, walking away from him thinking that the threat of imminent death the previous day had awakened a part of him I hadn't seen until now.

"Something happens to me when I see her – hear her – smell – or think about her. It's crazy!"

I understood. I felt the same way about Penelope but I hoped it wasn't as obvious.

I continued to explore the diner. Little did I know that as I was reading affirmations and studying photographs, someone had pulled an artifact from where it was affixed to the wall and was headed toward me armed with it. The sharp-looking black parasike was identical to the one the boy, whose hat was now in my possession, had flown on the night of my arrival.

One minute I was reading an affirmation and the next I was flat on the floor. It happened quickly and left me stunned. My body ached and throbbed. I got splinters as a result of grabbing the table in an attempt to break my fall. From the floor I looked up to see Darvon Damos, Jr. laughing condescendingly.

Alphia growled at him as she rushed to my side. She examined Darvon head to toe as if attempting to determine the deadliest spot for a bite.

"You'll never be as good as me. You think you can come into *my* world and take *my* position – but you're not going to get away with it. Go back to your dimension *Earth boy* – or you'll wish you had never burned that invitation."

Darvon tossed me the parasike he'd used to assault me.

"Here – you might need this – in your DREAMS!" he cracked, like a true bully.

This wasn't quite the thanks I'd expected for helping him earlier after he'd been accosted by a bluyole. Seemed a tad ungrateful. And, although I understood Darvon was upset, for some reason I was having a difficult time feeling badly in the *Downstream Diner*.

"He needs something – and I don't mean a burger," said Garby, in a threatening voice.

That peaceful, easy feeling was interrupted when I suddenly envisioned myself running after Darvon, hitting him repeatedly with the parasike's handle and stuffing metal bristles into his face. Uh oh. I'd lost control of my thoughts. They'd turned barbaric and honestly, I didn't feel that they were my own. Even though Darvon had injured me, the thought of retaliation didn't feel good. But, if these thoughts weren't mine, whose were they?

I'd never do the things these thoughts suggested and being that my homework involved keeping a log of my thoughts I hurried to find better feeling ones. I thought about how Darvon would be given some sort of consequence by Hemp, Maya, or the owner of the diner. Instead of dwelling on him and what had just happened I ignored the reality entirely and resumed reading the uplifting affirmations on the stool beside me.

"What are you doing?" asked Garby, extending a hand to help me up from the floor.

"Reading."

"Huh? How can you just sit there reading affirmations after what just happened?" he asked, dumbfounded.

At that very instant, and much to both of our surprise, a parasike that was hanging on the wall took off of its own accord and exited the diner through the front door at incredible speed. Whizzing sounds and strong currents of air trailed behind it. Alphia followed it, zigzagging her way beneath tables and chairs.

"I wouldn't miss this for a bucket of freshly grilled, grass-fed sirloin clawcon," she said, keeping her eyes on the obviously enraged parasike.

The place fell silent. All eyes turned toward the parasike. Seconds later everyone went back about their business as if nothing had happened. All the while thumping sounds, moans, groans and pleads echoed through the diner.

Alphia cheered. When she returned she happily reported that Darvon was being attacked by the parasike.

The front door creaked open. Darvon was almost unrecognizable with torn clothing, dangling teeth, bloody scratches, and a blackened eye. He swayed drunkenly as he stood in the diner doorway.

"This isn't over – *Earth boy*," he yelled madly, through swollen lips. He was then escorted away by two soulguards in a security auraplane.

"Did that broom thing just attack Darvon – or, am I imagining this?" asked Garby.

I sucked a drop of blood from the spot where I pulled a splinter from my finger.

"You're not imagining it. That broom thing did attack Darvon – and it's called a parasike."

"Oh! Good then," said Garby, smiling oddly as he hopped up on a stool and chugged lemonade. Pulling his journal from his duffel bag he wrote frantically.

It was at this moment that I realized the attack on Darvon played out exactly like the thoughts I'd had about him a few moments earlier.

From the corner of my eye I saw Hemp walking toward us with the bloody parasike clenched in his hand. He placed it on the table.

Garby and I retreated.

"It's ok," said Hemp reassuringly.

I wasn't reassured.

"I see you and Darvon are going to be good friends," he winked, as he rested his hand on my shoulder.

"The best," I said, playing along.

"Life brings many opportunities for battle, Levi. We must focus on peaceful resolutions." Hemp pulled up a stool.

"Did you read that somewhere?" I asked, looking through the affirmations on the shiny tabletop.

"No – but it would make a nice addition wouldn't it?"

Hemp drew a turquoise marker from his pocket. He handed it to me. "You do the honors."

I searched for a blank spot on the tabletop.

"What's up with Darvon?" I asked, as I wrote.

"Everyone has a past. Everyone has a story. But, our reality – our future – depends on which story we tell. Darvon lives in the past remembering and recreating painful scenes from his childhood. He was bullied by the one who should have protected him – his father. Like all of us, he has the power to change. One must ignore reality and find better feeling thoughts in order to change it. Better feeling thoughts create better feeling experiences. I'm not saying it's easy but we all have the freedom to choose the thoughts we think."

I know what it felt like being bullied by one who should have protected me. Darvon and I had something in common. An unanticipated compassion for him washed over me as I extracted more splinters from my fingers.

"I'd like to introduce you to Hiwinzin," said Hemp, pouring himself a tall glass of lemonade.

"Hi-who?" I asked, my eyes scanning the surroundings.

"Hiwinzin," said Hemp, holding up the bloody parasike.

"Hiwinzin's a parasike?"

"One could say that," said Hemp, struggling for the right words. "A great old school sifter known as Hiwinzin once owned this parasike."

"Hiwinzin's a sifter then – not a parasike?" I asked, trying to understand.

"He *was* a sifter. He's no longer with us. You see, artifacts, including parasikes, are infused with at least part of the residual spirit of the original, deceased owner."

This was just another strange concept I failed to grasp.

"I don't understand," I said, reaching out to touch the parasike.

"It is confusing. Well – when we leave our bodies – the essence of who we are has to go somewhere. It often goes into the things we enjoyed most in our previous existence."

I sipped lemonade as I tried to process Hemp's explanation.

"Are you saying that Hiwinzin's essence came through his parasike and attacked Darvon?"

"One could surmise that."

"Don't you think that attack was a bit of an overreaction?" I asked.

"Yes, my boy. But that's what happens sometimes as a result of misdirected thought."

I soon learned that Hiwinzin and Darvon's father had a falling out and then Hiwinzin had a falling off, so to speak. Hemp told me that rumor has it that Hiwinzin was pushed off the Cliffs of Doom.

"So – Darvon's father killed Hiwinzin? But – what does this have to do with me?"

"Darvon's father lost his solarshay position as stabilizer to Hiwinzin. Poor sportsmanship runs in the lineage."

Garby's eyes widened. He leaned in so as not to miss a word.

"Darvon's father killed Hiwinzin *for a team position?*" asked Garby, shocked.

"Yes. Yes he did. The extent to which some athletes will go when tempted by the bittersweet nectar of fame and fortune never ceases to amaze me."

I couldn't help wondering if Darvon was now considering killing me for the very same reason.

"Hemp, I think I heard – whoever was having thoughts about attacking Darvon – I think I heard them before it happened. They just kind of danced through my head but they didn't feel like my own. Does that make sense?"

"Makes perfect sense, my boy. It's called telepathy – and yours is obviously kicking in."

"But – whose thoughts were they?" I asked, visually examining the faces of those around me for a clue.

"Telepathy is a complex issue. Sometimes it's difficult to ascertain to whom thoughts belong."

Hemp's answer seemed evasive and wasn't at all helpful. Perhaps I'd never discover the source of those thoughts. I would just know that somewhere out there someone harbors intense hatred for Darvon.

Just then, the others joined us at the table and I welcomed the distraction. We all spoke briefly about the attack. I didn't bother mentioning my telepathic experience.

"Have you guys been writing your thoughts in your journals?" asked Penelope, sitting on the stool beside me.

"Not yet," I said, trying to get thoughts of Darvon and his father out of my head. "Have you?"

"Yes – and I'm going to need another journal soon."

Penelope showed me over three pages of thoughts she'd written in the past fifteen minutes. I read a few entries.

"You can't know all my thoughts," she said, snapping the journal shut just as I started to read a thought she'd had about me.

A few new team members arrived along with Mobert and Sner. Everyone introduced themselves. All searched for menus but there are no menus, or waitstaff, at the *Downstream Diner*. The only available dinner option is the veggie burger supreme with a side of organic sweet potato chips. I was starving and it sounded delicious.

Just then a plate with a juicy burger and pile of chips appeared on the table in front of Hemp. Sounds of surprise erupted around the table.

"Visualize a plate in front of you if you'd like to eat," said Hemp, stuffing a napkin down the neck of his t-shirt. "The chef is highly intuitive. Just ask for *The Special* – and say, *thank you.*

"No kidding! That's how it works?" asked Garby, flabbergasted.

"That's how it works," said Hemp. "Just close your eyes and envision your meal."

One by one plates with veggie burgers and frosty mugs filled with green lemonade appeared on the table. Raw excitement charged the air. Everyone was able to manifest dinner – everyone except Garby.

"Where's mine? This visualization thing isn't working," he protested, concentrating so hard that his face turned scarlet.

"I think the problem is that you really want a sirloin steak – and that's not an option here. Focus. Be specific," said Hemp, squeezing ketchup on his burger.

"I do! I do want a sirloin steak," said Garby, disappointment oozing from his whiny words. It took Garby a good ten minutes longer than the rest of us but eventually, and with sweat on his brow, he manifested dinner.

"Do you hear - what is that?" I asked, shushing the others.

Faint yawning sounds erupted from our plates.

"Ah, yes. Naptime's over," said Hemp, pointing.

One by one, chips stretched and squirmed beneath the penetrating glare of disbelieving eyes.

"Why – how are they doing this?" I asked, astounded.

"They're Fickle chips – the brainchild of a very special chef. He thought them into existence. We're fortunate tonight. No duds," said Hemp, examining plates. "I've had lazier batches that were far less fun. Their energy level depends on the thoughts of the chef as they're being prepared."

This was a bizarre experience. I wasn't accustomed to having to catch and eat things that move. My chips were especially mischievous.

Several of them burrowed themselves inside my shirt pocket. Others hopped from plate to plate.

Alphia sat strategically on my lap, waiting with her head hidden beneath the table. At just the precise moment she sprang forward and nabbed a chip as it dipped itself in ranch dressing.

Some of Penelope's chips hid themselves behind her lemonade. When she lifted it to drink they ran up her arm and screamed. She flung her glass across the room and it smashed against the wall. Luckily, no one was hurt. Soon we all broke into mad laughter. It was an experience I will never forget.

Following dinner Sarabella and Garby went to look at trophies. Mobert and Sner headed outside with two cute female nelf singers from the band. Penelope headed to the restroom as the new team members went to find the dance floor. Alphia napped on my lap.

Hemp pulled a small box from a turquoise beaded bag dangling from his shoulder. He placed it on the table in front of me. It was wrapped in paper that had a splash of every color imaginable and topped with a curly silver bow.

My eyes lit up when I saw it.

"What is it?" I asked, shaking it gently.

"Happy Birthday," said Hemp.

It wasn't my birthday. I told Hemp this, hoping that I could keep the gift regardless.

"Every day is one's birthday in Ceres because every day we're growing and learning something new about ourselves."

I couldn't argue with that. I shook the box, again.

"May I open it?" I paused with the bow in one hand, the box in the other.

"Yes! It's yours to open."

Hemp propped his feet up on the table. Today he wore pink and purple striped toe socks with hurache sandals.

Lifting the lid, I reached inside and pulled sparkling purple tissue paper from the box to reveal the thing I wanted, and needed, most – an ESPY watch.

"Wow! Thank you. It's perfect. How'd you do this so fast?" I asked, wrapping the band around my wrist and fastening its shiny silver lock.

"Passion," said Hemp, sucking up the last of his lemonade through a curly straw.

I was beyond thrilled. I would now know when Orable is in the dimension.

But my relief faded as quickly as it came.

"No – it can't be!" I gasped, as I turned the face of the watch toward Hemp.

CHAPTER FIFTEEN

THINK-A-VIEW

Hemp held my wrist and looked at the watch. The face was black. That could only mean one thing - Orable was near. Fearful thoughts poisoned me with panic. My body malfunctioned.

"It's new and still acclimating. No cause for alarm," said Hemp.

What a relief.

Hemp explained that when I put the watch on it had to adjust to my frequency as well as Orable's. I watched as it finished acclimating and returned to a beautiful shade of amethyst.

Shortly thereafter I mingled and chatted with some of our new team members. We all ended up dancing in a large circle with everyone holding hands under the direction of the eclectic band members. After a few hours of fun we retreated to our cottages.

The next day I wore my ESPY watch to solarshay practice elated that at any given moment all I had to do was look at it for reassurance.

Darvon Damos, Jr. wasn't in class. I learned that he'd been sent to the *Beverly Soared Center,* a thought abuse treatment facility, for three days, as a result of initiating the diner brawl.

The stadium was cold and dark that day, even with the doors open. Garby and I arrived early, in uniform. I took a seat beside him on the bleacher. Sarabella settled in a few rows away. Garby jumped up the instant she appeared and darted over to sit beside her. I almost took this personally. I followed Garby and again sat beside him with my thought journal in hand. I had filled ten pages with my thoughts and their corrections since breakfast. Unable to write fast enough to keep up with thoughts needing correction I realized there's quite a bit of random drivel going on in my head.

"This thought journal – great idea – don't you think?" I asked.

As I looked up I saw Garby painting Sarabella's toenails. Words failed me but I'm sure my facial expression spoke for itself.

"It's a pedicure," said Garby, winking flirtatiously at Sarabella.

I wrote in my journal and ignored this irritating event best I could.

"That was an amazing demonstration yesterday, Sarabella. You're really good," I said.

No sooner had I said this than her hair turned a very soft and pretty shade of pink.

"It's quite elementary," she said, holding a small bejeweled mirror and pair of tweezers in front of her face.

"My hair color is irrelevant," she snapped, just as I was about to ask why her hair changes color.

"I like pink," said Garby, trance-like and practically drooling.

"Is the game making sense to you, Garb?" I asked.

"Sort of. It's the whole controlling my thoughts thing that concerns me. I like the thirty-day training vests though," he said, blowing on Sarabella's toenails.

Sarabella looked up at me for the first time since I'd arrived.

"You really should get rid of that hat," she said, pointing to the place where it was attached to my duffel bag. "I can't believe you insist on keeping it now that you know to whom it belongs. Carrying that thing around is like trying to sail with an anchor down."

"You gave it back to me. You even went out of your way to get it."

"What are you guys talking about? Whose hat is it?" asked Garby, trying to grab it. I moved my duffel bag out of his reach.

"Remember – she drinks too much crater water," I whispered.

"I thought about it after I gave it back and regretted it. I should have burned it," she said, adjusting cotton balls stuffed between the bases of her toes.

As I looked at Sarabella I couldn't help wondering why that brain had been placed in such a beautiful body with such a beautiful face. I immediately wrote that thought in my journal – along with a correction.

I liked the hat and planned on keeping it. I promised myself not to wear it but wanted to keep it as a souvenir. The only way I intended to part with it was by returning it to its rightful owner.

Sarabella told me the initials V.S. on the front of the hat were definitely not the boy's initials but rather the initials of Orable's teen army – *The Virusian Soldiers*. She told me repeatedly that carrying it with me could be detrimental to my well-being.

Penelope arrived and walked up the bleachers toward us. A tinny stomping sound echoed through the chamber with each step she took. "Nice hat," were her first words.

Sarabella shot a burning glare at her that went unnoticed to all but me.

"Oh my – your hair – it's pink – I mean it was pink – but now it's turning red," said Penelope startled.

"My hair color is irrelevant," snapped Sarabella.

It was apparent by the look on Penelope's face that she was shocked, curious and wanted to know more about Sarabella's hair color phenomena – as did we all. Together we watched (and I'm pretty sure our jaws were dangling) as her hair returned to its original shiny shade of black licorice. We couldn't help staring. After several *mind-your-own-business* looks from Sarabella, Penelope broke the silence.

"Did you guys check out the tournament archives on your *T-View?*" asked Penelope, elated.

"T-View – what's that?" I asked.

Penelope said it was sort of like a miniature television except you think about what you want to watch and it appears on the screen. I wanted one. I reached for my duffel, as did Garby. A wave of disappointment washed over our faces as we searched inside our empty bags.

"You're the class assistant. Why didn't we get *T-Views?*" asked Garby crankily, accidentally knocking over Sarabella's nail polish with his foot and causing a thick stream of hot pink enamel to drip over the edge of the silver bleacher.

"I'm not responsible for your thoughts," she said snootily, passing her hand over the spilled polish and causing it to disappear.

Garby, Penelope and I exchanged impressed looks.

"So – you're also the janitor," said Garby, snickering.

Sarabella stared at him, blankly.

"If you want a *Think-a-View* you have to attract one by being in vibrational alignment with it," she said, yawning.

Our faces must have revealed bewilderment because Penelope looked at us pitiably.

"I think what Sarabella's saying is that the *T-Views* weren't in your bags because you didn't *think* them in. I have an idea. Zip your bags. Think about the *T-Views* being inside and then open them again."

I zipped my duffel bag and concentrated. After waiting a good twenty seconds I unzipped it. Much to my amazement there it was. I pulled the glossy metallic box from inside.

"How'd you know to do that, Penelope?" asked Garby, pulling a sparkly *T-View* from his own bag.

"I figured it out yesterday by accident. These bags seem to respond to your needs. You just ask for something and it's in there."

"I need a red Lamborghini," I said, looking expectantly at my duffel bag, trying hard not to laugh as I unzipped it.

"She said it responds to your *needs* – not your wildest fantasies," said Sarabella, peering at me from the corner of her eye. "And more specifically – the bags respond to your solarshay needs."

"I saw solarshayers do some crazy moves – how'd they get so good?" asked Penelope, twisting the cap off a bottle of *Mindfire* she pulled from her duffel bag.

"It's no big mystery. They practiced – visualized themselves doing those moves," said Sarabella, walking awkwardly down the bleachers with cotton balls still stuffed between her toes.

"Penelope held up a chilled bottle of *Mindfire*. "Anybody want one?"

"Yes, please," I said.

"Me, too," said Garby, reaching inside her bag.

Penelope pulled Garby's hand out at once.

"That's for Levi," she said, handing the bottle to me.

Garby shot me an envious look.

I shrugged awkwardly.

"Hey – let's all watch the archives tonight at our place," said Garby, excitedly.

"Sounds like a plan." I stole a secret peek at Penelope.

Just then a whizzing noise echoed through the chamber. It sounded like a bomb falling. Garby, Penelope and I ran outside. Looking up in the general direction of the sound we saw something flying toward the stadium.

There zipping across the sky was Maya. Within a few seconds she crashed into the same elder bush she crashed into the day before, and the day before that.

"Does she always crash into that bush? It's the only one on the field," asked Garby, dumbfounded.

"Always," answered Sarabella, plucking cotton balls from between her toes.

"Good afternoon," yelled Maya, popping out of the elder bush. Marching toward the stadium she paused beside the *Bin of Bane* and pointing said, "Weed the gardens of your minds. Leave all limiting thoughts behind." She then turned and entered the stadium. One by one we followed her lead and headed inside.

I was happy to learn that Darvon wasn't going to be in class. I had enough to focus on with trying to avoid lechucks, bluyoles, the cosmic qualm and assuming my role as stabilizer.

It was a productive practice session. Our team, the *Levitators*, won all matches against opposing teams. We wore vest #3 which meant there were twenty-seven remaining vest-assisted days of flight.

I actually felt grateful that nightly homework involved writing in my journal. It was helping me to become aware of, and improve, my thoughts. Resultantly, I was in a better mood much of the time.

Later that evening, Garby, Penelope, Sarabella and I ordered take-out from *The Downstream Diner* and headed back to our cottage to watch archieved solarshay tournaments. We all pulled *T-Views* from our duffels.

"What are you guys doing?" asked Sarabella, rolling her eyes. She tossed a multicolored, beaded pillow from the couch to the floor then walked toward the wall opposite the couch. She flipped a switch and the wall opened.

I practically collapsed in awe at seeing the magnificent device.

"Wow. Wow!" said Garby, gawking. "It takes up the entire wall. That's awesome! It's like we have our own theatre! All we need now is buttered popcorn."

Sarabella told us to put our miniature, mobile versions away.

We decided to have dinner before embarking on our tournament-watching marathon. During dinner Penelope's eyes followed my wrist as it moved between my mouth and plate. I grew self-conscious.

"Your watch – it doesn't have any numbers or hands – or anything. Why?" she asked.

"No numbers, huh." I said, winking. "Well, it's a – numberless, telepathic watch made by – The Handless Brothers – incorporated."

Everyone stopped chewing and turned toward me.

"It's just like Hemp's ESPY lamp," said Sarabella, brushing her hair with a clump of toothpicks she grabbed from a sparkling blue candle holder on the glass coffee table. She then returned them to the holder.

"Noooo – NO!" said Garby, his face wrinkled with repulsion and confusion.

Garby plucked the tainted toothpicks from the holder and handed them back to her. Sarabella looked at him as though she had no idea why he was upset about this.

"It's an ESPY watch, Penelope" I said, tilting the face of the watch toward her.

"What's an ESPY watch?" Penelope leaned in anxious to know more.

"A forecaster," I said, distracted by her scent and how cute she looked in her faded jeans and fringed accessories.

"What does it forecast?"

I had a dilemma. I wanted to tell her and the others what I'd heard the clawcons say but I didn't know if it was a good idea. I also wondered if Hemp would approve. I didn't want to cause anyone unnecessary anguish. At the same time, I didn't want to hide information that just might save their lives.

"Well – have you guys heard of clawcons?" I asked tentatively.

"Only from you," answered Garby.

Penelope shook her head, *no*.

"Of course," snapped Sarabella plucking a bunch of still sleeping

Fickle chips from Garby's plate, with her toes.

Garby tossed me a questioning look and shook his head disapprovingly. He then pretend-coughed into his fist, "Hhh – crater – water."

"Do you guys think I'm stupid? You do realize that I'm aware every time you make fun of me, right? I know you think I drink too much crater water. Truth is, neither of you drink enough. Otherwise, you wouldn't make fun of me."

"Just don't put your feet in the food – okay?" pleaded Garby. And by the way he said this it was apparent the attraction he felt for her was evaporating.

"Can we please get back to clawcons? What are they?" asked Penelope, twirling her hair.

"They're big bird-ish things. But they – umm – well..."

"Honestly, Levi. Spit it out," blurted Sarabella.

Without giving me a second to speak she revealed my secret.

"Levi overheard one of the clawcons say Orable would be abducting twelve more sifters in two weeks – and that was four nights ago, Monday."

"No way! Talking birds told you this?" asked Garby, stuffing chips in his mouth. "I've got to see this. Show us! Show us what they look like – on the big screen."

Alphia's ears perked as she appeared from beneath the coffee table.

"Trust me. You don't want to know. You don't want to see these horrible, squawking, drooling, carnivorous, child-eating predators the size of – school buses," she said, shaking off goose bumps and tucking her nose beneath her paw.

I didn't want to think about clawcons. I didn't want to remember the nightmarish ordeal but at the same time I wanted the others to know what they look like in the event they should encounter one.

"So – how does this work, again?" I asked, pointing to the enormous *T-View*.

"Oh. It's *very* complicated," said Sarabella, rolling her eyes. "Close your eyes and imagine whatever you want to see on the big screen, but wait…"

She removed the lid from a small woven basket on the coffee table and pulled out a silver ball the size of a golf ball. She held it high for all to see.

"…you have to hold this *thought nub* while visualizing otherwise thoughts of those around you compete for airtime. It can get quite confusing."

"Oh – it's sort of like a talking stick – only for thinking," said Garby, amused.

Sarabella had never heard of a talking stick so I explained that a talking stick is used when a group of people are together and each one takes an uninterrupted turn sharing. The stick is passed from person to person. Only the person holding the stick can talk.

"Yes, then. I suppose that's a decent comparison," said Sarabella placing the nub in the palm of my hand.

It felt cold and heavy, especially for how small it is. As I wrapped my fingers around its smooth surface I could hear it hum ever so quietly. I closed my eyes and thought about clawcons. Within seconds a scene from my nightmare appeared on the *T-View*.

"Wow! These *T-Views* are awesome. Those birds are mammoth – and scary-looking. Look at that. That's you right there," said Garby, running up to the screen and pointing at the image of me. "You mean one of these guys actually spoke?"

"It was more like – I heard its thoughts," I said.

"This can't be real. It was just a bad dream," said Garby.

"Unfortunately – it's very real. The upcoming abductions were predicted by Priscilla Omena," said Sarabella.

"Who's Priscilla Omena?" asked Penelope.

"The most renowned interdimensional psychic ever – never been mistaken."

"Oh – come on. It's just a prediction. Everyone makes mistakes," said Garby.

Sarabella laughed hysterically.

"It's just a bad dream. It's just a prediction. Yesterday you said it was just a vest and you nearly killed yourself without one."

She had a point and I was beginning to think she was a lot smarter than I'd first assumed.

"This is *terrible* news. What should we do?" asked Penelope, on the edge of tears.

"The only thing we can do. Be aware of our thoughts at all times and learn how to fly," I said, handing her a small package of tissue from my duffel bag.

"We're just a bunch of Earthlings," said Garby. "I'm from Pennsylvania – the land of *coal miners* and *Quakers*. We're no superheroes. We can't defend ourselves against this guy's powers."

" You're sifters," corrected Sarabella.

"Right. Great. We're on Horrible's abduction list. None of us can fly. We have what – twenty-seven more days of training vests? There's no way we'll be ready for this attack. We're sitting pigeons – waiting ducks."

"Backwards – I – I think you got that backwards," mumbled Penelope.

"Would you like to go back?" asked Sarabella.

"Back where?" asked Garby.

"Home. You can return anytime you'd like."

Each of us looked at the other gravely. After a long minute we all shook our heads, *no*. I have to admit I considered it but I soon realized I had no interest in returning. For the first time in my life I felt like I had an opportunity to do something that mattered.

"Then everyone *please* stop your whining. You chose to be here and you choose to stay. I suggest you focus your energy and create the reality you want."

"Hypothetically speaking – if Horrible knocked down our door right now – how do you suggest we protect ourselves? Do we just find a better feeling thought and he goes away? Is that how this works?" asked Garby, tossing his hands in the air.

"His name is *Orable* not *Horrible* – and all I can tell you is that we attract what we think about. Worrying is the habit of attracting the unwanted," said Sarabella.

"This is a conundrum, isn't it?" asked Garby, trying to catch a Fickle chip with his toes.

Sarabella excused herself. She ran across the living room.

"Hmm – maybe I should start drinking some of that crater water," said Garby as he watched her effortlessly soar out the front door.

The remainder of the evening was spent watching thoughtcasts of previous tournaments on the *T-View*. I was grateful for the small couch because it gave me an excuse to sit close to Penelope. We each took turns holding the *thought nub* and images on the *T-View* shifted between our thoughts. All eyes latched on to players representing our assigned positions. Penelope followed the airators, I followed the stabilizer, and Garby followed the satiator.

"Holy Fickle chips, Levi! The stabilizer never gets to rest," said Garby dramatically.

"Thanks for pointing that out, Garb," I said smiling at Penelope as I grabbed the thought nub.

"Look at that satiator, will you!" I teased, my voice filled with dread. "Boy – does he have the pressure on him. Team members drop like *flies* if he doesn't get to them in time. Most loses seem to be blamed on a lousy satiator."

Garby seized the nub. I snatched it away, again.

Back and forth went thoughtcasts between close-ups of the satiator and stabilizer.

"Will you guys *stop* it!" pleaded Penelope, from where she sat squished between us.

Garby and I laughed.

"I'm glad I don't have a position with your levels of responsibility," said Penelope, pausing the *T-View* just as the airator was about to be sucked into a bluyole.

"What are you talking about? You provide oxygen. I'd say that comes with a high level of responsibility."

I couldn't have agreed more. Penelope blushed.

The three of us watched tournaments until we could no longer keep our eyes open. Once Penelope fell asleep Garby and I went off to our rooms, but first I covered her with a fluffy blue climate-controlled blanket I found in the hall closet. I locked the front door, blew out candles, and dimmed lights. She rolled over with a smile. Beautiful thoughts danced through my head. I wrote them in my journal. They required no correction. Penelope was the best feeling thought I'd had all day.

CHAPTER SIXTEEN

THE ENCHANTED CUPCAKE

The following morning we awakened to a knock on the front door. It was Sarabella. Brushing away a large clump of lilasuckle vines that hugged the stone cottage she peeked in the bay window and knocked vigorously on the glass.

"Good morning! Rise and shine. There's a whole dimension out there waiting to be enlightened with your thoughts!" she yelled through the glass.

Penelope rose from the couch to let her in. The large circular wooden door creaked open. Yawning, she invited her in.

Sarabella made her way to the door careful not to step in the vibrant, overflowing flower bed.

Garby and I padded down the hallway from our bedrooms and seated ourselves beside Penelope on the couch. Alphia slept in on the back porch.

Sarabella yanked on a long, thick rope and up went the blinds. Sunlight scattered tiny rainbows across the room through beveled glass.

Garby put sunglasses on and headed to the kitchen where he

made a lot of noise. He returned with four glasses of bright burgundy juice and handed one to each of us.

"Carrot juice with kale, parsley, apple, turmeric, beet and a bit of garlic. All organic. I'm on a cleanse."

"Where'd you get all that organic produce?" asked Penelope.

"Didn't you read the instructions on the refrigerator door? It works sort'a like how duffel bags work. You think about what you want and – well, it…"

" – it provides you with what your body needs," interjected Sarabella happily.

"Yeah – it wasn't *exactly* what I wanted but it's surprisingly tasty."

After we drank our nutritious breakfast we got dressed and walked to the *Enchanted Cupcake Café*, a popular stop on the way to *Morblid's Museum* where we would attend our first *History of Grey Thought & Antagonistic Artifacts* class.

As we strolled down crooked paths framed with thick foliage in vibrant shades of green and blue Penelope pointed playfully at my feet.

"I will always chose comfort over fashion," I sang, dancing across the path in front of her in my climate controlled slippers.

She laughed and danced beside me.

When we arrived at the café the first thing I noticed was a bookshelf. On that bookshelf sat several copies of the familiar, and ungodly bright yellow book, *Mastering the M-Field Through Solarshay* by Maya Solarshay.

"She said it was everywhere, didn't she?" asked Garby, picking up a copy and leafing through it. We headed to a table in the far corner.

"Wait a sec," said Garby, searching his pockets. I don't have any money. Even if I did it probably wouldn't be any good here. How do we pay for stuff?"

"I almost forgot. Here are your *Requisite* cards for purchases," said Sarabella, pulling three shimmering violet-purple cards from her shoulder pouch.

"They look like credit cards. This one has my name on it. What's the limit?" asked Garby, flipping the card over and back again.

"No limit. These are designed specifically for sifters participating in the *Selective Thought Studies* program."

"No kidding!" beamed Garby, "I could get used to this. This is a *very* generous dimension.

"You may use your *Requisite* card to purchase food while dining out – household items – luxuries – or whatever you believe will make you happiest."

"So, the card – it never runs out?" I asked.

"That's correct."

"And, we don't have to pay it back?" asked Penelope.

"No. But – there is one, teeny, tiny catch."

"I knew it. I knew there had to be a catch. You know what they say – if it seems too good to be true," said Garby, deflated.

"The limit doubles daily and you have to spend your limit every day." Sarabella pointed to the lower right hand corner of the card.

"Right there – see? It says you have twenty dollars."

"What if we don't spend our limit every day?"

"The card reboots and begins again at twenty dollars."

"Wait. What? It forces us to spend money we don't have to earn – or pay back? That's the catch?" asked Garby.

"Precisely."

"So – can we save it?" asked Penelope.

"No saving. Just spending," said Sarabella. "It's part of your abundance training."

"No doubt I'm getting an A+ in abundance training. Spending money is one of my *best* skills," said Garby. "Not that I've had much practice."

"It's a lot harder than you think. I mean – spending huge amounts of money every day," said Sarabella.

"Not for me. It has always been my dream to be really, really, *really* rich!" admitted Garby.

"I'm pretty sure that's everyone's dream Garby," I said, pulling out a chair for Penelope and then taking a seat of my own. "And speaking of dreams that reminds me – I had a dream last night. I can't remember all the details but it was about a girl and a book she wrote. She was a prisoner of Orable's. Her book went missing. Everyone was trying to find it. She knew secrets about Orable – his thoughts – his motivations – his plans – as if she were inside his head."

"Good story – but it was just a dream," said Garby.

"There you go, again. *Just* a vest. *Just* a prediction. *Just* a dream. You really are *clueless* as to how things work here – aren't you? Even after what you've experienced so far." Sarabella shook her head disappointedly.

"Are you saying the book he dreamed about is real?" asked Garby skeptically, pulling a menu from between the crystal napkin holder and frosting dispenser in the center of the table.

Garby, Penelope and I exchanged questioning glances before

settling in on Sarabella.

"Oh, you'd like to hear from the crater-water-drinking-ditz now would you?" she asked, stuffing a curly straw with chocolate chips she'd plucked from her muffin. "Fine. Yes. The book exists."

"I knew it. I knew it!" I shouted, grabbing a white cupcake with green icing and purple sprinkles from a tray floating beside the table.

Sarabella snatched it from me at once.

"We are at the *Enchanted Cupcake Café*. Have you read the ingredients?" she asked urgently. "One should always read the ingredients before putting anything in one's mouth," she cautioned, pointing to the word "WARNING" printed in bold red letters across the top of the menu.

Cupcakes are pretty innocuous, or so I thought. I baked them with my mom a few times. Never imagined a little flour, sugar, baking soda, butter and milk could be dangerous enough to warrant a warning. I read it nonetheless.

WARNING: Choose your cupcakes wisely. There are two types: regular and extraordinary. While made from all-natural, organic ingredients and infused with the daily recommended allowance of all vitamins, minerals and nutrients, some cupcakes contain ingredients that are *unpredictable* in affect. Extraordinary cupcakes may open portals to other dimensions, alter one's physical appearance, and the list goes on. We do not recommend consuming extraordinary cupcakes: before class, prior to operating an auraplane, if you'd like to remain in the dimension, or anytime you need to get anything mundane accomplished.

"Now – do you understand?" she asked, handing me a brown cupcake with chocolate frosting and pink sprinkles. "Here – eat this one. Plain ole chocolate. We can try the extraordinary kind another day. We haven't much time before class. You want to know about the book – I'd like to tell you about it."

"Right," I said, devouring my *ordinary* cupcake. "So – it really does exist and it really does contain useful information?" I asked, sipping organic vanilla almond milk from a frosty mug.

"Yes it *really* does – and yes, it *really* does. Unfortunately, it's also *really* lost."

When she said this I realized that everything in my dream must be accurate but thought it best not to share it in its entirety just yet.

"We should look for this book," suggested Penelope.

"Hope is good," said Sarabella, scraping frosting with a hot pink painted fingernail. "But, many have tried and failed."

"We're in a dimension full of telepaths. What about that Priscilla Omena lady you told us about last night? She's a psychic. Can't she help?" I asked.

"It's not that simple. Look at your class syllabus. You had this dream because you're intuitive. On a subconscious level you knew it would be the topic of today's class."

We scrambled to find our schedules as Sarabella plucked chocolate chips from her muffin.

Penelope found hers first and tore apart an ordinary berry muffin, iced with pale pink frosting, while scanning it.

"Look – she's right," said Garby. "It says right here our first class this afternoon is about a missing book. And, look at that will you – the book's title is – *A Mender's Mind, by Agrestalia Mender.*

My heartbeat quickened at hearing the name – Agrestalia. It was the name of the girl who had come to me in my dream.

"We *need* to find this book so we can free the sifters," I said, looking at Garby.

"*We?* asked Garby, fidgeting with a cupcake. "You mean – YOU. And honestly, Levi, we don't even know them. Maybe they're happy with Orable. We should just leave well enough alone."

"You can't mean that. They're being held against their will, locked up – told what they can, and cannot, think?" I snapped.

"Hmm – we spent ten years like that. It's called school," said Garby, half-joking.

Penelope and I tilted our heads in thought.

"I don't have to know them to want to help them. Truth is none of us knows what they're being forced to endure. If you were one of them wouldn't you want someone trying to free you?"

Garby reluctantly agreed that this was an excellent point as did the others.

When it was time to leave we argued over who was going to pay the bill, each of us thrilled about our newly acquired abundance.

CHAPTER SEVENTEEN

OBSESSIONS

The four of us arrived outside the museum's front gate about fifteen minutes early for class with dozens of enchanted cupcakes stuffed inside our duffel bags.

I grabbed the cold, rusted bars of the entrance gate intending to jump over the monstrous thing but Penelope kicked it open as I leapt. I fell hard.

"Oh – no! So sorry! I didn't know you were going to jump!" Flushing with embarrassment she tossed her duffel bag on the lawn and ran over to help me up.

"It's ok," I offered, brushing dirt from my knees and soaking in the softness of her touch.

"Klutz," came a small, squeaky voice from the grass.

I looked at Penelope. I had to think twice about it but was sure she hadn't just called me a *klutz*. "Did you hear that?" I asked.

"Hear what?" she asked, pushing cords of silky hair behind her ears.

"Who said that?" I shouted. I spun around. My eyes raked every inch of the manicured lawn.

173

"Who said that?" came a tiny mocking voice. "I said that *lead* foot. Me. Yoo-hoo! Over here!"

"Now – *that* I heard," said Penelope, her eyes darting here and there.

"Me, too," said Garby.

Sarabella sat on the sidewalk smoothing the heels of her feet with a sheet of sandpaper she borrowed from Hemp's workbench last visit. She couldn't have been more disinterested.

Penelope and I spun in opposite directions, our backs pressed together.

"Over here *stupid*," called the voice. It sounded similar to the voice I'd heard at the crater – the voice that had told me not to drink the water. It, too, had called me stupid.

A patch of lilasuckle grass beside Garby's foot shook violently. A tiny creature poked its head out from between blue blades of grass. Standing in the center of a large flower resembling a sunflower, except that it was pink with a much shorter and thicker stem, was a tiny green bug with orange wings and turquoise hair. It stood the same way superheroes stand when posing for paparazzi. Its hands were propped on tiny hips; its chest puffed proudly and its chin angled skyward. The purple velvety scarf draped around its neck caught in a vine causing it to gag and cough.

"What are you looking at?" it asked in a hard-hitting voice. It took a clumsy step toward me and nearly choked itself with its scarf.

I was speechless.

"Never seen a *think bug* before? Are you from Earth – or somewhere equally uninformed?" asked the bug bitingly.

"Yes, I am. Actually – we all are." I was surprised it knew about Earth.

"So – what's a stink bug?" asked Garby, making a curious face at the bug.

"No. No. NO!" shrieked the bug, as it stomped madly through the flower. It's scarf now severely tangled in the vine and its feet covered with fuzzy pink pollen.

"I am not a stink bug. I am a think bug. Think. Think. THINK! It figures you're from *Earth*. Earth folks are the only *aliens* with a complete disregard for *any* life form other than their own – and often – *not even their own*. Do you see this grass? DO YOU?" it roared, without allowing us time to respond. "It's FULL of life. And you just roll around in it like you don't even care. You nearly KILLED me!" it yelled caustically, pointing to its tangled scarf and twitching wing.

I apologized as I reached over and untangled its scarf. All the while it glared skeptically at me. I had a feeling it considered saying *thank you* but thought better of it.

"Haven't you heard of paths, walkways, or sidewalks? They're made for *morons* like you who cannot fly."

"What's your problem?" snapped Garby, taking a step toward the bug. "Stop yelling at my friend. He fell down for crying out loud."

"Who asked you – FAT BOY?" said the bug brazenly.

"Fat boy? Fat boy!" screeched Garby, his eyes bulging with indignation.

The bug zipped across the field. Garby zipped after him.

"You can't catch a think bug – STUPID!" yelled the bug right before it appeared that Garby had captured it in cupped hands.

"So – no one can catch a *stink bug,* huh?" whispered Garby, pressing his hands together to secure his capture. He tried to reason with his miniature prisoner.

"Don't you think you're too small to be such a bully?"

When the think bug didn't answer Garby opened his hands to steal a peek. Excitement drained from his face at seeing the bug wasn't there.

"It's okay, Garby," I offered. "You probably would've squashed the little guy anyway."

"Well – that *was* the point," whined Garby, searching desperately for the bug.

"Can't catch a think bug," sang the little bug harassingly, as it buzzed through Garby's hair.

Hovering just out of Garby's reach it goaded, "The four of you are on your way to class. One of you obsessed with food, another with crater water, a third with Levi – the fourth with finding a book." It then laughed hysterically as it tumbled through the air.

Each of us looked at the other. The think bug had our undivided attention.

"I know where the book is – and you don't. Ha, ha, de, ha," it sang, childishly. The bug made a rude gesture at Garby then vanished.

"Twisted bug," muttered Garby, straightening his t-shirt.

"Twisted – but smart," I added, searching through flowers for him.

"Maybe not so smart. Maybe just nosey. Probably been following us around listening to our thoughts," complained Garby.

"Maybe," I said.

Not wanting to be late for class the four of us gave up the search and made our way toward the entrance of *Morblid's Museum* with Garby mumbling the entire way.

The building was definitely more interesting than *Ordin Acres High School* and it felt much less prison-like without all the bars on the windows. As I admired the architecture my thoughts returned to the words of the think bug. It was obvious it was referring to Garby as the one obsessed with food, Sarabella as the one obsessed with crater water and me as the one obsessed with finding the book. Although, until this moment I hadn't realized it was an obsession. The only shocker was that the bug said Penelope was obsessed with me. I had no idea but I didn't mind this at all.

Penelope was the first to make it to the top of the crooked museum stairs, her face flushed with what I assumed was embarrassment at her crush on me being exposed. She reached out to open the door and something terrible happened. She let out an ear piercing scream. I ran up the stairs to help her but it was too late.

CHAPTER EIGHTEEN

ANTAGONISTIC ARTIFACTS

P enelope screamed a second time. Instead of her grabbing the doorknob, the doorknob had grabbed her. Six long furry fingers, longer and hairier than tarantula legs, wrapped themselves around her hand, twisted her arm and dragged her inside before slamming the door.

Garby and I rushed the door. There was a lot of pleading and struggling from behind it.

"Penelope – you alright?" I yelled, my fist pounding thick elder wood panels.

There was a large hole in the place where the doorknob should have been. When I bent to peek through it I felt stabbing sensations across my forehead. Dozens of razor-sharp fibers, like cactus spines, embedded themselves deeply into my skin. I tried to pull some of them out but I just kept stabbing myself with the others.

"Let her go right now – *whatever* you are!" demanded Garby. He turned to look at me and as he did I saw fright in his eyes. "What are all those things in your forehead?" he asked worriedly.

"Just get the door open!"

Garby and I took turns rushing the door. There were periods when we stood together kicking until we could kick no more. Flushed, dripping with sweat and winded, I was relieved to hear the raspy voice and encroaching footsteps from inside the museum.

"Stop scaring our new students, Bonkrod. Release her...at once."

"She grabbed me first," said a second, surly voice.

The door squeaked open eerily. Out of the darkness appeared the silhouette of a stout man in tattered boots.

I gasped as Morblid, the owner of *Morblid's Museum for the Grey Arts*, appeared in the doorway. Enormous purple eyes with green pupils pierced the air. Blood pulsed through serpentine veins beneath ashen grey skin. Short wiry hair jutted out in every direction giving the appearance of his having had too many cups of coffee.

Penelope stood beside me trembling, a look of terror stuck on her pale face. She had several scratches on her hand from where Bonkrod grabbed her.

"I apologize for the unfortunate...incident," offered Morblid, raising his eyes to meet mine. "Welcome. Do come in."

Morblid removed a screwdriver from a tool belt tied around his waist. He unscrewed Bonkrod from the door, his movements slow and deliberate.

"You've just been demoted to back door doorknob until you learn to be a bit more welcoming and..." said Morblid, tossing Bonkrod into a hemp sack. He tied the string in a double knot and tossed it over his shoulder. The sack wriggled and Bonkrod complained.

"They're early for class. I thought they were thieves! Let me out of here you bloodless sack of skin," protested Bonkrod, grabbing

Morblid's grey t-shirt through the woven sack.

"This is what my museum is all about," said Morblid proudly, as he held the sack high in the air for all to see.

"Over the years I've collected enchanted artifacts from twelve dimensions. Most are quite…unpredictable. But their behavior tends to improve over time with…" he said, placing the sack on a rocking chair beside the door. The chair rocked erratically across the marble floor. It was obvious that Bonkrod was having a tantrum. Morblid urged him to take deep breaths and regain his composure.

Bonkrod yelled something incomprehensible.

Morblid apologized to Penelope and the others for his artifact's rude behavior.

Bonkrod screamed, "I'm NOT sorry. Your guests should learn to knock – or ring a bell. You don't just go up to someone's museum and grab the doorknob! It's rude."

"I hate to admit it – but he has a point," mouthed Garby.

Penelope and I tossed Garby looks of disdain.

"It's a museum – not someone's house – we're students here," whispered Penelope.

As though in slow motion, Morblid turned and plucked the hairs from my forehead with pliers. I felt warmth drip down the middle of my nose. Morblid placed the hairs in a silver pill box and slid it inside his jacket pocket. He then turned toward Penelope and using the same pliers extracted several of Bonkrod's hairs which stuck out like porcupine quills from her hand. He tossed them in the trash. There were still a few stubborn hairs that refused to be plucked.

"They'll dissolve on their own in just a few minutes, if…" said

Morblid, holding Penelope's hand in his.

I leaned in toward him waiting for the next word but it never came. I wondered if anyone else had noticed Morblid's tendency to not complete sentences.

"If what?" I asked impatiently.

"No if – but…" said Morblid, tossing me a questioning look.

I wanted to grab him and squeeze the next word from him.

"Come in. Come in please – and do…" he said, closing the front door.

"Garby. Doesn't that drive you crazy? Have you noticed he doesn't finish?"

"Doesn't finish what?"

"Exactly!" I said. "I'll never be able to sit through an entire class with this guy."

"Write that in your journal," said Garby, winking.

"Oh. Thanks a lot. That's helpful," I said sarcastically.

"Do come…this way," said Morblid, grabbing Bonkrod's sack from the rocking chair and motioning for us to follow him.

Straining to see through darkness my eyes were drawn to multicolored slivers of light pouring into the room through stained glass windows. As my eyes adjusted I saw large iron-barred display cases scattered across the lobby and against walls. Seemingly endless hallways stretched from the lobby like twisted trails through a foreboding forest. The air smelled musty. It weighed heavily upon my chest.

As I followed Morblid I heard ticking and clinking sounds coming from a display case on my right, moaning and groaning from another on my left. Large metallic contraptions hung from the walls. Crooked shadows crawled unnervingly across the ceiling. I flinched as flashes of light and glowing orbs bounced between floor and walls. Inside the orbs were faces; some laughed, some cried, others screamed.

Goosebumps scuttled up the back of my neck sending an icy explosion through my body. The sound of my slippers flopping against the cold marble floor echoed around me. Suddenly overcome with nausea I realized it was the same way I'd felt during an eighth grade field trip to the *Museum of Man* while walking through the *Exhibit of Torture and Intolerance.*

"Did you see the faces inside those bubbles?" I whispered to Garby.

"Yes – they're *the* most bizarre things I've ever seen."

Garby, Penelope and I huddled as we followed Morblid.

"Figures," said Garby, urging us to look at Sarabella who had stopped to converse with one of the orbs.

Penelope and I found this no more, or less, shocking than the myriad of strange and unusual things that were transpiring all around us.

Morblid's gait was lopsided. One of his legs appeared at least four inches shorter than the other. He stopped abruptly, opened a small circular door and motioned for us to follow him. He was the only one who didn't have to duck to enter the classroom.

"Take a seat wherever you'd like. The best learning takes place when one is…comfortable."

I felt incredibly satisfied at hearing Morblid complete a sentence.

Morblid's classroom was unlike any I'd ever seen. Anticipating low ceilings based on the size of the door I was pleasantly surprised to find the room had high ceilings. Leathery, grey couches arranged in a circle, with matching pillows and plush foot stools created a feeling of unity and comfort. Randomly scattered desks, reminiscent of those from classrooms on Earth, added a familiar but uncomfortable feeling. We unanimously preferred Ceresian classroom décor.

Garby, Sarabella, Penelope, and I plopped down beside one another and elevated our feet on stools.

"This is how school should be," said Garby, "Except - without all those creepy things floating around the lobby and without those moaning things in cages. And – definitely without Bonkrod."

I nodded my agreement as I turned to see several classmates arrive. I felt relieved at not seeing Darvon Damos, Jr.

"My name is Morblid Gorman. I'll be your *History of Grey Thought & Antagonistic Artifacts* teacher," he said, writing at snail's pace on the chalkboard. "The purpose of this class is to help you understand the *origin* and *significance* of grey thought. Grey thought forms are unfortunately the most common. My museum is *full* of antagonistic artifacts I've collected over the years. Each and every one of them exists as a result of grey thought – and some are quite moody. The *Selective Thought Studies* program does not encourage grey thought. We simply spread awareness of its subtle intrusion and disempowering effect upon you. We hope your blossoming awareness will inspire you to choose thoughts of other shades and higher vibrations."

Pointing to a shelf that spanned the entire length of a wall, floor to ceiling, he announced, "There on shelf #3 sit fifty copies of my book – and your new best friend – *The Little Book of Pink & Purple Thoughts*.

He handed out copies.

"All thoughts have a vibration. Grey thoughts are of a low vibration. Pink and purple thoughts are of a higher vibration. Grey thoughts drain the spirit – weigh it down with guilt and fear. Pink and purple thoughts inflate it with hope, love and joy."

Morblid pointed out the fact that in most dimensions a lot of time and energy is spent developing muscle and focused upon external beauty while little to no time is spent developing the power of the mind.

"My book is a tool designed to help you defend yourself against the energetic drain of grey thought energy."

He grabbed a chunk of pink chalk and wrote on the chalkboard:

A Mender's Mind

By

Agrestalia Mender

Garby elbowed me. My heart beat faster at seeing this.

"I'll begin today's class by exposing you to what is – in my opinion – one of the most influential non-grey thought artifacts of our…time."

Morblid rolled a squeaky grey cart to the center of the room beside his desk. On the cart was a toaster-sized display case. He removed the sparkling purple cloth draped over it.

"This is also a tool designed to help you defend yourself against the energetic drain of grey thought energy. The only problem is that the original is… missing. This is a replica," he said, pointing to where a book sat encased in a block of material resembling Plexiglas.

"The original was once briefly in our possession but vanished before we had the opportunity to read it. In short –," began Morblid, taking a seat on his desktop, " – the original holds secrets to unlocking the power of…the mind. Its secrets – once revealed – will render Orable powerless. It is best that no one touches it. Our local psychic, Priscilla Omena, is working on telepathically recreating its original content. Vibratory sensations of others could interfere with her…perception."

Morblid picked up a framed photograph from his desk and held it high for all to see.

"Priscilla's working on a top-secret case in Dimension 12. Otherwise, she would have joined us. Lovely, isn't she?" Morblid beamed as he gazed adoringly at her image.

Priscilla's smile was intoxicating. Her deeply set ocean blue eyes, mesmerizing. One could almost hear the tinkling of what must have been hundreds of tiny bells and chimes sewn around the neckline of her dress.

On the couch behind me sat Shane Fargone scratching facial stubble. Due to an overactive metabolism he appeared lost in jeans and t-shirt several sizes too large.

"What could happen if someone touches it?" he asked, stuttering.

Morblid peered worriedly over black and white zebra-striped spectacles as he returned the photograph to his desk.

"This would depend on *who* touches it – the position of the moons at the moment it is touched – the *intent* with which it is touched, and…"

And that is all he said.

"There he goes again," I griped, cracking my knuckles without realizing.

Morblid resumed speaking.

"Vibrationally, it would disrupt the flow of information from the ethereal source. Who knows what would end up coming in as a result of the energy of the one who touches it. There are endless possible scenarios – most of which would be…unpleasant."

Morblid stood eyeing the class curiously. No sooner had he opened his mouth to speak than there was an explosion outside the classroom door. Smoke trickled in through cracks in stone walls. A gooey substance flooded the floor. Garby jumped onto the couch. I joined him but only after I felt something warm and wet fill my slippers. Whatever it was smelled of vanilla and reminded me of my great grandmother's house.

By now, many of the others had tried to climb up on the couch with Garby and me but their feet were stuck in hardening goop. Mass panic brewed. Lights flickered and went out plunging the room into darkness.

"Today's not *the abduction* – is it?" asked Garby, quivering.

"It's not supposed to happen for another nine days," I said, wondering if the clawcons had lied. I grabbed my wrist to look at the face of my ESPY watch but my wrist was bare. An image of it sitting on the dresser beside my bed flashed through my head.

"Great," I complained, from where I stood sinking into the couch cushion in the dark.

Feeling vulnerable and angry at my forgetfulness I sat in the dark listening to the urgent complaints of classmates. Waiting for lights to come on I felt icy fingers wrap themselves around my head. It felt as if a dam broke inside my mind. I was drowning in my worst fears. I tried to open my mouth to scream but it was no use.

CHAPTER NINETEEN

TO TOUCH OR NOT TO TOUCH

Melted candle wax rushed the museum floor. In the hallway a six-foot-tall candle with a two-foot-long wick sputtered smoke and ash across the lobby. Two suns shone through a freshly burned hole in the ceiling. Red emergency lights flashed. A siren wailed. Coughing and grumbling sounds from artifacts permeated smoky air. Metal clanked against metal and glass shattered. Screaming orbs bounced between walls. Display cases toppled.

Inside the windowless classroom lights continued to flicker. Flashes of fright-filled faces blinked in and out of darkness. I looked around to see who had grabbed me but saw only flashes of classmates struggling to free themselves from wax.

"Was that you, Garby?" I asked frantically.

"Was what me?"

When the lights stabilized I intuitively knew it wasn't Garby or any of my classmates who'd grbbed me. As I rubbed the chill from my neck I discovered a tatty grey glove on my lap. The initials V.S. were embroidered on its front side. I stuffed it into my jacket pocket not wanting anyone – especially Sarabella – to see it. I was 99.9% sure it belonged to the boy on the parasike. *What would have happened if the lights hadn't come on when they had? Should I tell Morblid? Was that a failed abduction?*

Initially, I considered searching the museum but assumed that whoever had done this would be long gone. Besides, there were more pressing matters at hand. Candle wax continued to flood the room and the museum was on fire.

I grabbed a flickerlight from Morblid's storage cabinet. I had spotted them at the beginning of class and wanted to be prepared in the event the lights went out again. Although I'd never used one they seemed simple enough. I recalled Hemp's instructions. *Hold it and visualize bright light.* I did. It worked.

Morblid peeked inside the classroom.

"The fire is under control. Remain calm and stay put," he instructed, then scurried down the hallway.

I stared at the little book. It looked so vulnerable sitting there. *If Morblid doesn't want anyone to touch it why did he remove the lid? Should I, or shouldn't I touch it? What's the worst that can happen?*

An inexplicable compulsion washed over me the moment I saw it - like obsession at first sight. If I could be sure that touching it would be helpful I wouldn't have hesitated. But a slew of possible catastrophic scenarios flooded my mind. I weighed the consequences. There were too many unknown factors to make a logical decision. I tried to stop myself but curiosity was winning. *Is anyone watching?*

Looking aroud I saw classmates dangling from bookshelves while others sat on chairs they'd piled on desktops. All were busy discussing options. It seemed that everyone was too preoccupied to notice my next move.

Hopping across the ocean of wax I landed on Morblid's desktop beside the display case. I reached inside and touched the book. No sooner had I done this than Morblid entered the room coughing, covered in soot. I practically flew from the desktop to the couch, my palms now cold and clammy. *That was close.*

Morblid helped a few bookshelf-danglers find more comfortable locations then climbed up on his desk and announced, "I'll clean this mess up later. Feet up until the wax…hardens. For those of you already stuck please extract your feet from your shoes. I'll dig shoes out…this evening." He blew his nose ferociously into a tissue and squatted. As he looked at the book in the display case his face scrunched into a perfect picture of confusion. He shot a questioning, horrified look across the room. His eyes passed over each of us the way a scanner scans purchases at a store.

In an attempt to avoid Morblid's laser-like glare I bent to assist a classmate. Before my head resurfaced he announced, "I'll need help cleaning up after class…Levi."

My heart filled with dread.

"Okay," I said, regretfully.

CHAPTER TWENTY

THE ABDUCTION

I would have to wait until the end of class to know for sure whether or not Morblid knew I touched the book - but I assumed he did. He continued teaching in spite of the wax which by now had hardened enough to walk on.

"Sorry about all the commotion," he said, standing atop his desk. "One never knows what to expect with a lobby full of grey-thinking artifacts."

Paging through lesson plans he announced, "Since we're short on time I'll summarize."

He paced three stunted steps across the desktop chewing on the arm of his eyeglasses.

"Orable will block all attempts to find the missing text. The fewer empowered minds there are in the dimension, the happier he'll be. Until which time the book is found and Agrestalia's secrets revealed, most minds will remain obedient masses of...tissue."

"Do you think it's possible for someone to find the book," asked Penelope, twirling a glittering pink pencil between her fingers.

"Possible – yes. Likely – no. Death is, unfortunately, a probable fate of any who dare seek it. Most are unwilling to assume such…risk."

"We're all going to die anyway. May as well be with purpose," I mumbled beneath my breath.

Morblid's eyes zoomed in on me the way a camera lens zooms in on a brilliant scene. The timekeeper changed positions indicating class was over. Everyone exited except me.

The afterschool experience was nothing like I'd anticipated. There was no punishment or ridicule. Instead, I found Morblid to be as genuinely interested in learning about me as I was in learning about the missing book.

"Chocolate covered pyropede?" asked Morblid, offering me something that looked like chocolate except that it had twelve legs, six on either side.

"No. No thank you. Just brushed," I lied, thinking that based on its appearance, whatever it was must taste, at best, worse than dreadful.

I gagged as I watched Morblid pop one into his mouth. There were horrible cracking and crunching sounds as he chewed. I grew queasy at imagining the insect's skeleton being crushed beneath the pressure of his jaw.

Morblid wasted no time getting to the point.

"You touched the book, Levi. Are *you* aware that *I'm* aware that you touched the book?" he asked, taking a silver toothpick to his chocolate-tinted, fang-like teeth.

"I wasn't until now."

"Hmm. Are you aware that you *didn't* touch the book?" asked Morblid.

I was beyond confused and couldn't help wondering what kind of game Morblid was playing.

"Truth is, Morblid – I did. I *did* touch the book."

Morblid walked over to the bookshelf and returned with a book identical to the one on display. It, too, was encased in a block of material similar to Plexiglas.

"No, Levi. You *didn't* touch the book. Do you think I'd be fool enough to tempt twenty overly curious sifters with the real thing?"

"I didn't touch the book?"

"No. You touched a replica."

"I touched a replica – of a replica?"

Morblid nodded.

"Wow. What a relief. I regretted touching it as soon as I had – you know?"

"I know," said Morblid, placing the real replica on the table.

"Have all your curiosities about the book been…quenched?"

"No. No they haven't. I don't understand why the real book is so difficult to locate," I said squirming, as I watched him mercilessly devour another pyropede. "I mean – there are telepaths everywhere. Why can't someone find it?" I stared at Morblid anxious to hear his response.

He stared back. "If only it were that…simple."

"I think I know where it is – sort of," I offered.

Morblid slid his eyeglasses down his nose then removed them with a snap. "How could you possibly know this?"

"I had a dream."

I shared my dream with Morblid. I told him that in my dream a girl identified herself as Agrestalia and informed me that her book is in an attic in another dimension.

"Really? What did she look like?" asked Morblid.

I didn't know what she looked like because I'd only seen her from the back as she sat writing in a room devoid of color.

Morblid pulled a chair from beneath an elongated table beside the bookshelves. He tapped it several times. "Have a seat, Levi." He then got a chair for himself and proceeded to interrogate me.

Specifically, Morblid inquired about my dreams. He asked how many I'd had, how often I have them, when they started, and what percentage of them come to pass. Based on my answers Morblid concluded that my dreams are forecasts.

"So – Agrestalia came to you in a dream and told you the book is in an attic in another dimension?"

I nodded.

"It couldn't have been Agrestalia – because of the thought-block."

I tilted my head questioningly.

"Agrestalia's incredibly bright and highly intuitive. She's an enormous threat to Orable. She knows things about him that no one else knows so Orable placed a thought-block on her. He figured this would buy him enough time to find and destroy her book. If she speaks of its contents before the book is destroyed – or the incantation deactivated – she'll lose her ability to speak."

"That's messed up," I said.

"Couldn't have said it better myself," agreed Bonkrod, from where he sat still sacked on Morblid's desk.

Morblid and I looked questioningly at the sack.

"Agrestalia wouldn't risk losing her ability to speak. She has too much to say. So, the question is – who is pretending to be Agrestalia and wanting to communicate with you – and why?"

This new piece of information threw me into a deep state of contemplation. I had no clue who the girl in my dream could be or why she came to me. I was relieved when Morblid suggested I not concern myself with this missing piece for the time being.

"Sometimes in life we just don't know the answer – and that's ok." Morblid suggested that I focus instead on learning how to access parallel dimensions – a skill crucial to survival in Ceres – or anywhere for that matter.

"There are several ways one can access parallel dimensions, Levi. I will reveal these to you but you must promise not to attempt to access them without my approval. At least, until you complete solarshay training and are able to fly without the assistance of a vest."

I crossed my fingers beneath the table and promised.

"One can access parallel dimensions via the *Ethereal Revolving Doors,* through specially crafted vibrational funnels such as the one over the crater and..." said Morblid, walking toward a large grey metallic refrigerator. As he opened it a burst of chilly air wafted across the room. I shuddered at the sudden drop in temperature.

Morblid grabbed a small pink box from the third shelf, closed the door, and placed the box in the center of the table.

"And – what?" I asked, leaning so far forward that I nearly fell out of my chair.

"Cupcakes," said Morblid, removing the lid from the box.

"Cupcakes?" I repeated, wondering if Morblid suffered from short-term memory loss.

"I'd love a cupcake but what's the third way to access other dimensions?"

"Cupcakes," said Morblid, opening the box and removing a small pink cupcake with pale purple frosting. He placed it on the table before me.

"Ok – I'll have a cupcake."

"No," said Morblid, blocking my attempt to take it. "This is the third way to access parallel dimensions."

"Oh – right! The extraordinary kind," I said, smiling.

"Levi, extraordinary cupcakes pale in comparison to my little pink and purple commune cupcakes. These cupcakes take you wherever you want to go. It's just that…"

I waited for the next word. Inside my head I screamed – *it's just that what?*

"…returning from parallel dimensions *with* objects is a little tricky. Historically, there were only two manifestarians fortunate enough to possess such ability. Even if one were to locate the book, it would most likely spontaneously combust upon crossing and we'd all be left in the dark…forever more."

Morblid explained that Agrestalia had found a loophole in Orable's plan. Although Orable prohibited her from speaking about the book, he hadn't prohibited her from placing a *thought identifier* on the book. Thought identifiers determine whether or not something is in the proper hands. If it's not in the proper hands it registers the frequency of the thoughts of the unpermitted holder and switches hands. Since thought can only attract like thought, the object – in this case the book – somehow makes itself available to an individual with similar, lower vibrational propensities.

"Honestly, Levi, I'm of the opinion that this is a major flaw in her plan. There are several other ways she could have protected the book but she chose this one. She's very bright. I can only assume she has her reasons."

"I agree. It doesn't make sense. If it's already in the wrong hands, it just switches to another pair of wrong hands?"

"Precisely," said Morblid, rising and pushing his chair beneath the table.

I tried to make sense of Agrestalia's decision. I thought aloud.

"Well – if the book keeps switching hands no one would have enough time to read it – or destroy it – or do anything with it. They'd just know about it and always wonder what was inside it."

"You're right, Levi," gasped Mobert. "It's like she created an elusive literary hot potato. When finally it accidentally lands in the right hands…" began Morblid.

"It'll never *land* in the right hands, Morblid. It'll have to be *taken* from the wrong hands."

It was at this moment that something shifted inside me. I was now determined that I would be the one to do the taking.

Morblid peered knowingly at me over the rim of his eyeglasses.

"Yes – well – as long as *the taker* is properly prepared, Mr. Levy."

I gnawed a thumb nail.

Morblid walked around the room snapping his fingers while chanting, "*Mess recedemus. Mess recedemus. Mess recedemus.*"

Sections of wax spiraled into the air and vanished. The coat of soot on the walls turned into a glittery grey liquid that pooled and poured itself down the floor drain in the center of the room.

"Wow! Why didn't you do that earlier? You could've stopped the wax from flooding the room in the first place," I said, astonished by the paranormal cleanup.

"I could have, Levi. But, magic is largely...misunderstood. Menial demonstrations such as this only serve to further its misunderstanding."

Morblid continued to snap his fingers. As a result of his chanting, "*Foramen amplius. Foramen amplius. Foramen amplius,*" the hole in the ceiling repaired itself before my disbelieving eyes.

"Magic isn't always *obvious* – like visualizing something one day and getting it the next. One doesn't recognize these events as magical, but this is the most powerful magic of all. And it's all up here," he said, pointing to my head.

I wanted what Morblid has. I snapped my fingers several times trying to emulate him.

"Oh – the snapping doesn't do anything. It's just for dramatic effect," laughed Morblid, winking. "It's the intention. The belief. The focus." Morblid paused to stare at the timekeeper.

"Goodness, time flies when you're..."

He left the sentence unfinished and started another.

"I'll walk you home. I'm afraid my auraplane's at the station getting an overhaul."

"Why does everyone use auraplanes when they can fly?" I asked, tossing the strap of my duffel bag over my shoulder.

"Rather odd isn't it? Why do Earthlings drive cars when they can walk – or ride bikes? Thought propelling requires focus. Focus requires energy. Most seasoned thought sifters, shifters and manifestarians choose to save their energy for grander pursuits. Flying is a skill most reserved for emergencies."

The answer made sense to me. As we were leaving Morblid handed me a box with one commune cupcake inside it.

"When you feel a calling I'd like you to experiment. Go to the *Fields of Possibility* and locate the *Hag Stone*. It's one of many secured portals. Eat the cupcake – then walk through the portal with a destination clear in your mind. Just be sure to stay within our dimension. I cannot recommend you travel elsewhere until you can thought propel. You can take up to four friends with you on this dimension surfing adventure. Keep them closeby. They'll need to be within ten feet of you to experience the same effects as you. The journey will last about an hour. You'll automatically return to your original location when the time's up. Perhaps you and your friends can go to the crater for a midnight swim. Consider this an extra credit assignment."

"Wow! Really? Thank you, Morblid. I can't wait to try this," I said, carefully stashing the cupcake inside my duffel bag.

After I helped Morblid cover artifacts and lock doors and windows we headed to Sifter's Village. Along the way we admired the two blue moons and talked about the chocolate-covered pyropede factory Morblid planned to open. I was relieved to learn that the crunching I'd heard was crispy rice filling and not insect exoskeleton. I pretended to enjoy the rest of our conversation but my mind was preoccupied with the missing book.

When we arrived at my cottage I bid Morblid goodnight, went inside and wrote in my journal. An hour later I fell fast asleep mid-sentence, pen in hand.

I spent the next eight days studying my solarshay manual, watching archived tournaments and reading Morblid's *Little Book of Pink & Purple Thoughts*. We were now wearing vest #12 in solarshay.

Darvon Damos, Jr. was released from thought rehab but went right back in after initiating a fight during solarshay practice. This time he pushed me into a bluyole after kicking Garby into a lechuck.

I'd often stay at the museum after class. I'd help Morblid organize files, dust cabinets, mop floors and feed and groom artifacts. Caring for the artifacts was a task worthy of a small army and I now understood why Morblid lives at the museum. The artifacts are like family to him and like most families – it's a highly dysfunctional one.

One day after class Morblid and I talked about Agrestalia's book and read affirmations from *The Little Book of Pink and Purple Thoughts*. We tossed covers over the artifacts' cages and stoked the fire in the pit. Covers blew eerily and wind whistled through cracks in stone walls. When we finished tending to *The Unpredictables* – my new nickname for the artifacts – Morblid walked me home.

We stopped by *The Downstream Diner* to indulge in warm spiced chai and to bask in the optimistic surroundings. Upon leaving the conversation became so engrossing that midnight slipped by unnoticed. Preoccupied with finding the missing book I'd forgotten that tonight was to be the night of Orable's alleged attack.

As we passed the *Enchanted Cupcake Café* on the way to *Sifter's Village* we saw sifters young and old huddled around a holoport outside the café window. Lifelike images hung in the air. With so many bystanders it was almost impossible to tell who was, and wasn't, part of the broadcast. *Oohs* and *aahs* pierced the cool night air. Some clapped their hands to their cheeks in shock. Others gathered their children and ran to their cottages leaving valuables behind.

Moving closer to the holoport, with an unobstructed view, I spotted the newscaster, Lilith Chatters. Wrapped in a multicolored crocheted poncho she paced between large chunks of ship scattered across the shoreline. The oversized bell bottoms of her jeans flapped erratically in the wind. With her poncho blown up over her head she yelled, "This is Lilith Chatters with *Sifter's Network News*. The event we predicted occurred just moments ago. For you skeptics out there – please keep in mind – we psychics are powerless to prevent such events. We merely predict and report them."

Lilith's face wrinkled in pain as grains of sand struck her eyes. Coughing, she pointed to piles of debris.

"This is what's left of the infamous ship, *The Illusiara*."

As I watched the broadcast I felt a tug on my shoulder.

"No," I shouted, at seeing my hat being pulled from my duffel bag. I reached into the holographic image but each time I did the image bounced back rubber-like. The wind blew the hat over Lilith's face. She peeled it off and continued.

"At the moment there are eleven young sifters reported missing." Her voice grew louder with each gust. "Wait – excuse me – another – there are now twelve missing sifters."

I looked at the blackened face of my ESPY watch. *It works but what good is it now?*

Holding the baseball hat in one hand and grabbing a twisted piece of railing with the other, Lilith hoisted herself onto a serrated piece of ship the size of a compact car. She continued her broadcast. The camera followed her as she wobbled to the place where a book sat smoldering. She picked it up and coughed. Charcoal flakes drizzled onto the deck.

"Here is one of the burning books left behind."

She held up a small pink and purple book. Smoke curled into the air as she turned charred pages.

"Oh – you mind-wrecker!" howled Morblid, at the holographic image.

For the first time, I thought I saw a tint of pink wash across Morblid's ashen face. "What just happened?" I asked.

"That's my book is what just happened! Orable has his soldiers searching for copies. Orders are to burn every last one of them."

A close-up of the book revealed the title, *The Little Book of Pink and Purple Thoughts*.

Morblid fumed and Lilith continued her broadcast.

"This wasn't his first and won't be his last attack," she said, as a gust lifted her poncho like a sail and blew her across the broken deck.

"Orable *must* be stopped," she roared, then disappeared. The wind blew her away. The holoport showed the camera going back and forth searching for her. It finally landed upon a mass rolling across the sand. It was Lilith.

The camera zoomed in for a close-up. With smudged lipstick and mascara, and wind-teased hair with seaweed jutting out here and there she cried, "Oh – my aching back. We're not still filming – are we?"

"Rolling," came a faraway voice from one of the *SNN* crew.

"Oh, my – well…" said Lilith, regaining her composure and

202

resuming her broadcast from where she kneeled in a puddle of sea water, "…the cosmodent has placed our dimension on Amethyst Alert. All portals will remain closed until further notice. If anyone sees, hears, or senses anything unusual please call the D.I.A. at 1 (800) Find-Orable. Back to you, Vladimir."

At the end of the broadcast *Sifter's Network News* played a clip from the abduction. It showed twelve Virusian Soldiers flying on shiny black parasikes. Each soldier had a sifter sitting beside them handcuffed to one of their wrists.

My heart sank as my eyes fell upon their grey uniforms, matching boots, gloves and baseball hats with the initials V.S. embroidered on the front. They looked exactly like the one I had – the hat that was now in Lilith Chatter's hand. I didn't want to believe it belonged to a Virusian Soldier but this was getting increasingly difficult.

"Well – it looks like Orable got his dozen," grumbled Morblid with disgust, analyzing the holographic image hanging in the air beside us. "It's just a matter of time until he gets what he deserves."

The dreaded moment had come and gone. I felt empty inside. Although relieved I wasn't one of the abducted I felt guilty that I was free while others weren't so fortunate. I walked completely around the holographic image of a close-up of one of the abducted. As I watched a tear slide down the boy's unfamiliar face my heart ached.

CHAPTER TWENTY-ONE

DEAD BUT FAMOUS

The following morning I organized a meeting with my friends at the *Enchanted Cupcake Cafe*. Garby and Penelope were visibly upset about the abductions. This wasn't the first abduction Sarabella witnessed and she couldn't help feeling a bit numb to it all.

I was infuriated by what I considered Orable's act of madness. More than ever I wanted to find Agrestalia's book. I devised a plan and would try to get the others to assist.

I told Garby, Penelope and Sarabella what Morblid had said about my dreams being forecasts. I also told them about the three ways one can access parallel dimensions. Of course, Sarabella already knew this. I then ordered four extraordinary cupcakes from the waitress-less tray that paused beside our table.

Garby put two and two together.

"So – what you're saying is – you want all of us to eat extraordinary cupcakes – so we can travel to some unfamiliar, and likely dangerous, dimension – to search for a book that may, or may not, be in one of tens of thousands, or perhaps millions of attics?"

"That's right," I said, realizing how ridiculous this sounded but holding my position nonetheless.

"And – you think this is a *good* idea?"

"Yes," I said, trying to disguise the doubt in my voice.

Garby, Penelope and Sarabella took turns giving three solid reasons why this was *not* a good idea. Their reasons made perfect sense but they failed to change my mind. While I wasn't convinced this was a sound plan it was the only plan I had. I firmly believed that doing something was better than doing nothing.

In an attempt to persuade them to help me I resorted to using guilt and I did this quite well. Referencing last night's broadcast I asked them to close their eyes and remember what they'd seen. Painting graphic images with my words I concocted all sorts of scenarios depicting the kinds of torture and the suffering the abducted may be enduring.

Calling their attention to the cooler where dozens of enchanted cupcakes sat waiting to be joyously devoured I pointed out the fact that Orable's Virusian Soldiers – who were in fact typical teenagers like ourselves – would never have the pleasure of eating any of them.

This went on for about half an hour. Finally, Garby and Penelope broke down and agreed to help.

"I don't know how you talked me into this. You could probably sell snow to an Eskimo," said Garby.

"There's one Eskimo who won't buy my snow." I pointed to Sarabella.

"It's not a good idea," she snapped. "You're risking getting yourselves killed, or worse – captured."

"Well – that's not helpful," I winked, hoping to remind Sarabella of the reality-impacting properties of thought.

"Are you in or not?" I asked urgently.

"No," she said flatly. "I am not *in*."

While disappointed I understood her not wanting to participate. She would have been risking a lot. She could lose her position as class assistant if something happened to one of us during the journey. I hated to admit it but she would have been helpful. My confidence was low at realizing she wasn't going to help but my determination high.

Penelope agreed to meet me and Garby at our cottage the following evening. We would indulge in extraordinary cupcakes and surf parallel dimensions together. To everyone's surprise Sarabella joined us. Boy was I relieved.

Garby stopped by *The Downstream Diner* and grabbed some late dinner for us - thrilled to be able to use his *Requisite card*.

The four of us ate in silence. Following dinner we went off and dressed quietly for our mission.

Garby squeezed into an old pair of jeans and green t-shirt – both of which he grabbed from the dirty laundry. Sarabella sat on the edge of the couch. She slipped her feet into a pair of insulated boots that operate on the same principle as our climate-controlled robes and slippers.

"Sarabella – what's with the change of heart? I thought you weren't coming," said Garby, appearing as though half his face were happy and the other half disappointed.

Sarabella rubbed a clump of glittery body cream up and down her arms. "I'm here because it's my job to protect you all – from yourselves."

Penelope, Garby and I exchanged curious looks at her appearance. I couldn't understand why she was wearing such a tiny dress on an extra-dimensional trip. I tossed her a sweater and suggested she might need it later.

"Which reminds me – your closets will provide you with clothing. All you have to do is stand in front of the door and think about where you are going. The closet will register your thoughts and design your outfit based upon your visualization – and its interpretation of it. When you open the door your ethereally designed, altered-to-perfection attire will be ready to wear.

"Why didn't you tell us this earlier? We just grabbed whatever we could find!" complained Garby, who then raced to his closet.

"While this is an *amazing* thing for which I'm appreciative – we don't have time for this now", I said anxiously, following Garby in close pursuit.

We all watched as Garby stood in front of the closet. Based on his scrunched facial features it was apparent he was in a state of deep concentration. When finally he opened his eyes - and the closet door - a large brimmed straw sunhat tossed itself at him.

"Did you see that? Huh? Did you? This is *awesome!*" roared Garby.

He put it on and tightened the strings until his cheeks bulged like a chipmunk on an acorn hunt.

Staring at him I spontaneously shook my head, *no*. I couldn't help questioning the closet's stylistic interpretations.

" The closet designed it for me. We're a team," said Garby, pointing to the hat. "It comes – or I don't."

"Wear it if you want to look like – a lost tourist," I cautioned, as I laced up a pair of black and purple sneakers designed by my closet.

Penelope took to her closet and came out looking beyond cute in camouflaged pants and matching green sweater. I liked how the closet painted in a bit of blue here and there so her outfit would blend with the Ceresian terrain. Just then the closet tossed out a hat. "Oh – I do hope it came out like I imagined it," she said, crossing her fingers. She caught the hat, looked at it, and gasped. "Oh my! That's exactly how I envisioned it!" Her voice squeaked with joy. Penelope tied her hair back in a knot and donned the black baseball hat with the initials *FB* painted on the front.

"What does the FB stand for?" I asked.

"*Freedom Brigade* – our soon-to-be-formed *Virusian soldier-freeing army*. Of course – you'll be the leader. I know how determined you are to find Agrestalia's book and free Orable's prisoners and you're going to need help."

Soon the closet tossed out three more identical hats. As Penelope handed one to each of us she shared several of her ideas about how the brigade could help.

"That – is *such* a sweet idea," said Garby, tossing his straw hat on the couch and donning the hat Penelope had just given him.

"I thought you two were a team," I said, pointing to the insensitively discarded straw hat.

"We were – but we make a better team," he said, positioning his new hat just so.

"Faculty shouldn't wear such a thing," said Sarabella, as she reluctantly put one on.

We all smiled appreciatively.

I thanked Penelope for her support and generosity before heading out the front door. The others followed.

"We don't know how to thought propel, yet. Does this concern any of you?" asked Garby, closing the door behind us.

Sarabella rolled her eyes.

"We don't need to know. We walk like we have for the past fourteen years until we find the book," I said, draping the strap of my duffel bag over my shoulder.

"You mean – *if* – *if* we find the book," said Garby, snapping the top off a banana and tossing the peel into a nearby bush. "Why can't we just stay here and eat the cupcakes?"

"I learned that the best results happen when you eat them in the *Fields of Possibility* and then walk through the hag stone."

"The *where* – and do *what*? Hag stone? You never said anything about a hag stone. What's a hag stone?" asked Garby frantically.

"A secured portal," I answered.

"Have you thought about all the things that could go wrong?" asked Garby, tossing his hands in the air.

"What could go wrong? And why would I want to think about that when we're learning how our thoughts influence what happens to us?" I asked, straightening Garby's hat.

"If my thoughts are going to influence what happens to us it's important to prepare for the worst. Would you like a list of all possible things that could go wrong – so you can be prepared?"

"No, Garb. I don't want a list. I don't want to expect the worst," I said, picking up the candy wrapper he just tossed and stuffing it into his shirt pocket.

"What we think about is what we attract? That's what Maya's been drilling into our heads," said Penelope.

"*Drilling* – into our heads? That's such a disturbingly graphic analogy. How else could you say that?" asked Garby.

"You know what I mean – teaching us," said Penelope.

"She has also been *teaching us* that some sifters never learn how to fly because they never learn how to direct their thoughts. I think I may be one of those," said Garby, popping open a bottle of *Mindfire*.

Sometimes, the things Garby says frustrate me beyond the point of normal frustration.

"I'm going to ignore you from now on whenever you say something negative," I said, taking a deep breath.

"The two of you may never speak again," interjected Sarabella.

Garby made a rude gesture at her as she turned away.

"We should have brought elevests," said Garby, "We could have practiced flying – and walked less."

"Maybe we should walk more and talk less," I suggested.

"You're not allowed to take vests home. You'd get proscribed and have to retake the whole training next semester," warned Sarabella.

"*Proscribed?*" repeated Garby. "That sounds painful."

"She means suspended," offered Penelope.

"Oh! Why didn't you just say so?"

"Is that why Darvon's taking the class again?" I asked.

"Darvon's repeating the class because he has so much anger he's unable to make it past the training vest portion of solarshay."

"That's what I figured," I said.

Garby ran bull-like through the fields attempting to fly.

"Hey, Garby! Make yourself useful. Where's the map?" I asked.

"I have the map." Garby, burped the word *map*, letter by letter.

"Study it and figure out the best point of entry."

"To what?" he asked, stupefied.

"The *Fields of Possibility*, Garby."

"Right," he said, unraveling a heavily crinkled map.

Just then something whizzed through the air and crashed into Garby's forehead above his right eye. Whatever it was left a glowing turquoise streak across his forehead.

"What was that?" asked Garby, dumbfounded.

"What *was* that?" asked a mocking, nasal voice through the darkness.

Garby pulled out a flickerlight. He tried to visualize light but his anger just made it flash like a strobe light. He swept the unsteady beam across every inch of the ground.

"Hey *fat* boy. Up here," said the little voice harassingly.

"It's that nosey *stink* bug," said Garby, turning and aiming the still blinking light at the nearby trees.

"Off trampling carelessly through the grass yet again? This time trying to find the *unfindable* book whose secrets you hope will unlock the *cages* of your minds."

The bug's voice was dark and foreboding. I felt a cold rise within.

Garby picked up a stone and as he was about to throw it at the bug I grabbed his arm and stopped him.

"Hey – little bug. What do you know about the book," I asked, to the trees, not knowing exactly where he was.

"Stop calling me that!" came a voice from somewhere within the foliage. "My name is Airaldo," he said indignantly, curling his tongue around the "r". Leaves shook and a branch wiggled. On that branch was Airaldo. He marched out to the end of it all the while aiming a length-of-his-body twig at me.

"Okay then – *Airaldo*. What do you know about the book?"

"Oh, Airaldo – share your vast knowledge about the book. We need you, Airaldo. Only you can save us, Airaldo!" he said dramatically, as though auditioning for a part in a movie. Practically laughing himself to death he gasped for air.

"Airaldo – when you want to stop playing games and contribute something intelligent – let me know," I said irritably, picking up my duffel bag and urging the others to move forward.

Airaldo zipped through the air and hovered just inches from my eyes. He was so close that as I looked at him I could feel my eyes cross.

"Intelligent? Pfff. How ironic. An *Earth boy* wants ME to say something intelligent. Fine!" he cried indignantly, tossing his tiny scarf. Buzzing, he flew one full rotation around my head then perched himself atop my shoulder.

"You won't need the book when you meet Orable, Levi. You will find only what you take with you," he whispered in my ear.

Our eyes locked.

"We're on a very important mission. We don't have time to waste on your silly – unoriginal riddles," I cracked, twisting my head uncomfortably to see him better.

Airaldo waived his hand through the air dismissively.

"Ah – I didn't think you'd get it – idiot."

He then took off so fast that a miniature twister trailed through the air behind him. I watched as he disappeared into the woods, buzzing and grumbling.

"Let's not waste any more time on that bug," I said, motioning for the others to follow me.

"I think he's trying to tell us something, you know – without telling us," said Penelope.

"Maybe, but I just don't get it," whined Garby, scratching his head.

The four of us walked a good twenty minutes while talking mostly about Airaldo. When not talking about Airaldo, Garby managed to find something to complain about. He spent a great deal of the trip talking to himself about how he'd be better prepared the next time he would cross paths with - *Airaldo the Annoying*. He focused hard for a good sixty seconds then pulled something from his duffel. It was a bottle of natural bug repellent. The label read: *Bug Off & Be Gone*. It was a mixture of essential oils including: lemon, rose, citronella, cinnamon and castor oil. He stuffed it inside his jacket pocket.

Finally, unbeknownst to all but me, we arrived at *Scurry's Station* – the station that repairs, buys, sells and trades new and used auraplanes. Free-floating street lights hovered twenty feet in the air all around the lot's perimeter. It was much brighter than I hoped it would be.

"Where are we – and why are we here?" asked Garby, his voice uneasy.

"We're at *Scurry's Station*. We're going to fly to the *Fields of Possibility*."

Everyone complained. Questions overlapped.

I made a shushing motion then checked to see if the captain's bedroom light was on. It wasn't. Motioning for the others to follow me I crouched spy-like through the aisles between parked vehicles. Pressing my back against an auraplane I surveyed the place for movement. I spun around to the next vehicle. Making my way across the lot I ducked beside the last auraplane in the lineup.

Garby was close behind. He tried to mimic me but as he approached an auraplane he tripped over a large yellow tool box. The sound of unfamiliar Ceresian tools clanking, bounced off what must have been more than two hundred auraplanes parked there.

"Watch where you walk," I whispered, in a pleading voice.

"You sound like Airaldo" criticized Garby, dramatically curling his tongue around the "r." "Isn't there a security guard or something?"

"It's past midnight. The station closes at ten," I whispered, checking my pendant. "Ole Cappy already downed a forty of Lawanda's and passed out. His bedroom is above the station at the end of the lot. We're borrowing an auraplane from this end so we don't wake him."

"La-what? Cappy who? How do you know all this? And – you mean *steal* not borrow."

"I've done my research. And, no – I mean borrow. Stealing is when you don't put something back. Technically – this is borrowing," I half-joked.

"You should be a lawyer. You can make a lot of money twisting truth," said Garby, tripping over a creeper sticking out from beneath the auraplane. Several *Dimension 11* candy bars fell from his pocket.

"We're going to have to fly without headlights," I said, gathering candy bars and stuffing all but one of them back into Garby's pocket. I handed one to Penelope. She thanked me. Our eyes met and we exchanged smiles. I soaked in the warmth of the powerful magnetic current that passed between us.

"Do you have the flickerlights, Garby?" I asked, reluctantly peeling my penetrating stare from her beauty.

"Yes – but I have something even better. I brought one of Hemp's everlasting candles."

"Let me see that," demanded Sarabella. "That's strange. I've never seen one quite like this. It must be a new and improved version."

"Nah – it's old. I grabbed it from the museum."

"You – did – WHAT?" screeched Penelope, Sarabella and I in unison. The three of us stopped dead in our tracks.

Sarabella's hair turned grey at once. We knew enough by now to just ignore this temporary cosmetic phenomena.

"I grabbed it from the museum. What's the big deal?" Garby tossed the candle in the air.

"Are you CRAZY?" I asked, catching it as it descended.

I had a sudden urge to shake Garby by the ears but didn't.

"It's probably got some kind of grey spirit attached to it. It's an antagonistic artifact from who knows where which does who knows what. Whatever you do – don't light it."

"Oh – it's just a candle," said Garby flippantly. "Morblid likes regular candles. I peeked into his office – it's full of them!"

"*It's just a* – that's a dangerous phrase," warned Sarabella, shaking her head regretfully.

I couldn't help worrying about the candle but I had so many other things to focus on that I pushed it out of my mind best I could for the moment.

"What about snacks? Did you guys bring any?" asked Garby, his stomach growling.

"Snacks? We ate before we left. We haven't been gone more than thirty minutes. You just had a banana – a candy bar – and a *Mindfire*," I tallied, patting Garby on the back. "I thought you were doing a cleanse."

"This is a special circumstance," said Garby, adopting an awkward stance with his arms propped wide on chubby hips and his chest puffed rooster-like. "Be prepared," he yelled, in a strained sort of voice.

I couldn't help bursting into laughter. Penelope stifled giggles. Sarabella rolled her eyes.

"What's so funny? When you go camping you should always pack enough food and H_2O for at least seven days. I know this because *I was a boy scout.*"

"Why are you still thinking about everything that could go wrong? Do you *want* to be stranded for a week?" asked Penelope.

"No – but at least I'm prepared for it."

"I'm going by myself next time," I murmured, rummaging through my duffel bag, wishing I hadn't invited Garby.

Penelope picked up tools and gently returned them to the toolbox before joining Garby and me inside the auraplane. Sarabella climbed in last, or so it seemed. Out of nowhere came Alphia.

"I told you to stay home and keep an eye on the cottage," I reprimanded, a worried hand against my forehead.

"You're not the boss of me. Besides, I won't be left behind – again.

Being that you have a tendency to not return from trips I figured I'd save myself the heartache and accompany you in the first place. Now – move over – pet."

"This can't be happening."

"It's not a big deal. It's actually quite convenient. Now we have an offering for the clawcons should we encounter any," laughed Sarabella.

"That's very funny. If I were a bit less civilized – say a Chihuahua maybe – I'd bite your ear off."

"You haven't a clue – the things I could do to you," breathed Sarabella darkly.

Alphia growled and hid beneath a seat.

"How do you start these things? Where's the ignition?" asked Garby, in a booming voice.

"*Shh*, you're talking way too loudly – they're motion activated and voice controlled," I whispered, from where I sat in the pilot's seat.

"Oh – you mean sort of like the water faucets in fancy restrooms back home?" asked Garby, fascinated.

"Sort of like that, Garb," I said in an appeasing, exasperated voice.

There was a moment of actual silence. One could hear the wind whistle through the, well, I'm not exactly sure what.

"Everybody ready?" I mouthed.

All nodded.

Alphia barked.

We shushed her.

"Take us to the *Fields of Possibility*," I whispered, leaning into the control panel. Sweeping the palm of my hand across a small screen caused the auraplane to rise. It hovered a few feet above ground making sounds as though it were downloading information. Red numbers flashed on the dashboard: 15, 14, 13, 12. When it reached the number 1 the auraplane shot straight up into the air. It ascended so quickly that the resulting force snapped the frayed seatbelts and the four of us hit our heads hard against the roof.

Alphia, being under my seat, hit her head on the underside of it. She whimpered then complained about my piloting skills. As I rubbed the ache from my head I remembered my first auraplane ride with Sarabella. It had been a rough one but this was far worse, with jerking and clanking sounds emanating from somewhere beneath the rusted hood. I didn't know much about auraplanes but I knew enough to know that what was happening wasn't normal. All the dipping, rising, shaking and swirling had me petrified – inside.

"We're not going to make it you know. We should go back," warned Sarabella.

"Where's your usual optimism?" I asked, pushing buttons on the panel, one of which resulted in the dispensing of a large pile of chocolate covered raisins. Garby and Alphia battled over them.

"We can't go back. We're on a very important mission," I said as the auraplane whirled then dropped several feet before leveling off.

Color drained from Garby's face. He grabbed a barf bag from inside his duffel bag.

"Is this thing going to do this the *entire* trip?" he asked, his face wrinkled with nausea.

"I don't think so," I lied.

"Why are we flying so low?" asked Garby, as the auraplane brushed the tops of several uprooted, black elder trees.

I hesitated for a moment trying to think of a good lie. The truth is that I was afraid the auraplane would, at any second, stop working entirely and plummet to the ground at incredible speed, leaving us all, well – dead quite frankly.

"He's flying low because he knows we could crash at any moment. Odds of surviving a three-story fall are much better than a thirty-story fall."

Sarabella then nodded at me as if to say – *you're welcome.*

"Thanks a lot. Now everyone will panic," I complained.

"So – we're all going to *die*? I will have spent my last living moments – *barfing*?" asked Garby, crumpling up one of his wax-lined, vomit-filled bags and tossing it out the window.

"Will you *please* stop that," I shouted, at seeing him litter for the umpteenth time.

"What does a little litter matter if we're all *dead*?" countered Garby, grabbing a fresh bag.

Penelope trembled. She opened a notebook and started to write but the ride was so bumpy she ended up scribbling.

"How can you write at a time like this?" shouted Garby, his stomach gurgling.

"I'm writing a happy ending – to this ride. If it's true that we create our experiences with our thoughts – it'll work," she said, writing frantically. "Someday – back on Earth – the story of our adventures here will be a bestseller."

"That's great, Penelope. We'll all be famous! *Dead* – but *famous*," cried Garby, heaving into the bag.

"Are you okay?" asked Penelope, rubbing his back.

"Never felt better."

Garby stuffed his face into the bag and moaned.

"I'm sorry you don't feel well, Garby," I offered.

"What about me? I'm not in my usual merry, let's-go-chase-squirrels-and-chew-rawhide kind'a mood myself you know?" complained Alphia, shooting Sarabella a nauseated look.

Garby mumbled something inaudible then heaved.

"Let's all focus on a safe landing," pleaded Penelope.

The auraplane jerked, puttered, clanked, and spewed forth grey smoke. I tried to appear calm to minimize panic but inside I was terrified.

Twenty minutes had passed and to my amazement we were still airborne. Garby threw up five times. Penelope filled four and a half pages in her notebook.

"Prepare for landing. I repeat. Prepare for landing," came a choppy computer-generated voice from the control panel. But instead of descending, the auraplane ascended. After several minutes of this it began losing elevation so rapidly that I couldn't breathe.

There was a jolt and the glove compartment snapped open. I caught a bunch of envelopes as they fell. Between them was a pilot's license belonging to – Morblid Gorman. My heart sank.

"Oh, no! Morblid said his auraplane was in the shop," I yelled, dumbfounded, as I stared at the license.

Garby grabbed it from me.

"Nice photo of Gorman – don't you think?" he asked sarcastically. "Well – that explains the *toolbox*. Out of all the auraplanes we could have *borrowed*, we take the one with the toolbox beside it," said Garby, just before the wind ripped a barf bag from his grip.

Pages of Penelope's notebook flapped wildly as currents of air twisted the vehicle. Her fingers grew pale where they clung to the spiral binding. Her new, closet-designed *Freedom Brigade* hat was sucked from her head by the mouth of the wind. Her ponytail pointed north as the auraplane continued to fall.

I pleaded with the voice activated screen.

"Please – slow down for a soft landing – please," I begged, over and over while maintaining an air of false calm. Inside, my heart pounded against my rib cage.

Eardrum piercing noises erupted. I couldn't believe my eyes. The vehicle was splitting in two, mid-air. A zigzagging fracture crept across the floor snapping the titanium screws from their bolts. One hit Garby in the side of the head.

"OW," he wailed. "Why me? Why am I always the one to get hit by flying debris?" His face flushed.

"Look out!" I screamed, pointing to the ever-widening fissure. An eerie whistling sound permeated the air as wind blew through it. Horrified, we clutched the frame of the auraplane and each other as we watched the ground grow nearer.

"It was nice knowing all of you! Maybe we'll see each other in another dimension once we're all DEAD," cried Garby, heaving.

CHAPTER TWENTY-TWO

THE APPEARIDIAN SEA

T he pieces severed leaving me, Sarabella and Alphia in one half. Penelope and Garby in the other. The impact was explosive. Four air bags inflated sending booms across the canyon. Thick smoke trickled out between buttons on the control panel. A fire ignited beneath Penelope's seat. She reached into her duffel bag, pulled out a *Mindfire* and poured it over flames. It sizzled. Someone coughed.

"Who said we wouldn't need to know how to fly? Who didn't want to hear my list of all possible things that could go wrong?" asked Garby, from where he lay pressed against sand beneath an airbag.

"Stop it, Garby. This isn't the time for more of your negative thinking. You thinking about all the things that could go wrong probably *attracted* this," I suggested, as I pulled a pocket knife from my jacket and stabbed airbags. "Is everyone ok?" I asked, rubbing soreness from my neck.

"*Well* – if we're going to play the *blame game* – I'd say you need to learn how to make better choices and develop better powers of observation. There was a fricking toolbox by this one – *duh*," retorted Garby, kicking a deflated airbag.

"I don't want to argue. It's a waste of time and energy. Just stop being so negative – will you, please? It affects me," I said, reigning in my anger.

"You're not exactly, *Mr. Optimistic*," cracked Garby.

"No – but I'm trying to be aware of my negative thoughts – unlike you. I'm trying to focus on what I want – not on what I *don't* want."

Garby and I went back and forth for a few more verbal rounds until we agreed that we were both frustrated by our inability to direct our own thoughts.

With the exception of minor bruises everyone was in good condition considering the scope of the crash. Silently, I assessed the situation.

The auraplane's totaled. How will we get back to the station? At some point the captain's going to notice it missing. How will I explain this to Morblid? What are we going to do if Orable shows up?

I recalled the day I crashed into the bleachers during solarshay practice. Maya stared coldly into my eyes and said, "Adapt, evaluate, improvise, overcome, uncomprehend – and sometimes yodel." I thought she was crazy. But now, it seemed as good advice as any. I had no idea when yodeling would help, but I was trying to keep an open mind. Even if it helped by adding a bit of humor to the situation to keep worrisome thoughts away I was willing to try it.

Penelope exited the auraplane, the bells of her jeans charred.

"Where's Sarabella?" I asked, searching for my duffel bag beneath deflated airbags.

"*Teach* flew away before we crashed," said Garby bitingly. "She didn't even *try* to help us."

I called out to her without response.

"I'm sure she's ok. She's probably giving herself a manicure perched somewhere in a tree," I said half-jokingly.

"I don't see any trees. Do you see any trees?" asked Garby acerbically, looking around at desolate landscape.

I sized up the surroundings and shrugged. In the distance sat an enormous ship tilted on its side and broken into several pieces. A chunk was missing from the hull below the waterline. Its sails torn and twisted. Carved into the wood was the name: The Illusiara.

Garby still lay upside down beneath a deflated airbag clenching an unused barf bag. "I can't believe we lived through this," he said, staring off into space.

Penelope bent so she too was upside down. "I wrote a happy ending – remember?"

"Hmm – if this is your idea of a happy ending I'd hate to hear your idea of a *tragedy*," said Garby, rolling his eyes.

"You can get up now, Garby," said Penelope, offering a hand.

"I know," he said, standing. "Item #254 on the list of all possible things that could go wrong. The list no one wanted to hear," he said, pointing at the smashed auraplane. He stepped toward the Illusiara.

"Wow – it looks way worse in person."

He climbed up on the same piece of ship where Lilith Chatters stood during the emergency bulletin.

"I'm Lilith Chatters and this is the Illusiara. Don't count on your thoughts getting you out of this one," he announced, in a mocking, high-pitched voice. He swept his arms around dramatically toward the ship, took a step back and fell off the precariously perched wreckage.

Luckily, he landed in soft sand.

"I guess I'm still a little dizzy."

"Excellent impression," said Penelope, clapping.

"How far are we from the *Fields of Possibility?*" he asked, brushing sand from his jeans.

I reminded Garby that he had the map. Pulling it from his duffel bag he unrolled it and reported that he had no idea where we were let alone where the *Fields of Possibility* could be. He corrected himself when he came across a drawing of a ship with the title – *The Illusiara,* beside it. He estimated that we were about twenty miles south of the *Fields of Possibility*, a bit south east of the *Uprooted Forest.* Knowing this didn't help. Without a compass we were clueless as to which way was north, south, east or west. I considered asking my duffel bag for a compass but unfortunately, the bags only respond to our solarshay needs.

"I'm going to buy us all a compass with my *Requisite* card if we survive. I can't believe I came out here without one," said Garby, gazing worriedly across the barren basin.

As I looked at the ship my curiosity spiked. Since we were there I suggested we explore it in search of waiting-to-be-found treasure.

"How are we supposed to get up there?" asked Garby, craning his neck back as he looked up at the largest piece of ship.

Sarabella appeared out of nowhere and pointed to the enormous hole in the hull. "Through there," she said, without even so much as a driblet of remorse in her voice.

"Oh – *Sarabella.* How nice of you to join us!" said Garby caustically. "You just flew away while we stared death in the eyes. What is it they say about captains who abandon ship?"

"I'm not your captain. I warned you that this was a bad idea."

"Well – you're not the best role model, either," griped Garby, wriggling his noise. "Besides, you said it's your job to protect us from ourselves."

"You're alive – aren't you?" snapped Sarabella, just before she flew into the massive hole in the hull.

Anger turned Garby's cheeks fire-red.

Alphia shook her head, *no,* at seeing Sarabella do this. Pacing, she protested, "Where there are *holes* there are predators. The bigger the hole the bigger the predator. THAT is a large predator hole. Let's just… yell. Hellooooo – anybody here?"

Everyone stopped talking and listened for a response.

"That was easy. See – no one's here. Let's go find the hedge stone," yapped Alphia, running back toward the destroyed auraplane.

"You mean – hag stone," I said.

"I'm not crawling through that hole. Alphia's right. There are probably all sorts of creepy things living in there," said Garby.

"Look – there's a rope. It looks like it goes all the way to the deck," said Penelope pointing.

The rope was thick with large knots running to the top. Penelope pulled it hard. I pulled it a second time to its strength before climbing up a few knots. I jumped down and handed the rope to Garby. "You go first. It's sturdy. Shimmy up there."

Garby shot me an incredulous look.

"Why me? Oh – I get it. Send the fat guy up first to see if the rope breaks. No way. I'm not going."

"No – that's not why. You're the heaviest. If you make it up – we'll all make it up."

"Uh – right. Like I just said, send the fat guy up first to see if the rope breaks."

"Forget it then. You and Alphia can stay down here and be our lookouts."

I grabbed the rope and climbed up the knots easily. Once I reached the top Penelope followed. Sarabella was already there.

"Oh great – I get the moron," griped Alphia.

"Wha – I – I'm not a moron – you miniature, overpriced – whatever you are," said Garby.

"Yorkie – moron. I'm a Yorkshire terrier. You obviously know nothing about the royal pedigree of England."

The two chased each other in circles.

Above them, on deck, I yelled, "Hello. Anyone here?"

Penelope, Sarabella, and I waited but there was no response.

"Whistle if you see anything," I called, to Garby and Alphia below.

"I can't whistle. See?" shouted Garby, making a pitiable blowing sound while chasing Alphia.

"Yell then," I said, once again wishing I hadn't invited Garby, and remembering I hadn't invited Alphia.

The three of us assessed the moonlit deck. Penelope discovered a doorway leading to staterooms. She motioned to Sarabella and me. We each lit a flickerlight before descending the narrow staircase. Halfway down I saw words painted on the wall in turquoise:

All will see the water
Few will look beyond
One moment it is with you
The next it is gone

227

"I wonder who painted that," said Penelope.

"Whoever it was can't be far away. It's still wet," replied Sarabella, the tip of her index finger now turquoise.

"Let's hurry," I shouted, running down the stairs.

Flashes of light from the flickerlights traced the narrow stairway walls exposing enormous spider webs and freshly stirred dust particles.

Meanwhile, Garby paced the length of the ship below attempting to whistle. Pathetic, sporadic toots erupted from his lips as he walked back to where we had piled our duffel bags beside the fragmented auraplane. Reaching into one of the bags he pulled out a cupcake. He stuffed most of it in his mouth. A noise startled him and he froze. He looked around. His mouth dangled open and his eyes popped. He tried to scream but couldn't.

Alphia darted across the sand, bit Garby's ankle, jumped into an old battered rescue boat and hid beneath a tattered orange life vest.

As Garby howled in pain he heard her complain, "That was one tough ankle. I think I broke my *dentes canini*."

A second noise came louder than the first. It was an unnerving rumble. That's when Garby, without hesitation, climbed the rope. He ran across the deck looking for us then trailed the sound of our voices. Dashing down the stairway fast as he could resulted in him sliding most of the way on his backside.

We turned as one to look at him.

He devoured the last bite of cupcake, licked his fingers and stood there staring at us. His flickerlight cast dancing shadows across our faces reflected in the cracked mirror of an old nearby dresser.

"Geez – you guys look – *creepy*. Listen! Did you – do you hear that?"

he asked, panic escalating in his voice. "It sounds like a moan. It was a moan but now it sounds more like water. No – wait – yeah, it sounds like a wave. Sounds like a *big* wave – getting closer."

No sooner had Garby said this than the ship rocked hard from side to side. Debris rolled from one end of the cabin to the other. There was a lot of banging and clanking. The old wooden dresser slid across the floor and tipped over. Its mirror smashed into pieces, its drawers fell out dumping the contents at our feet. Water poured in through cracks in walls.

This can't be good, I thought, as I watched a porthole burst open from the pressure of rushing water.

"What's happening!?!" screamed Penelope.

The three of us ran up the broken stairway to the top deck and watched helplessly as hundreds of gallons of seawater flooded over it engulfing our feet, our ankles, our knees. We looked out over the place where just moments ago sat a barren canyon. How was it possible that it was now a raging ocean? The shattered ship was now whole with full sail snapping in the wind, enduring the cruelest of waves.

"How can this be happening?" yelled Penelope, just before a wave overwhelmed her.

"What's going on?" screamed Garby, grabbing iron railing.

"It looks like someone conjured up an ocean," I yelled, paralyzed with fear.

From the corner of my eyes I saw what must have been a dozen sifters being chased around the deck. I heard their screams and the splatter of their footsteps. I could even feel their anxiety. It was at that moment that I realized I was standing in the midst of an abduction.

Then, a boy ran right through me. I felt an icy chill and a peeling sensation ripple through my body. I knew something was terribly wrong.

"Garby – you just ate a cupcake, right?" I yelled.

"I ate a cupcake – but it was one of mine – a regular one," said Garby, as a large wave washed over him filling his mouth with sea water.

Penelope screamed. I turned toward the scream but didn't see her anywhere. Garby and I scurried around the deck and called for her. We heard her but the vessel rocked madly and tossed us to opposite sides of the ship. A tiny *help* beckoned from the sea. The ship rocked harder. Shadows flew overhead swooping up sifters from on deck. I recognized the black metallic parasikes and the embroidered lettering on their hats.

A wave hit me hard and I grabbed railing. It was slippery but I managed to work my way around to the other side where I could hear Penelope's calls for help. There in the raging water I caught a glimpse of her head bobbing in twenty-foot swells. My heart pounded as I watched abducted sifters, cuffed to Virusian soldiers, soar unnervingly above her. I'd never felt so completely helpless.

Trying desperately to hold on to the railing waves washed over the deck and tugged at me with a force so great I thought I might be sucked overboard. My eyes traced the deck for a lifejacket but I couldn't see. Salt water burned my eyes and a thick fog rolled through the air. Through the fog I caught glimpses of an old yellow life preserver. It was a good eighteen feet away. Getting to it would be risky. I'd have to let go of the railing, make my way across deck, and get back before the next wave hit.

Hesitating, I stepped away from the railing and slipped. I scraped my hands on the rough deck. Fresh cuts burned from salty water. *Must – get-up*. I flung myself across the deck, ripped the preserver from its hook, slid back to the railing, and tossed it toward Penelope. I watched helplessly as she tried to grab it. Each time she reached for it, it drifted farther away.

Silhouettes of soldiers flew across the double moonlit sky. Soon, I realized that I was seeing residual images of the abduction – in another dimension. This was a difficult concept for me to grasp being that the entire experience looked as real as the fear I felt.

"You can do it, Penelope," I shouted, as another wave pounded me. I wasn't sure if she heard me but I saw her kick like crazy.

Finally, she captured the preserver, slid it over her head and swam toward the ship. After securing the other end of the rope to the railing I began to pull and lift her from the water. She reached for my outstretched hand. Her fingertips grazed mine and then the rope snapped. A resounding "NO" faded as she fell. There was a large splash and she was gone.

Sarabella stood close by watching.

"Do something!" I shouted so fiercely that I could feel the veins in my temples bulge. "You can do all sorts of things. Why aren't you helping?"

"This is *your* manifestation – not mine. If I help, you'll continue to blame others for the experiences you choose."

Hearing her say this in this moment was infuriating. Just as I was about to give Sarabella a piece of my mind and tell her how ridiculous I found her reasoning to be mad laughter erupted from behind me. I turned to see an eerie shadow with the outline of a cape blowing wildly in the gusts. My eyes traced the shadow to the thing to which it belonged. It looked – inhuman.

As it moved toward me my heart raced. I couldn't tell which dimension it was in. I recalled the theory of dimension shifting and hoped this wasn't one of those rare, unfortunate occurrences. Morblid had said there are some dimensions through which one can travel physically, while others could only be observed through residual images of past events. I knew the soldiers were residual because one passed through me. I could only hope that the vision I was now having is also residual.

"That's Orable," offered Sarabella, just before she flew off into the night, her hair shifting to an eerie hue of midnight blue.

A small sound came and died unhappily in my throat. The *hate* I felt toward her in that moment consumed me. I fell faint and nauseous at my own rage.

Heavy boots clunked against slippery wood. I looked at my wrist. The face of my ESPY watch was jet black. I tapped it hoping it might change its mind – but it didn't. My thoughts fell upon all things dark. I grew lethargic and wanted to cry the nearer Orable approached. It was as if someone had pulled a plug and drained all hope from inside me. Maya and Hemp had warned me of this. They told me that outside forces can drain energy. That thoughts can be siphoned, absorbed, planted, and rearranged.

I stood on the still rocking deck facing an uncertain fate, feeling helpless and hopeless. I trembled. A million regrets flooded my mind.

What was I thinking? Why did I come here so ill-prepared? Why was I stupid enough to risk my freedom?

The sound of Orable's boots against the deck quickened.

Will Penelope survive? What will happen to her if I'm abducted?

The foreboding shadow enveloped me. A darker and colder world I'd never imagined existed.

And then, as fear consumed me, I felt the icy residual essence of Orable pass through me. I watched his silhouette run across the deck and soar over the raging sea on a parasike triple the size of the others. His condescending laughter caused hairs on my arms to stand at attention. As I watched his shadow fade into the darkness my breath deepened and my heartbeat slowed until the sound of Penelope's screams shook me back into the moment. My eyes fell upon where she bobbed in rippling swells.

"HOLD ON! I'll find another rope. Everything will be okay," I lied, as two monstrous waves smacked me. I scanned the deck for another rope or for anything remotely useful. *I could tie the sails together. No, that would take too long. I shouldn't have done this. I can't believe I talked my friends into coming with me!*

Just then Maya's teachings danced through my head. Her words lingered. I felt as if she were standing beside me shouting in my ear.

THOUGHTS ARE ATTRACTIVE. FIND BETTER FEELING THOUGHTS. PUT ON YOUR HAPPY.

Enormous waves pounded the ship. I could no longer hear Penelope's calls for help. *Am I too late?*

I tried to find a better feeling thought. Maya taught me that the best way to attract what I want is to *focus* on the desired outcome and *ignore* the current reality. Part of me thought the notion was ridiculous. But in this moment her advice seemed almost rational and I had no better option. So, I focused as hard as I could on ignoring the harsh reality. I envisioned the sea gone and Penelope safe in my arms.

Another wave hit me hard in the face. Spitting out a mouthful of salty water I focused my thoughts again. I refused to accept the current reality. I closed my eyes and imagined there was no raging sea. I did this until doubt got the best of me.

"This is so *stupid*!" I screamed and punched railing. My knuckles swelled and throbbed painfully. "But – I have to keep trying!" Closing my eyes I continued to ignore the oh-so-convincing reality. I did this for what seemed like an eternity but nothing improved. The nightmarish reality persisted. Again, and again, I focused my thoughts on how good I'd feel when the water was gone. I imagined myself looking into Penelope's eyes, holding her hand feeling relieved she was safe.

Shivering and delirious Garby rambled as he clutched railing.

Overwhelmed and unable to control my own negativity I had absolutely no patience for Garby's complaining. I lost it and blasted him, "Put on your fricking happy – like Maya taught us! I'm not always going to be around to try to save you. And you can forget about Sarabella helping!"

I kept one eye on Penelope as she bobbed farther out to sea and the other on the next approaching wave. As Garby and I tried to direct our thoughts a powerful jolt catapulted us over the railing in opposite directions. The last sound I heard was Garby screaming, "I can't swim!"

CHAPTER TWENTY-THREE

A CURIOUS CANVAS

Dark and still, the raging ocean was no more. *The Illusiara* was once again scattered in pieces across a barren terrain, her boards dry enough for kindling.

Headlights beamed through thick fog. Three suns peeked through the sad blue blanket of the night. An approaching auraplane landed quietly beside the chunk of ship where Garby stood last evening mocking Lilith Chatters. A man with silvery hair stepped out and started to search through rubble.

"Hello. Is anyone there?" His scratchy voice echoed but no one answered his call. With crooked cane in hand he limped to the wrecked auraplane I'd *borrowed* from his station.

Several of Garby's vomit-filled paper sacks were strewn across the back seat of half of the auraplane. My jacket lay crumpled in the front seat of the other half. The captain found Penelope's notebook and read an entry:

Levi is pretending there is nothing wrong with the auraplane so none of us worry. Not only is he incredibly handsome, smart and brave, but he has an amazing heart. I hope he asks me to the Sifter's Ball. ~~If we survive.~~ I mean, once we're back safely.

While the captain assessed the damage a small avalanche emanated from beside a chunk of ship. He limped over and poked at a pile of stones with his black metallic cane. Rocks scattered. A sneaker appeared through rubble. More poking revealed an ankle, and then a leg. Tossing his cane aside, he bent to remove rocks from the body then rolled it over. The captain wiped sand from my eyes.

"Are you okay, boy? You're not looking quite right."

"I'm – where – thanks," I mumbled, as I tried to sit up.

The captain assisted.

"Have you seen my friends? Where's the ocean?" I asked, in a panicked voice as I grabbed the captain's shoulders and shook him.

"You're the only one I've seen so far," said the captain, looking around. "And, the ocean was about twenty miles south last time I checked."

"Three friends – my dog…have to find them," I stammered, as I stood, then fell hard to my knees. Aching, but determined, I limped around the shipwreck trying to focus on the outcome I wanted.

The wind picked up and together we heard a repetitive banging emanating from the opposite side of the ship. We walked toward the sound. Dangling from the railing was Garby. His thick hemp belt had caught on one of the ladder hooks. It twisted around his wrist and held him fast against the ship. His hand was bloated and blue. His forehead was badly bruised from banging against the hull as his body swung back and forth. With the captain's help I cut him down.

Garby was unconscious. The captain pulled something from his pocket and placed it beneath Garby's nose. This caused him to cough and moan. It took him awhile to come around. When finally he did he was uncharacteristically quiet.

Alphia crawled out from beneath an old rescue boat with a life preserver wrapped around her. She ran toward me.

"You know I don't like water – especially BIG water. I don't even like baths in a tub," she complained, shaking the wetness from her fur.

I picked her up and comforted her, relieved she was alive.

A few minutes later I found Sarabella exploring a nearby cave. With only seaweed for clothing she danced and chanted while holding a black canvas as if it were her partner. Her hair color matched the sand.

Garby, Captain Scud Scurry, and I spent the remaining daylight hours searching for Penelope.

As darkness was about to fall the captain suggested we resume our search in the morning. While this made sense something inside me refused to give up. Mentally and physically drained I continued to reach for better feeling thoughts and to visualize the outcome I wanted.

Stopping by the wrecked auraplane to get my jacket, I saw Penelope's open notebook. I read an entry and a solitary tear cleared a path down my dusty face. When it hit the page it smudged the word, *maybe*. I stuffed the notebook inside my duffel bag and took a good look at the Illusiara. *What happened last night? Why did I risk the lives of my friends to satisfy my obsession?*

I looked again at Penelope's notebook. The word *maybe* was gone. It was at this moment that I remembered Maya's words: *There is no maybe. There is only I choose to, or I choose not to.*

With all the strength I could muster I visualized Penelope safe and well in my arms. I summoned the feeling that passed between us each time our eyes met. Staring beyond the Illusiara toward the barren reef-splattered basin I imagined her walking toward me. I sighed and tossed my head back in an attempt to stop tears from rushing. As I looked out to the place where Penelope once bobbed at sea movement caught my eye. Something small and faraway was walking toward me. Squinting, I hurried toward it. The closer I got the more hopeful I grew. *Are those camouflage jeans?* I ran toward whatever it was.

Penelope's jeans were torn. A shredded headband dangled from her neck. Shoeless, the soles of her feet bled. Her eyes were red and swollen from sea water. The life preserver still hung around her waist, its frayed rope trailing behind her. She shivered. The sea had swept her miles from shore until suddenly there was no sea. She walked all night and dared not stop, terrified that at any moment it could return.

Elated, I reached for her hand just as I imagined I would. Wrapping my jacket around her I picked her up and carried her to the captain's auraplane. I couldn't help wondering if my thoughts had anything to do with her unlikely survival.

Everyone hugged her and chattered at once. None of us said anything of importance. We were all just happy to be alive and together again.

"My hat – it's gone," she muttered, through salty tears.

"I'd give you mine but I lost it as well. It's ok. I'm sure the closet will design new ones for us," I said, in a comforting voice.

The captain helped the four of us, and Alphia, inside.

Sarabella stuffed the canvas she found behind the back seat.

During the ride to Scurry's Station, Sarabella waved her hands over everyone's bruises and sore spots. In an instant they were gone. By the end of the trip we were all like new.

The hot topic involved Garby's eating of the commune cupcake that Morblid had given to me. Garby insisted that he *hadn't* eaten it but when I unzipped my bag the commune cupcake was gone. I fumed. It was irresponsible.

Garby apologized and explained how the light from the moons distorts color. "All the duffel bags looked the same," he argued defensively.

"Does moonlight also distort *size*?" I asked, zipping my duffel bag. "Commune cupcakes are about half the size of the enchanted ones, Garby!"

"Oh – that's why I was still hungry," he muttered innocently.

When I raised the topic of Orable the others were stunned.

None of them had seen him or any part of the residual abduction.

The captain explained that consuming a commune cupcake outside a secured portal, like the hag stone, could be disastrous. He said that I was the only one who'd seen Orable because I was the only one thinking about Orable.

Each of us had an entirely different recollection of the events that evening based on the thoughts we were thinking at the time. Penelope had been worried about drowning so that's what she experienced. Garby had been worried about losing a limb. Whatever it was that was foremost in each of our minds had become our reality.

We sat in silence for the remainder of the trip contemplating the power of commune cupcakes and our own thoughts.

I recalled Hemp's words: *Worrying is the art of attracting the unwanted.* I could think of nothing I wanted more than to become master of my thoughts. I knew it was the only way I could build the life I want.

When we finally arrived at the station the captain provided us with food, a place to shower, and beds for the night.

"I recommend none of you speak of this – to anyone," he warned, explaining that giving it attention would only bring more of the same.

We agreed.

Before turning in the captain asked for a few minutes of my time in private. Once we were alone he handed me a small white box. I opened it to discover a shiny copper ring engraved with the phrase:

The only wand you'll ever need is a better feeling thought.

I recalled having read that phrase somewhere at the *Downstream Diner. I* slipped the ring on. It was a perfect fit.

"It's really nice, thanks. I don't wear much jewelry. Are you sure you wouldn't rather give it to one of the others?"

"No, Levi. I think you'll make the best use of it. It isn't a fashion statement. It's – quite practical. It neutralizes thoughts so that others either can't hear them – or makes it so that others hear a *distortion* of what you've thought. Sometimes it's best to keep certain thoughts to ourselves." The captain winked.

I was unsure if I'd just been complimented or if this was the captain's way of telling me my thoughts, in particular, are a liability.

I graciously accepted the ring curious if Hemp had invented it. I asked the captain several questions about it, and specifically whether or not there was anything it required such as special storage, or charging.

The captain smiled. "It requires your wearing it."

"Good. I can handle that," I said, relieved. "Are these sold at the *Thought Depot?* Maybe I can get some for my friends."

"No, Levi. You'd be hard-pressed to find another like it anywhere."

"Really? Why are you giving it to me then?"

"It chose you – but only because you asked for it."

"What?" I asked, baffled. "I didn't ask for it. I didn't even know you had it – or that it existed."

"You put a lot of thought energy into wishing your thoughts couldn't be heard by others. So – you attracted the ring. We get what we ask for, Levi. The answer isn't always obvious – or in a form we recognize as the answer. That's why it's important to pay attention to subtleties."

"Right," I said, confused and amazed. I mulled over what he'd said and we soon rejoined the others.

The captain made the four of us promise we would never again *borrow* an auraplane from his lot without asking permission.

We agreed.

Garby offered to pay for the damage with his *Requisite* card. I argued that I should pay for the damage because it was really my fault. Penelope argued that she should pay for at least half the damage being that she agreed to come along. Sarabella cleared her throat in a dramatic way.

"While it's generous of all of you to want to help – none of you can. Remember, you have to spend your limit daily and when you don't the cards reboot to twenty dollars. Thus, you each have access to twenty dollars. I'm sure the damage exceeds your collective sixty. You really should practice using your cards though. You can order online through the *Cosmic Web*.

Our faces simultaneously drooped with disappointment at learning that we couldn't pay for the damaged auraplane.

The captain excused himself and turned in for the night. He suggested we do the same. We headed off to our rooms. Penelope and Sarabella would share a bedroom. Garby and I would share another.

I tossed and turned where Alphia and I lay on the upper level of the hand-carved elder wood bunk bed while Garby snored below. Thoughts of how terrible it felt being in Orable's *residual* presence battled with the fun thoughts I was having about future *Requisite* card purchases. Random thoughts about the *Appearidian Sea* squeezed themselves in here and there. *How could an entire body of water vanish?* It seemed to me that no matter how powerful thoughts are the water would still have to go somewhere. The fact that I stepped into another dimension and watched a residual version of the abduction was mind boggling.

My head spun as I lay in bed staring through the skylight at the twin moons. My mind replayed the evening over and over until finally, much to my relief, I fell asleep.

In the morning the five of us hopped into the captain's auraplane and returned to Sifter's Village. At some point during the trip Sarabella pulled her newly found frame from behind the seat and held it on her lap.

"Why, out of all possible souvenirs, would you choose *that*? There were so many pretty shells back there," said Garby, critically.

Sarabella rolled her eyes.

"I have to agree with Garby on this one. It's a black frame with a black canvas. Looks like someone started to paint – but never finished. Why would you want it?" I asked, polishing my new copper ring with the hem of my t-shirt.

"Yeah. It's just a…" began Garby, catching himself before he finished the statement that would have sent Sarabella into a tizzy.

"It's an *artifact*. Morblid's going to be thrilled. It's the canvas Darvon Damos, Sr. and Hiwinzin fought over on the Cliffs of Doom. Hiwinzin died because of it," she said, dusting it off with the sleeve of Garby's sweatshirt.

Garby pulled his sweatshirt from her at once, "Stop it. I don't want any *doom* rubbing off on me."

Penelope gulped and began to write in her journal.

The captain explained how Darvon Damos, Sr. had lost his position as stabilizer to Hiwinzin and how Hiwinzin subsequently lost his life to Darvon Damos, Sr. "He's well connected – he got off Scott free!"

Garby and I already heard this story. Hemp told us about this tragic event at the *Downstream Diner*.

"Darvon lost his position as stabilizer to *you*. I worry that…"

"Don't say it. I don't want to hear – or think it, Garby," I snapped, uncomfortably aware that Darvon may want to kill me just like his father killed Hiwinzin.

My thoughts rewound to the evening at *The Downstream Diner* when Hemp had alluded to the rivalry between Hiwinzin and Damos, Sr. but Hemp hadn't mentioned anything about the canvas. Why?

"Hiwinzin died because Darvon Damos, Sr. killed him for a position as stabilizer. What does the canvas have to do with anything?" I asked, confused.

"Hiwinzin was going to expose Darvon's portal empire."

"What?" I asked, more confused than a moment ago.

"Hiwinzin had reason to believe Darvon was misusing portals. They were being sold as art. It was a way for Darvon Damos, Sr. to get on the inside of wherever and whoever he wanted – to gather information. Damos has a lot of friends in dark places," warned the captain.

"At one time there were a slew of these. White ones, grey ones, and of course, black ones like this. They're windows to other dimensions based upon their color," said Sarabella, adoring it.

"Can you PLEASE move that thing over there?" asked Garby impatiently, pushing himself as far away from the frame as possible. He practically crushed Penelope against the door in the process. "If they're windows to other dimensions based upon their color I don't imagine *black* opens into *friendly fairyland.*"

Garby, Penelope and I barely took our eyes off the canvas while discussing the merits of tossing it out the window.

"No one's tossing this priceless artifact out the window. So – *back off,*" snapped Sarabella, her hair morphing into a dreadful shade of blood red.

Just then an image appeared on the canvas.

We all gasped.

CHAPTER TWENTY-FOUR

PORTALS

Our eyes locked upon the image and followed it as it ran toward the front of the canvas.

"Excuse me. Excuse me! I couldn't help hearing all the commotion. What's going on out there?" came a voice from the canvas.

The image illuminated the canvas like a 250-watt bulb. A man dressed in white jeans, t-shirt, baseball hat and matching white sneakers scanned our faces as though searching for someone in particular.

Garby practically fell out of the auraplane.

Penelope jumped onto my lap. *Maybe that frame isn't so bad after all.*

Alphia's head tilted from side to side. She growled. "Who's this dude?"

"Who are *you* and where did you find this portal?" asked the man urgently, pointing north, south, east and west from where he stood inside the canvas. "*Where* did you find it? *Who* found it? Tell me at once!" He rushed forward.

"Relax little man. I found it last night during the – storm. It was buried in the sand," volunteered Sarabella. She pushed the little luminous man back farther into the frame with her pinky.

"Where is he?" asked the man, rushing forward.

"He – who?" asked Sarabella, pushing him back, this time a bit farther.

"Hiwinzin. The last time I saw him he was just about to…" The man paused for a moment. "…please – tell me he didn't."

All eyes went to Sarabella.

"He did. He's been dead for more than a decade," she said gravely.

"NO! And, for ten *years?*" shrieked the man, taking a seat in the center of the canvas and planting his face in his hands. After a reflective moment he stood and paced. "What has become of the portals? For years I've tried to access this dimension but all I could see was an endless wall of sand."

We looked expectantly at Sarabella as though she had all the answers.

"You were buried. I mean – the portal was buried. I don't know what happened to the others," she said flippantly, pulling the frame closer to get a better look at him.

The man grew agitated. He droned on about how he couldn't believe the inhabitants of *Dimension 11* weren't using portals.

"Who are you?" asked Sarabella, examining the sides and back of the frame.

"Special Agent Spelzig is all I can tell you," he grumbled, pacing back and forth looking as though at any moment he would jump out and start hitting someone.

"This portal must be placed within Orable's tower on Incantation Island. Do you know of anyone prepared for this critical mission?" he asked, standing and propping his hands on his hips.

"I don't know anyone *reckless* enough to consider it," said Sarabella, dusting sand from his little white sneaker with a makeup brush.

"But – this is urgent. And you mean *courageous*, not reckless. Simply put – if you don't want to end up extinct or catatonic like the lower dimensions, this portal needs to be placed inside the tower at once."

Spelzig glared at us with a mad twinkle in his eyes.

There was a long, tense period of silence. I could no longer bear it.

"I'll do it!" I eagerly volunteered, raising my hand.

Garby shuddered.

"NO – no, no, no he won't. He can't."

Garby pulled my hand down at once and leaned challengingly into the frame.

Special Agent Spelzig ignored Garby and turned to me.

"Boy, can you thought propel? What is your current level?"

"NO – he can't thought propel. He's a level *no-can-do,* about to go on training vest #15," said Garby protectively, pushing me out of Spelzig's view.

"I can do this," I said, breaking away from Garby's grip and arranging myself so that Spelzig and I had a clear view of one another.

"Maybe *after* you learn how to thought propel," snapped Garby worriedly.

"I appreciate and admire your willingness and optimism. How fast can you learn, boy?" asked Spelzig, hope blossoming in his voice.

"I – I don't know," I said, pushing spirals of hair away from my eyes frustrated that I didn't already know how to fly.

Spelzig's face lit up. "I have an excellent idea! Hang me on your bedroom wall. I shall help you prepare. In no time at all you'll have this portal within Orable's Tower and he won't even know it's there," he said, breaking into maniacal laughter.

Garby looked at Spelzig the way a police officer looks at a murder suspect. "You know – Mr. Spelzig, is it?"

Spelzig nodded, *yes.*

"Luckily for Levi this canvas belongs to Sarabella over here," he said, pointing. "She's giving it to Morblid to add to his collection of psychotic artifacts at the museum. I'm sure there's no way she'd *ever* part with it. Isn't that right, Sarabella?" asked Garby, in a menacing voice.

Sarabella and Garby stared unflinchingly at one another until finally she turned abruptly toward Agent Spelzig.

"In the name of progress you can *borrow* it," she said, handing the canvas to me.

Garby fumed. He tugged on my sleeve.

"We need to talk. We don't know *anything* about this dude – or the canvas. I don't want this hanging in our cottage. We should toss it – and him, over the cliffs."

"Extinct or catatonic, I say! The choice is yours," blurted Agent Spelzig, before vanishing into the canvas.

Shortly thereafter we arrived at Sifter's Village. The captain dropped Penelope and Sarabella off first. Garby and I last. As soon as we exited the auraplane we argued and began a tug-of-war with the canvas.

The captain looked on knowingly and bid us a goodnight. He smiled an odd sort of smile and I couldn't understand what was so amusing.

"Would you two please stop this? You're embarrassing me not to mention delaying my dinner. I'm famished," grumbled Alphia.

"I can't believe I'm even touching this shady imposter of fine art," said Garby, infuriated and red in the face. "Look at us fighting over it. See what it brings out in people? Good thing we're not standing on the edge of the *Cliffs of Doom*. Put it in the trash RIGHT NOW!"

"FINE," I submitted, walking toward the compost pile and recycling bin at the edge of the walkway. "Are you happy?" I asked calmly, leaving the frame propped against the bin. I walked toward the cottage, my beady emerald eyes glaring scornfully at Garby. I slammed the screen door so hard it came off one of its hinges.

"Yes – I – I am happy," said Garby, baffled.

Alphia walked toward the canvas and lifted her leg. I saw her do this from the corner of my eye.

"NO! What are you doing? Don't do that, Alphia!" I yelled.

"Busted", mumbled Alphia, lowering her leg disappointedly.

"You're female. Why'd you do that?" I asked, frustration dripping from my words.

"I – I was just stretching," she lied, rolling her eyes as she strutted into the cottage through the special doggie-door I'd cut out for her.

I hurried to my room. I waited and listened behind the closed door until I heard Garby enter his bedroom and close the door. I then tiptoed through the living room and ran outside to get the canvas grabbing a cupcake from the kitchen counter on my way back.

Sitting on the edge of my bed holding the canvas I contemplated hanging it on the wall but knew I needed to put it somewhere out of Garby's sight. As I contemplated a good hiding spot I repeatedly called out to Special Agent Spelzig to no avail. I slipped the canvas inside an oversized pillowcase and slid it beneath my mattress.

Most of the morning I spent doing absolutely nothing - something I hadn't done in a long time. Lying in bed in my climate-controlled lime-green robe I felt grateful that everyone survived the ordeal two nights ago.

Throughout the day I pulled the canvas from its hiding place and called for Agent Spelzig without response. I ordered a computer game, *World of Thoughtcraft,* from the Cosmic Web with my Requisite card. It arrived within minutes. I heard a knock on my bedroom window and when I opened it there was a violet-purple beam displaying the game.

"Delivery for Levi Levy. Please place the palm of your hand, along with your Requisite card, here for authorization," came a voice from inside the beam.

I placed the palm of my hand, along with my Requisite card, inside the beam as instructed. The game slid onto my hand and the beam vanished. Several minutes passed before I could fully grasp what had just happened. I stood there, stupefied, holding the game in midair long after the beam had disappeared.

This delivery was a bizarre and wonderful thing. I told Garby about it immediately and he ordered a game as well. The balance on our requisite cards doubled and we laughed so hard we nearly cried.

I returned to my room and ended up playing the game for hours stopping only for bathroom breaks and to heat up leftover pizza. I devoured a blueberry cupcake with pink icing that I'd grabbed from the kitchen counter earlier.

Shortly thereafter, at exactly 11:11, I heard faint music and stomping. *Could that be Agent Spelzig?* I pulled the frame from beneath my mattress and propped it against my pillow. I removed the pillowcase to discover the canvas was black and barren.

The noise came again. This time I was sure it wasn't coming from the canvas. It seemed to be coming from the wall behind the bed. After returning the canvas to its hiding place I ran into the hallway to see if there was another room next to mine, or a closet I managed to overlook but found nothing of the sort. Returning to my room I pushed my bed away from the wall and drew back the decorative beaded curtain that served as its headboard.

A glowing orange light poured through a hole that appeared to be made for a skeleton key. As I ran my fingers across the wall I felt a ridge. I raced to the toolbox beside my dresser. With screwdriver in hand I scraped putty from the ridge, stuck the screwdriver into the keyhole, popped the lock, and pried open the door. The hairs on the back of my neck stood.

Why hadn't Hemp mentioned anything about the cottage having an attic? Could there be a burglar up there? Is it possible that Agent Spelzig relocated from the frame into the attic?

"My guess is it's a predator. A raccoon. A skunk. Possibly a large rat. I can handle this," boasted Alphia, heading up the narrow green enamel stairway. She made it up five stairs before turning around.

"On second thought – *you* handle this one. I don't care for the dark and I've had a traumatic few days being a castaway and all. Night, night – pet."

"Good night, Alphia," I said, kissing her. I watched as she scampered toward her bed beside the living room fireplace. *And to think I was going to get a German shepherd instead,* I thought, as I closed the bedroom door.

I made my way back to the attic doorway, ran my fingers along the wall inside and found a light switch. When I flipped it on the bulb at the top of the stairway exploded. Bolts of electricity shot toward me. I ducked.

While smoke cleared I rummaged through my duffel bag searching for a flickerlight but couldn't find one. Instead, I grabbed a candle, lit it, and headed up. A sliver of orange light sliced the darkness at the top of the stairs. Classical music permeated the air. I recognized Rimsky-Korsakov's Capriccio Espagnol. It was a song that took me ten lessons, and my mother two hundred dollars, to master on the piano.

"Hello up there," I yelled.

There was no response.

Creeping up the stairway, through the flickering candlelight I noticed a pile of books on the attic floor and the back of what appeared to be a very thin woman bending over them.

"Excuse me," I said softly, climbing up another stair, my head now level with the attic floor.

The figure didn't respond.

Perhaps she hadn't heard me over the music. I watched her pick up books and stack them in her arms, all the while mumbling.

"Excuse me," I repeated in a louder voice. "Who are you and what are you doing in my attic?"

"Ehh," said the woman in a frustrated voice, dropping books as she turned to look at me. She snapped her neck awkwardly in the direction of the music and the volume dropped at once.

A surge of energy blew through the cool attic air. My eardrums vibrated. Good thing I hadn't been standing in her way. Based on the power I felt behind her neck toss I was certain I would have been thrown across the attic and ended up with at least one broken something.

"Your attic, you say? HA! This is MY attic, child. GO AWAY! SHOO," she said sloppily.

In the dim candlelight the woman appeared tall and slender with beautiful blonde hair pulled back into a sleek ponytail. She wore a red ankle-length crepe skirt and fitted spaghetti strap jersey. She had the posture of a ballerina with her chin angled skyward as if the air were better up there. When she stepped forward into the light I gasped. Darkness had been kind to her. The light revealed a tanned skeleton wrapped in wrinkled, barely-there skin with Scarlet-red lips and protruding horse-like teeth.

Without realizing I stepped down a stair, then another.

"This is MY attic," she said, through chattering, rotten teeth. "Be gone!"

"Who are you?" I stuttered, keeping my best eye on her neck. "Are – are you a ghost?"

"Who are YOU?" she asked, in a voice so loud I jumped.

"I'm Levi. I live here."

"So – *you're* Levi. I've heard of you," she growled, while pointing a gnarly finger in my direction.

I ducked. I couldn't help wondering what it was she heard about me and from whom. I watched cautiously as she lit candles, placed them on a cobweb-wrapped table and piled books on a shelf.

"California's a popular place this year," she said, without looking up.

She knows where I'm from?

As I watched her organize books I wondered if I was seeing a ghost in my own dimension or a residual image in another. Or, was I seeing something else entirely?

"I'm Suzanne. I'm a professional dancer," she bragged, twirling across the attic floor. Her skirt flared and an ocean of dust particles swam in the air around her. My nose spontaneously scrunched as the musty smell wafted toward me.

"So, you're a dancer?" I asked, squinting for a better look at her.

"That's right," she said proudly. "I won the senior division of the annual tango competition in Florida a few decades ago."

"Florida? You're from Earth?"

"Not exactly," she slurred.

She ended her dance with a bow so low it caused her wig to slip over her skull and fall to the floor. I could feel my eyes bulge at seeing this. This was creepier than seeing my grandfather's dentures fall into pasta fazool at dinnertime.

"So, you won a competition? You must be a very good dancer," I said patronizingly, picking her wig up and handing it to her not noticing the insects crawling out of it and up the sleeve of my robe.

"Well – thank you," she said too sweetly, shaking the wig and adjusting it just so on her skull. While combing the synthetic hair with foul spiral fingernails she asked, "Would you like to see me dance?"

"Well – not really. I – "

"Which dance would you prefer? The Tango? The Bosanova? The

Waltz? I do them all." She pulled a stack of old vinyl records from a dusty box and put a forty-five on a record player. She reached over, lifted the arm, and gently placed the needle on the record. Round and round it went. For an instant I was back at my great grandmother's house watching her do the same. Grainy sounds shot forth from timeworn speakers as a rusty needle traced dusty grooves.

Suzanne floated across the attic several inches above the hardwood. She stomped and twirled violently. Mixing so many dance forms together caused her to trip over her skirt and knock over a lamp. The lamp knocked down a plant and a compartment in the wall snapped open. Out poured at least a hundred more books. They piled on her until only her feet were visible.

"Are you ok?" I asked, rushing toward her, extending my arm to help her up. "Something similar happened to me just a few nights ago – except with rocks. Not fun," I admitted.

Suzanne looked at me quizzically but said nothing. She declined my assistance and as she pulled herself up by the straps of her blouse a surge of energy, similar to the one I'd felt moments ago, blew furiously through my hair. Every dust particle in the attic danced. Her bones rattled and shook like a loose muffler. I watched her body rise through the books as if they weren't even there. She blew her nose with her skirt, grabbed a bottle labeled *Lawanda's Herbal Tonic*, chugged, then slammed it down on an old chest. Dust swirled. She coughed.

"I'm guardian of these books," she spit with self-importance. "I must keep them hidden."

"*Hidden?* Why?" I asked.

"Good question," she said sloppily, chugging tonic and floating in my general direction. Her skirt gently swept the dusty attic floor. She was so close I could smell her breath. It smelled musky and medicinal.

"Can you keep a secret?" she whispered, her face just inches from mine.

Until this moment I'd only seen her from a distance. Finding myself face to face with her was *horrific*. I wondered if I was seeing bone, or melted skin covering bone. The sight and smell of her was nauseating but I tried my best to hide my revulsion.

"Can you – or can you *not* keep a secret?" she repeated urgently.

"I – I think I can," I said, noticing another rotting smell.

"You *think* you can? There is no *think* – child. There is only I can, or I cannot," she said matter-of-factly. She glowered at me suspiciously then glanced down the narrow attic stairway as though to see if anyone were listening.

For a moment I thought I'd heard Maya's voice ooze from Suzanne's words.

"Ok – yes. I can keep a secret," I said reluctantly, crossing my fingers.

"There are a lot of books here," she whispered.

I laughed spontaneously. I realized immediately that this was a *terrible* mistake.

"What's so funny?" she said scathingly, straightening her dress in a serious way.

"Well – it's just – I mean – the fact that there are a lot of books here isn't a secret – really – is it?"

"Never mind then, know-it-all. I won't tell you," she said, in a dark voice through yet a darker stare.

I swallowed hard and cleared my throat. "Please tell me," I said in an appeasing voice.

Suzanne offered me a swig of Lawanda's Herbal Tonic.

"No – no, thank you," I said, nauseated by the smell of her breath.

"I *was* going to tell you the history of these books, how they came into being and what's inside them. But – I really don't have the time," she said, scurrying toward the cabinet.

"I can help put them away if you'd like," I offered, moving closer to the pile. As I reached for a book candlelight lit up covers. They were all the same. The title read, *A Mender's Mind*.

My head spun at seeing this. I couldn't wait to tell Morblid. I was thrilled but puzzled at this vision. *Why are there so many copies of Agrestalia's book when there's only one original? Is the original here?*

It wasn't until this moment that I realized I was in an attic in another dimension - just like my dream had forecast. I thought back to the cupcake I'd eaten earlier. *Garby!*

I grabbed one of the books.

"DON'T TOUCH THAT," snapped Suzanne. But I already had it in my hand.

"Oh, no – it's too late," she roared, grabbing it from me. She tossed it angrily into the cabinet. A fury of wind blew through the air beside me.

"What! It's too late for what?"

"Your energy is on it. He'll *feel* you."

Her eyes fell upon my copper ring.

"Who'll feel me? What are you talking about?"

"Never mind."

Suzanne slammed more books into the cabinet.

I heard Garby call out to me. I was grateful for an excuse to make a getaway. I stuffed a book inside my shirt when Suzanne wasn't looking.

"I – I have to go now," I stuttered, turning to walk down the stairway.

Suzanne grabbed my arm. Curly, rotten fingernails dug painfully into my skin. I was certain I wasn't in a half dimension, or experiencing a residual event. I looked at my arm then looked suspiciously at her.

"That hurts. Please let go."

Suzanne's eyes crawled over me to the place where her nails, like rusty clamps, squeezed my arm. "Sorry. I misjudge my strength." Her apology oozed insincerity - but she loosened her grip.

"Don't tell *anyone* about seeing me. I'm hiding here from an abusive…ex-husband. You wouldn't want him to find and kill me – would you?"

"Not to be rude or anything but – aren't you already dead?" I asked, rubbing my arm where five red indentations appeared.

"Just don't say a word – to anyone. No one will believe you anyway. They'll just think you're weirder than they already think you are."

Really? I felt as though I'd just been sliced in half by the sharpness of her tongue. I walked sideways down the attic stairway without taking my eyes off her then bolted down the last few stairs and slammed the attic door behind me.

Keeping this encounter a secret proved too difficult. I told Garby everything, detail for detail, as soon as I got downstairs. I brought him into my room to show him the attic but the door was gone.

"I find it hard to believe you, Levi. But, I remember when you didn't believe me about the little girl in the pink dress. So – I'll give you the benefit of the doubt. Wait a minute. Did you eat one of the cupcakes I left on the counter?"

"I did," I said, baffled that the entrance to the attic was gone.

"Sorry – I should have told you they weren't ordinary."

"Yeah – you really shouldn't leave those around," I said, running my fingers across the smooth wall where only moments ago there had been a door.

"She has Agrestalia's book. At least a hundred copies of it."

"She – who? What are you talking about?" asked Garby urgently.

"The bizarre ghost lady in the attic. The only difference is that the covers weren't velvet like the ones Morblid has. I'll show you."

I reached inside my shirt for the book but it was gone.

"*What the* – I had one. I had a book. Right here inside my shirt," I mumbled as I ripped my shirt off searching for it. Buttons popped. One hit Garby in the eye.

"Ouch!' Garby rubbed his eye and looked at me skeptically. I could tell that he was growing increasingly nervous at my seemingly odd behavior. Just then a voice called out from beneath my bed.

"Master Levi – are you there?"

My heart sank. I'd tried contacting Spelzig most of the day. Why out of all possible moments did Spelzig choose this one to respond?

"Wow – voices carry. I can hear that shady agent calling you from the trash bin," said Garby, laughing as he headed toward the door.

"Imagine that," I said, practically shoving Garby out of the room. But, just as he was about to exit the voice came again.

"I repeat – Master Levi – are you there?"

Garby froze where he stood in the doorway. His eyes roamed the room skeptically.

"YOU DIDN'T! The canvas – it's in here, isn't it? You SNEAK!" he hollered, dashing to look under my bed.

"Wait – stop!" I pleaded. "Hear me out."

Garby crossed his arms in resistance but agreed to hear what I had to say. Then he would pour gasoline on the canvas and burn it in the fireplace.

I convinced Garby to give Spelzig a chance. We agreed to take it one day at a time. Spelzig would be given an opportunity to prove that he has good intentions.

Garby kept gasoline and matches close by at all times.

"Hello – I say – is anyone out there?"

CHAPTER TWENTY-FIVE

THE WIND CHAMBER

A week passed since the ordeal at the *Illusiara*. I hadn't heard from Suzanne the dancing ghost but for the one evening in the attic. No one, other than Garby, knew I'd seen her because I was too scared to tell anyone. I was determined to see her again and get my hands on one of those books. This would require eating more extraordinary cupcakes, so I stocked up.

Spelzig had been on his best behavior. Still, Garby's disdain for him persisted. I was relieved that Garby had refrained from dousing the canvas with gasoline. Nonetheless, I hid Spelzig's canvas in a different location each day in the event Garby should have a sudden change of heart.

I spoke with Spelzig at least once a day and typically right before bedtime. Spelzig dispersed words of wisdom that he promised would help me to become the dimension's most famous and respected sifter. I made it clear that it wasn't fame I wanted but freedom, for myself and others.

I appreciated that Agent Spelzig was supportive and patient about my ineptness. I couldn't help wondering if it was because he really didn't have any other options. It wasn't like there were sifters lined up volunteering for the task.

Spelzig was convinced that in just a few weeks, I'd be ready to venture to Incantation Island and implant his portal in Orable's tower so that he could begin an official top-secret investigation.

I thought Spelzig was being overly optimistic and the pressure to succeed felt overwhelming. I secretly hoped his assumptions about me were right but I was painfully aware that my skills were weak.

I kept a timekeeper on my nightstand and worked on improving my time-telling skills. My estimates were never off by more than two years. Hemp said this was very good. On the bathroom mirror I taped a reminder note: *Do not leave the cottage without your watch and ring.* Little good that did.

Lilith Chatters reluctantly returned my baseball hat. She insisted I answer 111 questions before reclaiming it. Although I was glad to have it back I no longer wanted to wear it. I realized it made me feel bad and the whole point of my participation in the *Selective Thought Studies* program, and sifterhood, was to feel good. I wasn't sure why I felt bad wearing it. I rationalized that it was due to my overactive imagination despite Sarabella's warnings.

I spent most of my time practicing solarshay. I was now on vest # 21. With each passing day and each progressive training vest I could feel the effects of my thoughts more, and more. It was getting harder to stay airborne. Crashes were numerous with fractures, sprains and bloody noses occurring daily. This kept Sarabella quite busy.

Darvon Damos, Jr. was as miserable as ever. He finished thought rehab at the *Beverly Soared Center* twice, and no less angry than when he'd entered.

I spent most of my free time watching videos of past solarshay tournaments on my *Think-a-View*. I was envious of how seasoned sifters made the sport look so effortless. Each night before bedtime I visualized myself doing what the best players had done in the videos. Nightly, I'd write my final thoughts in my journal and correct those needing improvement.

Memories of the first day of class and how I rescued Garby haunted me. I hadn't been able to duplicate even a fraction of the skill I exhibited that day. Our first tournament would take place in ten days and I would wear an uncharged vest – a vest that could be drained by my self-doubt as well as the ill will of others.

I couldn't help thinking that a crash resulting from the ill will of others wouldn't be nearly as humiliating as a crash resulting from my own out-of-control thoughts. On second thought, how would an observer know what caused a sifter's crash? It would seem that only the sifter could know for sure, unless the observer's telepathic skill was finely honed.

In my worrisome thoughts I envisioned Darvon Damos, Jr. whizzing through the air, swooping down, intentionally knocking me into a lechuck, or bluyole, all the while laughing. This was the exact opposite of what I wanted and I knew better than to imagine things unwanted. I couldn't help wondering why I kept doing this. It is so self-defeating. I had to do something *and fast*.

Spelzig's teachings were helpful but I needed more. Instead of hanging out at *The Downstream Diner* with my friends after practice every day, I started going to *Forest's Flying Chamber* (also known as the *Wind Chamber*) for private thought propelling lessons.

Forest's Flying Chamber reminded me of the car washes back on Earth except that the chamber skipped the wash and went right to the dry. Gusts of wind spit forth from thousands of tiny holes in the front wall. Two of the four chamber walls were made of a transparent material through which spectators were able to watch while seated cozily on fuzzy white couches in the lobby.

On the day of my first lesson I approached the couch where a young man watched a boy practice inside the chamber. He introduced himself to me.

"What's good? I'm Forest. Welcome to my chamber."

I remembered having seen a photograph of him inside a trophy case at The *Downstream Diner*. Little did I know that I was about to get a lesson from the *Ceres Scorpion's* #1 All Time Interdimensional Hall of Famer, Forest Phire.

I sat on the couch and watched the boy. He was having a hard time of it. Although we'd never spoken I recognized him from solarshay practice.

Forest excused himself and went into his office.

It was apparent the boy was unable to generate even the most basic uplifting thought for each time Forest turned on the air blowers the boy ended up compressed against the back wall.

I laughed. It was a reflex - totally unplanned. I felt *horrible*. I don't like laughing at the weaknesses of others because I know all too well how it feels to be laughed at. Still, I couldn't help it. The boy's facial expression made it impossible to keep a straight face.

Slouching into the couch I hid my face behind my duffel bag in the event I would inadvertently laugh, again. I watched as the boy tried over, and over, to fly. All of his attempts ended disastrously with him blown flat and hard against the back wall.

He gasped for air as he exited the chamber looking as though he were about to burst into tears. I wanted to say something encouraging but drew a blank. He walked to the exit looking deflated. He turned before closing the hallway door. Our eyes met and I could feel his disappointment. Then he was gone.

"Levi Levy," announced a female voice over the intercom.

Startled, I jerked and knocked my duffel bag to the floor.

"You may enter the chamber now. Please read the instructions on the door before stepping inside."

I read the sign:

1) Please leave all negative, self-defeating thoughts outside the chamber
2) Empty your pockets of all sharp objects
3) Use of this flying chamber may result in bodily injury and/or death
4) Enter at your own risk

How do they expect me to control my thoughts before I enter the chamber? If I could control my thoughts I wouldn't be here. This is going to be a complete disaster.

Forest entered the chamber and made a welcoming gesture for me to follow him. I took a deep breath and stepped inside hoping he wouldn't notice that my mind was filled with doubt. I also hoped Forest would, at the very least, provide a helmet. I realized I'd forgotten my copper thought-neutralizing ring and couldn't help wondering if Forest also has Hall of Fame-worthy telepathic skills. I then realized that it didn't matter. *The moment I'm unable to fly my negative thoughts will be obvious.*

"I like your sneakers," I said nervously, pointing to a larger but identical version of my own on Forest's feet.

"Oh – thanks. Maybe someday you'll have your own line with your initials," said Forest.

"I'd like that," I said, thinking about athletes from Earth who had their own product lines. It was at this moment I realized Forest must be the Ceresian version of a star athlete. This was both exciting and intimidating. I stood a bit straighter than before.

"Why are you here today?" asked Forest.

I was at a loss for words. I couldn't tell him I was there because I wanted to learn how to thought propel as quickly as possible so I could help put Spelzig's portal in Orable's tower. So, after a bit of thinking I said, "I need to have better control of my thoughts so I can charge my own vest. I also don't want to look like an idiot at our first practice tournament." And, both of these things were true.

"Try rephrasing that, Levi. Don't tell me what you *don't* want. Tell me what you *do* want."

"I want to be able to fly without using a training vest."

Forest placed his hands on my shoulders. He turned me so that I was facing the wall with thousands of tiny holes through which powerful blasts of air thrashed a boy moments ago.

"Lesson number one," said Forest, "Phrase your words as positively as you can. Even if you don't believe what you're saying, your subconscious mind and all the forces that can assist you will. Words – thoughts – and the feelings they conjure – are the most powerful weapons sifters have."

I liked the analogy and until that moment I'd never considered thoughts as weapons.

Forest showed me the proper flying position. He checked to make sure my knees were bent, my back arched, arms extended, and neck tilted skyward. Maya's voice echoed through my head. "Arms out – neck back – run – fly."

"How will you feel when you can charge your own vest – or better yet – fly without one, Levi?"

Every cell in my body reacted to this question. Fire raged through my veins. Into my head popped a vision of myself flying during class just before I'd realized Garby had lost his vest.

"Amazing," I said, "I'll feel amazing."

"Say it like you mean it. Yell it."

"I CAN FLY AND I FEEL AMAZING," I shouted.

"That's right. Keep saying it. Know it. Feel it. Don't try to fly – just know you can."

Forest exited the chamber. I could still hear his voice as it was pumped in over the intercom.

"I'll gradually increase the air flow. When you feel like you're losing your balance run into the wind and maintain the flying position. Close your eyes and visualize yourself flying. Enjoy your flight," were the last words I heard before a loud clicking sound signaled the intercom was off.

A gentle breeze crept into the chamber. It was refreshing and pushed air into my anxious lungs. The intensity of the flow increased over the next few moments just as Forest said it would.

Alone in the soundless chamber with only the gentle pressure of the wind and my thoughts I felt an unfamiliar peace. I closed my eyes and pretended I was flying. I didn't just hope I could fly, I knew I could. The wind grew stronger. It felt as though it and I were one. I basked in the incredible weightlessness. When I opened my eyes I was flying. I was wide awake, vestless, and flying. There are no words to express the elation I felt.

At the end of the lesson Forest gave me a pair of black sneakers with the initials F.T. embroidered in red thread on either side. I thanked him and put them on. They fit perfectly.

"Well done, Levi," said Forest, shaking my hand firmly. "The boy in the chamber before you has been here many times. This is your first time and you were airborne in minutes. You have incredible potential. It's a rare gift. I know because I've taught a lot of sifters."

I was speechless. Forest Phire, Ceres Scorpions' #1 All Time Interdimensional Hall of Famer had just told me I'm amazing.

Forest offered to give me a lift to my cottage but I politely declined. I wanted to stop by *The Downstream Diner* to see Garby and Penelope. I couldn't wait to tell them that I'd flown without a vest and that it felt amazing!

CHAPTER TWENTY-SIX

PARANORMAL INCLINATIONS

Aweek passed. I went to the Flying Chamber nightly following solarshay practice. I could now thought propel from the top of the bleachers to the bottom and back again without crashing. This was while wearing vest #28 which gave minimal assistance. I could do a "U" turn as well as Darvon Damos, Jr. and Darvon was not at all happy about this.

Anxious to get to my *History of Grey Thought & Antagonistic Artifacts* class I arrived thirty minutes early foregoing my regular breakfast at the *Enchanted Cupcake Café* with Penelope, Garby and Sarabella. Although my refrigerator and freezer were stuffed with enchanted cupcakes I asked Garby to bring another few dozen home. I intended to eat them until I found Suzanne.

In class, I learned why an entire dimension would want to read Agrestalia Mender's book. She was one of Orable's original abductees. Initially, like the others, she was forced to sit through disempowering lectures indoctrinating her into Orable's mind-numbing ideology. But as the days passed she began to ask questions. She disagreed. She challenged Orable's authority. Because of her, other captives also

269

started to ask questions. Her curious nature set a bad example as far as Orable was concerned. Resultantly, she was banned from class and chained to a bed in a small, private room on the top floor of the tower.

There through the circular barred window beside her bed Agrestalia heard the continuous and ever-so-depressing chatter from the Quote Moat below. Unlike the Thinking River, the moat stored and spewed the most disempowering thoughts imaginable.

Agrestalia was forced to spend most of her time alone but she used solitude to her advantage. She flourished despite the relentless and unavoidable background yak. She taught herself how to direct her thoughts regardless of outside circumstances. She learned how to glean information from objects by holding them – a skill commonly referred to as psychometry. In time, she learned how to materialize things she wanted. Being that Agrestalia loved to write, a pen and notebook were her first manifestations.

When Morblid finished speaking about her one could hear a pin drop. All eyes were glued to him hoping to hear more.

"You mean – someday we won't need our duffel bags?" asked Garby, who was seated on the couch beside me.

"Some of you won't need them while others..." said Morblid, and he never finished the sentence. He spoke more of Agrestalia.

"In addition to her being able to materialize objects she could transport them through time and space – a skill similar to the postal service. Of course – no stamps required with teleportation," joked Morblid. "As for all of you – your gifts will gradually...find you. One never knows which powers will develop, where they will develop, or when. Everyone gets something a bit different. Like kernels of popping corn, you never know which kernel will…blow."

Garby and I exchanged worried looks, as did most of the others.

Morblid turned on the holoport which cast a holographic image in the center of the room. The image was that of a little girl sitting on a swing in the *Fields of Possibility*. Her back faced the classroom. Long straight platinum hair blew in the breeze.

My eyes followed the swing's ropes to where they extended into the sky too far for eyes to follow. Agrestalia's colors were muted, her skin pale. Her light pink dress was the brightest thing about her. When she turned around Garby nearly jumped out of his skin.

"That's her! That's the girl!" he blurted, from where he now stood on the couch pointing at the image.

Agrestalia's penetrating, insightful eyes moved across the screen and focused directly on Garby. He trembled at her sight - but I found her intoxicating.

Morblid paused the holoport. "What did you say, Garby?"

"That's the girl I saw – the day my vest fell off at practice – the day I almost died!"

"Are you certain?" asked Morblid, pointing to a close-up of Agrestalia's eyes on freeze frame.

"Yes! Except - when I saw her – her skin wasn't so white – her eyes not so black. She was grey like she'd been dead for a while except she wasn't. Or, maybe she was because she was floating."

Many classmates shuddered and exchanged looks of shock.

Did she say anything – anything at all?" asked Morblid.

"Not that I remember. Wow. I saw Agrestalia Mender – in person," said Garby in a self-important voice.

"I have a second hologram I'd like to show you. It's the one in which she telepathically transported herself right before she…" Morblid paused for a moment before adding, "…crossed over." Perhaps you'd like to take a look to be sure it's the same girl you saw."

Garby nodded frantically.

After seeing the second image Garby was doubly convinced the girl he'd seen was Agrestalia Mender.

Morblid explained that seeing Agrestalia was a rare phenomenon and that it typically occurs during a near-death experience being that she is a gatekeeper to other dimensions.

"Few have lived to tell of seeing her," said Morblid, staring admiringly at her image. "I mean — outside of myself and a select few fortunate enough to have been invited to her house for tea."

I watched goosebumps march over Garby's arms.

"See — I almost died. I knew it! She was waiting for me," said Garby, his mouth dangling open.

"It's good to know you have a friend in another dimension," said Morblid, shutting down the holoport.

Whispers whipped through the musty museum air as we all tried to make sense of this.

For the remainder of class Morblid talked about the spontaneous onset of magical abilities — or paranormal inclinations - and how each of us would be affected by this phenomenon. He distributed a small book he authored entitled:

How to Deal With The Spontaneous Onset Of Paranormal Inclinations Without Losing Your Mind And / Or Your Friends

I opened the book and read the following:

While it's true that the majority of sifters develop the standard, common paranormal inclinations of thought propelling and telepathy (to various degrees), it is also true that each and every sifter will develop, over the course of their adolescence, (and occasionally delayed into adulthood) additional paranormal inclinations unique to them.

Fortunately, or unfortunately, these paranormal inclinations range from the practical and useful to the ridiculous and completely absurd based on one's focus and intention. Additionally, these inclinations appear through spontaneous onset giving one absolutely no warning. Please be vigilant as to this possibility while operating heavy machinery or standing at the edge of the Cliffs of Doom.

A few days later, our paranormal inclinations started to develop as Morblid promised. It happened to Garby first. One day, just minutes before the end of class a beautiful brunette in a Ceres Scorpion's cheerleading uniform appeared - of all places - smack dab in the middle of Garby's lap.

"Whoa," he said, jumping up from the grey leathery couch as though he'd been electrocuted, the poor girl hurled to the floor.

"Where am I?" cried the disoriented girl before vanishing.

Garby flung his hands in the air. His disbelieving eyes scanned the room. He wondered if the others had seen her.

Whistles and applause proved Garby hadn't hallucinated.

Morblid wasn't as impressed as our classmates.

"Based upon your reaction I will assume this is the first demonstration of your paranormal inclinations," said Morblid, chewing the end of a crystal quill.

"Is that what just happened?" asked Garby, shocked.

"Out of all possible paranormal inclinations – this is the one you choose?" asked Morblid, hoping Garby would have enough sense to say — *no, of course not.*

"I haven't decided, yet," admitted Garby, brushing off his lap as though brushing off the remains of a dead rat.

"Our paranormal inclinations — or potentials — develop as a result of our focus and attention, Garby. If you were to spend one tenth of the time you now spend fantasizing about girls focused instead upon a useful paranormal inclination you could accomplish...great feats. However — if you continue to allow your energy to *drift*, as just happened here, then the manifestation of beautiful girls will be the extent of your... power."

Most of the boys in class looked dazed and confused unable to comprehend how this could be a problem.

Morblid's shoulders drooped disappointedly.

"You are all free to go. See you...tomorrow," he said, waving a disconcerted hand through the air.

Several boys followed Garby into the hallway as he exited. They wanted to know how he manifested the girl.

"Do you know who that was?" asked Edyl Cartuff, practically drooling and looking up at Garby.

"Nope," said Garby, stuffing books into his duffel bag, his face still flushed with embarrassment.

"That was Becky Solowada. I've wanted to meet her friend, Julia Omo, since I got here."

"Never heard of either," said Garby, zipping a bag of pens and pencils and writing something in his journal.

"Can you do it again?" asked the boy. "Only this time — with Julia? Please. Put Julia on *my* lap."

Edyl handed Garby a photo of Julia and took a seat on the museum wall beside him all the while looking as though he worshipped him.

Garby looked at the photo of Julia, then at Edyl. Garby thought it was odd that Edyl had this personal photo of a girl he'd yet to meet and immediately classified him as a stalker. Still, when Garby looked into Edyl's hopeful, pleading eyes he felt his angst and wanted to help him.

"Look – I'll try this, Edyl – but only because I want you to stop bugging me," said Garby, snapping his journal shut. He looked at the photo of Julia then closed his eyes and tried to manifest her. It was obvious by the wrinkles on his forehead that he was really trying. Try as he might he couldn't do it.

"Sorry Edyl. No can do."

"Bummer," said Edyl walking away, his hopes crushed.

"Sorry, Edyl – it was a fluke," shouted Garby, "It'll probably never happen again."

Garby was wrong. Not only did it happen again but one evening as he was nodding off he accidentally manifested a group of swimwear models from *Dimension 10* at the foot of his bed.

As news of Garby's ability spread his popularity soared to near celebrity status. People gave him things for no reason and invited him to all kinds of fun events. Every sifter enrolled in the *Selective Thought Studies* program wanted to know him - to touch him - to breathe the same air he does.

Garby told me he had mixed feelings about his sudden popularity and his emerging power. He knew he had to get the embarrassing ability under control fast.

Next, my paranormal inclinations started to surface. One day between classes as I sat on the museum wall eating lunch, Kristin Paterson joined me. She was an unusual looking girl with braces and excessive facial hair. She sat beside me on the wall and stared at me affectionately while batting her eyelashes.

"Mind if I join you?" she asked, belatedly.

I didn't want to be rude but I preferred that she not join me. I silently wished I were somewhere else.

Just then there was a loud rumbling that apparently only I heard. In the blink of an eye I was gone. It was as if I evaporated. I saw Kristen fall off the wall, as she'd been leaning against me. Then everything went blurry. I soon found myself standing in the middle of a winding dirt road with mountains on one side and an ocean in the other. A sign announced:

Welcome to Somewhere Else

"Is this – *a joke?*" I shouted to no one there.

I tried desperately to transport myself back to the museum but since I had no idea how I'd transported myself there in the first place, I didn't know how to transport myself back. Nevertheless, I closed my eyes and visualized myself once again on the wall seated beside Kristen - a very difficult thing for me to *want* to imagine.

It didn't work because it wasn't what I wanted. Each time I opened my eyes I was still right there in the middle of the winding road beside the sign. I headed down the road toward the ocean until I saw another sign that read:

Morblid's Museum – 15 miles

"Fifteen miles!" I yelled, my words echoing through the canyon. It took me hours to get back but I arrived safely.

Penelope was the next to experience a surge of paranormal inclinations. She didn't manifest beautiful women or handsome men, cheerleaders or football teams – nor did she have to walk great distances each time she wished she were *Somewhere Else*. Penelope had a different challenge.

One day while shopping at *Darvon's Thought Depot* she picked up a calendar with photographs of puppies front to back. Secretly she wished she could have all of them. She showed the calendar to other customers walking by while making cooing sounds of wonder at the photos. As she made her way toward the register to purchase the calendar she was stopped by one of the clerks who said, "They're adorable – but they can't run around the store like this. They're tinkling everywhere – people might slip. We're liable you know."

Penelope turned around. Behind her, like ducklings following their mother, were sixty, perhaps seventy of the cutest Blue Frenchie puppies - ever.

The store's *Director of Telepathic Services* contacted Mobert and Sner per Penelope's request. The two arrived shortly thereafter in two white limo auraplanes. They transported the puppies to Hemp's house.

Later that day, Penelope, Garby and I arrived at Hemp's to discuss our emerging paranormal inclinations. We all spoke at once.

"What am I going to do with all these *puppies*?"

"What am I going to do about just disappearing to the middle of *somewhere else*?"

"What am I going to do with all these *girls*? I mean – well, you know what I mean."

Penelope and I shot beams of disgust at Garby.

"You don't even have a problem," I blurted.

"Oh – you don't think having every girl you fantasize about show up in the middle of class *on your lap* is a problem?"

"It's nothing compared to having to find homes for dozens of puppies – possibly every day!"

"You escaped Kristin Paterson. Like that's a problem?" asked Garby emphatically.

Hemp stuck two fingers into his mouth and blew hard. Puppies barked. Penelope, Garby and I stopped arguing. Hemp opened the back door and the puppies fled to the garden.

Hemp appeared overjoyed at our predicament which disturbed me as I would have preferred some empathy. I wanted Hemp to agree that what was happening to me, to us, was the worst thing that could happen to anyone - ever. Instead, he poured each of us a steaming cup of spiced chai and asked us to take a seat.

"Congratulations! Your paranormal inclinations are emerging. This isn't some sort of curse you know. When you first learn to do anything it takes time. It also takes doing it wrong in order to learn how to do it right."

"What kind of inclinations are these, anyway?" asked Garby, frustrated. "They're stupid. Useless. Not to mention – incredibly embarrassing." He gulped half his tea.

"These abilities are neither stupid, nor useless – even if you find them embarrassing," said Hemp. "But, I understand your frustration."

Again the three of us complained at once.

"Would you all calm down and think for a moment," offered Hemp calmly. "You've each just been given the opportunity to attract exactly what you want. And this is just the beginning," he said, filling a large wooden bowl with almond milk and placing it on the back porch.

"I think that's why we're afraid," I offered.

"The key, of course, is to focus your thoughts. What you think about most often is what you will most often get," said Hemp from where he sat on the back porch, puppies jumping over him.

After a lengthy pep talk we finished our tea, thanked Hemp and headed to our cottages.

"It's an awesome concept when you think about it. We can have whatever we want. We just need to be able to control our thoughts. It seems like it should be easy – but it's *unbelievably* hard," said Garby, admitting that an image of the Ceres Scorpion's cheerleading team had just popped into his head.

"Oh – no! I have to go," he shrieked, charging ahead.

After I walked Penelope home I returned to my cottage. I tugged on the screen door but it wouldn't open. I assumed this had something to do with the broken hinge but as I looked down toward where the door was sticking I saw a book wedged between it and the ground. A note taped to the front of it read:

> Levi,
>
> Sorry I missed you. Hope you are well.
> I found this in the wreckage and figured
> it belongs to you.
>
> Captain Scud Scurry

The book looked exactly like those Suzanne had in the attic that dreadful evening I'd encountered her. I went inside and closed the door. Sitting on my bed I studied it. The title on the front read: *A Mender's Mind by Agrestalia Mender*, but when I opened it there was nothing inside. Not a single word.

I stuffed half a leftover butterscotch cupcake (the regular kind) into my mouth and jotted a few words in my journal. I crammed the book into my duffel bag and headed to the museum to talk with Morblid.

When I arrived the gate at the entrance was locked so I jumped over it. The museum was dark except for one window on the third floor. I picked up pebbles and tossed them at the window. This sounds easier than it was. It took me several minutes, which seemed like an eternity, until one of the pebbles hit the window hard enough to make a sound. Eventually, Morblid appeared in the window enveloped by the golden glow of a lantern he held before him.

I held the book high in the air for him to see. He yelled inaudibly through the glass before disappearing. The sound of his boots clicking against the marble museum floors at full gallop grew louder and louder. When Morblid opened the door he looked at the book and hugged me.

"Come in – come in" he said, a toothy smile illuminating his face. Sticking his head out the museum door he surveyed the estate left to right before locking it behind us.

I handed him the book.

"Where, *oh where*, did you find this?"

As we walked across the lobby I told Morblid that I'd found it propped against the screen door outside my cottage. I told him that Captain Scud Scurry had left it along with a note.

Just then an orb floated aggressively across the lobby toward me. It screamed in my ear. My arm swung defensively and I unintentionally knocked the thing a good ten feet away but it came right back and screamed a second time. Morblid grabbed it and pitched it across the lobby. It made a slurping sound as it passed through the stained glass window into the garden.

"Captain Scud Scurry, you say?" asked Morblid, paging through the wordless book.

"Yeah," I said, wanting to tell him about the night we'd met, but thinking it wasn't the smartest idea. I didn't want to admit how irresponsible I'd been with the commune cupcake, nor did I want to confess that I totaled his auraplane.

"Captain Scud Scurry's been – disembodied – for some time now," said Morblid, opening his classroom door.

"No – he's not dead. He gave us all a ride back from…" I stopped speaking at once. I rubbed my ringless finger. *Oh! He probably knows.*

It was true. Morblid already knew everything about the traumatic evening on the Illusiara.

"Oh – he's dead all right," said Morblid. He was – I mean *is* my brother. He's in another dimension now. Wish you would have told me you were visiting him. I'd a come along." Morblid pulled a framed photograph of the captain from his desk drawer and placed it on the table before me. I recognized him at once and was at a loss for words.

"You know Levi, in a telepathic realm such as ours, the only one you can hide truth from is yourself. Unless you happen to have a powerful, thought-neutralizing, copper ring," said Morblid, winking.

Typically, I feel annoyed when others know my thoughts but in this moment I was relieved. I had so many unanswered questions and I wanted, needed Morblid's advice.

As I contemplated the fact that a dead captain had saved my life I realized Scurry must have been part of the commune cupcake experience. After a bit more thought I concluded this didn't make sense because I was able to touch the captain and communicate with him – unlike Orable and the Virusian Soldiers. I was confused.

"Hmm…yes, well. There were two entirely different things going on that evening, Levi. Garby ate the commune cupcake and when he got within ten feet of any of you – you were all pulled into the journey. You pulled my brother into the journey because you kept thinking about him. You were worried about him noticing that one of his auraplanes went missing and you imagined that he would find it – and so he did. As far as the touching thing, well, subconsciously you didn't want to touch Orable – and so you didn't – although you could have. Dimension surfing is a complex matter. It doesn't operate on a firm set of principles. Every situation varies."

I replayed the evening in my mind. I would have to get used to the idea that life in the dimension was unpredictable and that I wouldn't always have answers to its mysteries. I felt a sense of uneasiness rise within.

"So – how did you feel as Orable's residual essence passed through you on the ship?" asked Morblid, tearing open a bag of chocolate covered pyropedes.

"Horrible," I snapped, at remembering.

"Speaking of horrible – I see you've met my ex-wife," said Morblid, holding up the book.

"I did? Where?" I asked, gazing around the room.

"In the attic of the Pagani Mansion in Dimension 9," said Morblid.

"So, *that's* where she is! The Pagani Mansion – Dimension 9 - Wha - no! That's your ex-wife? *You're* her abusive ex-husband?"

"Abusive! Is that what the old battle-axe said?" Morblid fumed. "I lost a good part of a limb trying to save that ungrateful woman," he said, tapping on a prosthetic leg. "If I had it to do over again I'd keep the foot and let Orable have her!" Morblid pounded the table. Tonic in a nearby goblet splashed over its rim.

"I'm so sorry – about your loss, Morblid."

Morblid shrugged.

"So – your ex-wife – she's dead then?" I asked.

"Deader than a doorknob. No offense, Bonkrod," he said, turning toward the back door where Bonkrod was now stationed.

"None taken," replied Bonkrod, in a hoarse voice.

"She had about a hundred copies of this book," I said, picking up the replica and leafing through it. "I took one. I stuffed one in my shirt but when I looked for it – it was gone." I reached inside my shirt to show Morblid the exact spot where I'd stashed it. Much to my amazement – there it was. I was speechless as I pulled the book from my shirt.

"But – I – it – what's going on?" I asked disbelievingly.

"Ah – yes," said Morblid, taking the book from me. "If items don't spontaneously combust as they cross dimensional borders there is most often a delay in their materialization – the length of which varies depending on a host of factors. Could be minutes – could be years."

I was befuddled but thrilled by the book's appearance.

Morblid paged through it. It, too, was wordless.

"Let's get to the heart of the matter, Levi. We have two books here. Neither is the original, but we can take them to Agrestalia and she can tell us who made these copies and why my ex-wife, out of all disembodied spirits, has them!"

I thought this was an excellent idea and honestly, I couldn't wait to meet Agrestalia. But, the appearance of the first book baffled me the most because the note said it was found in the wreckage at the Illusiara. I had no clue as to how it got there. Nevertheless, I now had two copies of the book and was happy about it.

Morblid and I talked for hours. At some point he invited me to spend the night. Exhausted, I accepted.

When I awoke the next morning I stared at the ceiling trying to recall my dream. I dreamt of a cemetery where several ghosts sat around a coffin-shaped table playing a game. One of them had a copy of Agrestalia's book. I jumped out of bed and slid down the curvy iron railing that led from the guest room on the third floor to Morblid's classroom. The book I had taken from the attic was gone. I told Morblid about my dream.

"*Algor* - Arctic Algor Steeley!" he yelled. "One of the ghosts of Sprightly Cemetery. *Obsessed* with books. Thinks I'm a library. Squeezes into the museum through keyholes without my noticing. Takes books – never returns them."

"What would a ghost want with a book? Especially one without words?" I asked.

"Probably didn't bother looking inside. Most people judge a book by its cover," said Morblid, placing two amethyst goblets on the table. "I'm convinced that once we find Algor, we'll find our missing copy."

Morblid filled goblets with organic grandberry juice made from the berries of the grandiose trees peppering the museum grounds. He handed me a goblet.

"Drink this. Its self-esteem boosting properties will do you good."

Self-esteem boosting properties? I'd like a 12-pack, please.

"What's that you said?" asked Morblid, wiping burgundy stain from his lips.

"Oh, nothing. I – I didn't say anything."

"Hmm – I could have sworn – well, anyway, you know – I'm convinced Algor reads to escape the memory of his own murder."

"No! Really? How did it happen? Why? Who?" When?" I asked urgently.

"Many, *many* years ago, Algor was the chef at the once bustling but now boarded up saloon, *Thoughts & Shots*. Orable showed up one day demanding a hamburger. Being that sifters are vegetarian only veggie burgers were available. Orable threw a fit and locked Algor in the freezer. It was a Sunday night. The saloon was closed Monday and Tuesday. No one found him until the following Wednesday morning – his hands stuck to the freezer door handle, a box of veggie burgers clasped between his teeth," said Morblid, demonstrating Algor's death position then lowering his head in sadness.

"That's – that's awful," I said somberly, taking a seat beside Morblid on the couch.

"Algor wants justice. Can't say I blame him. The Minister of I.C.K. – the *Interdimensional Council of Karma* dismissed the case. He dismisses all cases involving Orable."

I wanted to meet Algor. Morblid explained that we could find him at the cemetery on a Friday night when the moons are full. He checked his ephemeris. We were in luck. The moons would be full that Friday - just two nights away. Morblid said we could stop by the cemetery on the way to Agrestalia's. It wasn't exactly *on the way* but Morblid said it would be a fun detour.

These two days dragged. With my duffel bag packed I was ready to leave at a moment's notice. When Friday finally arrived I walked to the museum to meet Morblid who was packing.

"Do you know proper ghost etiquette?" he asked, tossing a short, blue-green camouflage cape over his shoulders and buttoning it.

"Uh – no. I don't think I do. What is proper ghost etiquette?"

"Depends on the ghost. Sprightly ghosts like to play the *Game of Death*, and they're disappointed if you don't play with them. If you really want to get on their good side – and who wouldn't – you'll play."

"The *Game of Death*, huh? Never heard of it. I'd rather play the game of life," I said half-jokingly.

"Well – that's not a ghost's game," said Morblid gravely.

I swallowed hard.

"You'll love it once you get the hang of it. It's hilarious the way they catch everything on fire," said Morblid, tossing his hands in the air and wriggling his fingers as if they were flames. "Wait till you see the hearses – charred beyond recognition. Same as the bodies of the children inside them." Morblid burst into mad laughter.

I sat speechless, my eyes bulging. *Charred children? Everything on fire? Why is Morblid laughing? Morblid must be mad.* A small sound came and died in my throat.

"You look worried," said Morblid, stuffing his duffel bag with odds and ends.

"Well – yeah! It sounds terrifying."

"Trust me. You'll *love* it. Have I ever let you down?"

I shook my head *no* but I hadn't known Morblid very long.

"Right then. Off we go to play the *Game of Death*." Morblid laughed and that laughter echoed eerily through the museum halls. I felt queasy.

"I want to come along, too," came an excited voice from the hallway.

Startled, Morblid dropped the miniature ESPY lamp he was about to place inside his duffel bag. It made a loud crashing sound and broke into several pieces. I turned toward the familiar voice.

"Garby?"

"Nothing better to do than sneak around my museum hallways at midnight…eavesdropping?" asked Morblid, in a surly voice. "How'd you get in?"

"Bonkrod's friend, Kindra, let me in. I was just looking for Levi." Garby took a step back and apologized.

"Out of all possible places to look, you choose…?" asked Morblid.

"Levi – did you tell Garby you'd be here?"

I shook my head, *no*.

"How'd you know I'd be here, Garby?"

"Your journal."

"*My journal?* You *read* my journal?"

"You left it open on your bed!"

"Do *not* write events such as this in a journal," cautioned Morblid, fuming. "Mr. Vanderlin. You are too nosey for your own good. But since you are here and have heard our conversation, I'll put your…curiosity…to good use. You shall accompany us to the cemetery."

"Cemetery? Cemetery! I thought you were going to the diner for burgers!" Garby rubbed his growling belly.

"Me, too," came a second, then third voice from the hallway.

Penelope and Sarabella appeared beside Garby in the doorway.

"It's a cosmic calamity!" bellowed Morblid, a vexed hand against his forehead. "Well – looks like it's going to be an interesting evening." Morblid explained the *Game of Death* to all.

"I'm not going to any cemetery – to meet a bunch of ghosts – and play the *Game of Death*. So you can just forget it," said Garby, quivering.

"I'm not going either," said Penelope, trembling.

"Oh – if all the *neophytes* are going, I don't suppose I have a choice now do I?" grumbled Sarabella.

"If you're referring to *us*, no worries, because we *neophytes* – whatever that means – aren't going!" said Garby, in such a loud voice that several of the screaming orbs hovering about his head darted down the hallway and tossed themselves out into the garden through a stained-glass window.

CHAPTER TWENTY-SEVEN

THE GAME OF DEATH

Untamed winds rustled through the nearly naked trees bordering Sprightly Cemetery. The bamboo gate at the entrance rattled. Silhouettes of clawcons in flight crawled eerily over headstones. Morblid's auraplane with detailed skull and snake paint job blended with the surroundings. Skillfully maneuvering the vehicle through darkness without headlights he managed to find a perfect tree with a perfect view of the large circular pit below. The hoovering craft gently settled into the tree like an egg in a nest.

Beneath us, a phosphorescent light illuminated headstones and crooked trails that carved their way through the plots like drunken worms. As my eyes adjusted to darkness I could see the outline of a pit trimmed with boulders and partially roofed by branches of elder trees. A moan from within the pit floated through the crisp night air.

A transparent clawcon leaped to its feet and flew to the opposite side of the arena. Purple berries and blue leaves fell from its nest at the flapping of its wings. Thick white goop splattered below. The tree shook and the auraplane settled more deeply into the branches.

The monstrous beast landed in a tree not more than twenty feet away. Our eyes locked. I looked back and forth between the pit and the clawcon. My heartbeat quickened. I was sure I was having a panic attack.

Morblid assured me that the ghostly clawcon couldn't harm us. It was a good thing I hadn't yet seen the place where hundreds of skulls, with candles stuffed inside their eye sockets, formed a shrine on the far side of the pit - for my fright capacity was on overload.

Penelope, Garby and I leaned forward and looked down wide-eyed. Sarabella yawned and propped her bare feet against the peeling trunk of the tree cradling the auraplane.

Morblid whispered something about how he'd planted it fifteen years ago from a stem he'd clipped from an artifact dig in *Dimension 9*. He referred to it as a Manipulating oak.

Below us I saw a coffin lid propped between two headstones. I recognized it from a dream I'd had the previous night. The makeshift table held a flattish box and several shiny red ceramic goblets. Unable to get a clear view of the table I twisted branches together and bent them back. No sooner had I done this than the branches violently snapped forward and whipped my forehead. As I tried to silence the sound of my pain I felt a sharp jab to my back.

"Watch it buddy," the oak warned, in a foreboding voice. "Morblid's welcome to park his vehicle in my roots but don't start twisting my extremities unless you want me to start twisting yours."

Astonished - and bleeding just a little - I couldn't help wondering why Morblid hadn't warned us about this possibility.

Without hesitation Morblid apologized to the Manipulating oak on my behalf. I thought it should have been the other way around.

Sarabella removed her feet from where they were propped against the tantrum tossing tree. I pulled the hood of my jacket over my head and sank further into my seat careful not to touch the unpleasant tree.

"Oh – slipped my mind that you don't all know one another," said Morblid apologetically, before making belated introductions that I could have done without.

"Why are we up here – and not down there?" I whispered anxiously to Morblid.

"It's a sacred space. One must be invited if one is to…survive. Besides, I want to give you time to adjust…to the visuals."

"When can we go down?" I asked, with one eye on the tree and the other on the pit below.

"We'll know when the time's…right."

Morblid pressed an index finger against his lips and making a small shushing sound announced, "They're about to begin."

"Begin what?" I asked.

"Shh. The game," he whispered.

A sinister sounding voice cut through the silence below.

"Filthy bird did it again – right on the lid!"

I gasped as my eyes fell upon the ghost belonging to the voice. Icicle-like fingers reached across the coffin lid and pulled a long, shallow box toward itself. My eyes followed the hand to an icy blue arm attached to any icy blue body. This visual reminded me of a dry ice carving I'd once seen at a cousin's wedding, replete with fog. This was the ghost of Arctic Algor Steeley. A vision capable of producing haunting nightmares.

I whispered urgently into Morblid's ear. "That's him. That's the ghost I saw in my dream last night."

Morblid nodded knowingly.

Arctic Algor Steeley removed the lid from the box. It read:

The Game of Death
– A Game for the Whole Family –
Ages: Birth through Deceased
Unlimited players
A Barren Brothers Game

The *Game of Death* is a board game? I was shocked but relieved. *Why would a bunch of dangerous ghosts sit around playing a board game?*

"They need an occasional break from their rigorous haunting schedule," joked Morblid. "They don't play *all the time*. Only when the moons are full."

I looked down at my copper ring disappointed that it wasn't distorting my thoughts as the captain promised.

Morblid interrupted me mid-thought.

"It works – just not all the time. Like everything in life, it's imperfect."

The sound of Algor's voice pulled our focus away from the ring and into the pit below.

"Are you up for playing tonight?" asked Algor, staring into the plot of ground beneath a nearby headstone.

The plot burst into flames. An explosion rippled through the trees jolting the auraplane. Penelope gasped and grabbed my arm. I went lightheaded. Garby nudged me hard then whispered, "Your face. It's locked up with a silly grin. Focus! This is some seriously spooky shit happening right now."

I did my best to appear nonplussed by the magnetic rush of

Penelope's touch and deliberately changed my facial expression at once.

"Look at that thing, will you!" whispered Garby frantically.

I looked at what I assumed was a second ghost. It was a grotesque vision that burned itself upon my memory forever. Words sputtered forth from lesions in the neck of the ghost of, Blaze Barren.

"What color hearse do you want tonight, Algor?" asked Blaze, hacking. Blaze stuck a cigarette into a hole in his own neck.

"Blue," said Algor, holding his hand out expectantly.

Blaze tossed him an indiscernible game piece smaller than a dime. Upon contact it melted a hole through the palm of his hand, fell to the ground and disappeared into tall grass.

Algor searched for it complaining, "No offense – but don't you think *someone else* should hand out the hearses?"

Blaze looked back and forth between the melted hearses and daggers of fire flaring from his own fingertips. He pouted and pushed the box in front of Algor.

"They should make these things out of steel," he said, picking up a deck of cards labeled, *Calling Cards*. He shuffled them. The cards were singed around the edges but they were much worse after Blaze shuffled them.

Algor grabbed the cards. His eyes dripped pity. His eyelashes clinked.

"I'll shuffle – don't touch anything," said Algor pulling the game box away from Blaze.

"It's no fun playing a game without touching anything," griped Blaze.

Just then an ethereal voice sounded from beyond the pit.

"One of these beautiful twin-moonlit evenings you're going to burn the entire cemetery down. That's sure to raise the rest of the sleeping dead."

My eyes scanned the perimeter of the pit until I saw a third ghost. Wobbling toward the others was the ghost of Mire Sludgemore - a walking, talking mound of slug-infested sludge with moss covering just half his body.

Algor tossed him a hearse as he settled into a sloppy heap beside the coffin-lid table.

My bottle of *Mindfire* started to quiver from where it sat on the auraplane's dashboard. The floor vibrated. The sound of distant drumming grew louder. From the corner of my eye I saw a shadow crawl up the side of a nearby boulder. Shortly thereafter I saw the thing to which it belonged. A fourth ghost had arrived.

Veins and arteries pumped beneath its transparent surface. Dreadlocks dangled over dark shoulders and strands of wooden beads rested upon its shirtless chest. Wearing baggy, red, yellow and green, horizontally striped sweatpants, Earl Stoner, danced, drummed and chanted to his own primal rhythm.

Blaze mocked him. Sparks shot forth from Blaze's hips as he danced, causing fires to erupt in surrounding shrubs.

Algor extinguished them.

"Earl – *please* stop drumming," pleaded Blaze.

"I'm summoning the spirits of the cosmos, man." Earl swirled and drummed faster and faster. A 250-watt smile illuminated the darkness of his skin.

Blaze coughed. This caught a small pile of game money on fire.

Algor blew it out.

"All the hearses are burnt. How will we know whose is whose?" asked Mire.

"We won't – okay?" Just play the game already!" snapped Algor.

Just then a translucent form rose from the steam in the nearby hot spring. The form swayed in and out of focus as it expanded and contracted. The world appeared magnified as I looked through the fifth, and final ghost - Perdu Vaporous.

"Let's play already!" howled Perdu, stretching beyond the height of the trees, his voice ascending from baritone to soprano in less than a second.

"Oh – don't forget – everybody starts off with one dead body in their hearse. That's the rules – like it or not."

"That's the *rule*, not *the rules*. Grammar slammer," spit Algor, tossing everyone a second indiscernible object. This time it was a burnt peg, representative of a carcass, and it was supposed to fit into one of the melted holes in the melted hearses.

Just then Perdu touched Algor which caused his arm to melt.

"Oh – sorry! Didn't mean to *disarm* you! Ah ha ha!" laughed Perdu.

Algor's arm grew back instantly.

Penelope, Garby and I watched in amazement.

The five ghosts spun to see who would go first. Blaze won, having spun a nine. He moved his game piece ten spaces.

Algor eyed him suspiciously recounting spaces.

"What are you doing?" barked Algor.

"What do you mean?' asked Blaze innocently, blowing smoke rings as he spoke.

"You spun a nine – but you moved ten spaces."

"I think Algor's right. You did move one too many spaces," added Perdu, from where he sat boiling in the hot spring.

Algor counted the spaces again.

"Look, Blaze. You started here. You spun nine – but moved ten spaces. Ten rewards you twenty grand for dredging the lake and finding the bodies of those two little girls who went missing last July. But – you should be *here*," said Algor, pointing, "Host cemetery charity concert. Pay thirty-five grand."

"Oh! How could I have made such a *sensible* mistake?" asked Blaze dismissively.

"You need to practice your counting," suggested Perdu.

"Counting? You mean morals – values – principles! He cheated!" snapped Algor.

The two argued for several minutes until Algor realized that no one had chosen a means of death – a requirement of the game.

"How do you all want to expire?" he asked, "Sudden death or slow and agonizing?"

Garby and I gulped.

"No-brainer. Slow and agonizing. Why else would I smoke?" choked Blaze, as a grey cloud leaked from between foul lips. He lit five more cigarettes and stuck them in holes in his neck.

All agreed that slow, agonizing death was preferred.

Just then the wind howled and violently shook the Manipulating oak.

"Shh. I think I hear something foul," whispered Algor.

"Don't you mean smell?" asked Mire.

"Same difference. My senses merged during my expiration."

"You're probably hearing Morblid and a few of the sifters on their way to the *partay*," said Earl.

The ghosts exchanged dumbfounded looks.

"What *partay*?" they asked in unison.

"Must I remind you?" asked Earl, swinging dreadlocks.

"Remind? You never told us in the first place," said Mire.

"Short-term memory loss," said Earl proudly.

"But – we didn't decorate," said Perdu. "Let's slaughter a few clawcons. Make the place look festive!"

Penelope, Garby and I shuddered at hearing this.

Garby clasped his hand over her mouth.

"Are they hoping to communicate with the dead?" asked Blaze, laughing himself into a hacking frenzy.

"I heard they're looking for a book," said Earl.

Algor moaned and snuck away, sliding smoothly through the soil beneath his headstone.

"Why am I always the last to know?" complained Blaze.

"Hey, it's a partay – remember? Let's act like we're having a miserable time – so as not to disappoint our guests," begged Perdu.

The five argued. Then for no apparent reason they ran around looking for places to hide.

"Shh. I think they're coming," said Blaze.

"Are we playing die-and-seek?" asked Perdu, snickering.

"Shh. They're here. Scramble *death breath*," said Blaze.

Mire flattened himself against the ground. He blended with the dirt.

Blaze sat in the hot spring with Perdu, the combination of which created an enormous amount of steam. Earl climbed a nearby tree and reclined comfortably on a thick branch while cradling his djembe.

"See – I told you we'd know when the time is right. We've just been invited," whispered Morblid who then started the auraplane and glided into the sacred circle below.

We all reluctantly climbed out of the auraplane and stood around the *Game of Death* careful not to step on graves. Morblid asked us to pretend that we had no idea the ghosts were hiding nearby. It was an awkward few moments.

I sat on the boulder where Algor had been seated just minutes ago. This was a mistake. The temperature of that bolder was so cold that I jumped up feeling as though I'd been electrocuted.

Blaze laughed at seeing this which gave away his hiding spot. One by one the others revealed themselves. Each tried, unsuccessfully, to live up to their reputation as cruel and dangerous entities.

We assured the ghosts that we were extremely frightened. When they tired of their faux scare tactics we all gathered around the coffin table.

Morblid made introductions. There was a brief period of small talk.

Blaze was an entertaining host. The only problem was that he had to stay at least ten feet away from everyone or else clothing would catch fire. He gave off such intense heat that my copper ring scorched my finger even though he was a good three feet away. I removed it and put it in the pocket of my jeans. Ironically, as the night wore on and the temperature dropped, we were all happy to have Blaze around.

Mire poured fat goblets of *Stomped & Bottled* grandberry juice that

Morblid makes from berries he picks from trees on the museum grounds. Earl placed a large tray of warm buttered soul cakes on the table and we hesitatingly indulged.

Perdu invited everyone to join him in the hot spring but none of us had planned for a night in the ghost's Jacuzzi. Perdu ended up soaking solo while Earl played the djembe. Algor was nowhere in sight until Morblid mentioned the missing book. The topic must have hit a nerve with Algor because the ground beneath my feet shook madly as Morblid spoke the words – *missing book*.

I propped my feet on the coffin lid. A blast of bone-chilling cold blew my way and frost formed on my eyelashes. As I moved closer to Blaze seeking warmth, I bumped into Algor and fell hard. Algor bent so that his eyes were level with mine and just inches from my face. I wanted to scream but my lips and tongue were numb from the cold and I couldn't get a word out.

"Just a little F.Y.I for ya. I see that freak fly over my cemetery at least twice a week. I watch him whip those kids when their parasikes aren't held at a certain angle or when they speak without asking permission. I – more than ANYONE – want you to find Agrestalia's book and put an end to that tyrant."

Algor then whipped furiously around the cemetery. He circled back and landed beside me.

"When you're ready to put that canvas portal thingy in the moron's tower – I'm your ghost."

"How do you know about that?" I asked, trembling.

"I wouldn't be a very *interesting* ghost if I didn't snoop around and spy on people's most intimate moments – now would I?"

"I – I guess not," I answered, taking an uneasy step back.

Algor's ethereal body expanded. Shooting over the trees it curled back toward me and slid into the ground beside a nearby headstone.

Faint complaints echoed beneath me like voices through a tunnel. I pressed my ear against the hole and heard Algor shout in agitation, "They can accuse me of being a bad chef – unable to produce a proper carnivore's burger to save my life. But a *book thief* I am not!"

Just as I removed my ear from the hole Algor shot out of it. This resulted in a flurry of snow that covered me with a thick layer of white powder. I shook it off as I stood trembling - my lips blue.

"If you really want to find the original book, submerge yourself in the Thinking River – and inquire," he whispered, as he returned the borrowed book to me and floated away. He turned around abruptly.

"You know – I really have to stop judging a book by its cover. There aren't any words – or even pictures in there," said Algor disappointedly.

I laughed and thanked him for returning the book as I sat quivering. Penelope noticed this and motioned for me to join her where she sat on a boulder, close enough to Blaze to keep herself warm, and far enough away to avoid catching herself on fire. We sipped warmed grandberry juice and as we did I realized that Algor wasn't so bad after all.

Looking around I noticed Garby sitting on the rim of the hot spring, daydreaming. He looked so relaxed and content. I hadn't seen him like this, well, ever really. Unfortunately, this didn't last long because suddenly, out of nowhere, the ghost's Jacuzzi was full of girls in bikinis. Startled, Garby fell backward.

Writhing in pain, the girls jumped out of the near-boiling water – their bodies lobster red. As each stood and saw the ghosts they screamed bloodcurdling screams. One by one, the traumatized beauties vanished. They just popped out of existence like bubbles.

Garby apologized for this unexpected materialization, his face flushed with embarrassment.

"No apology required," said Morblid, shaking his head disappointedly as he helped Garby up from the ground.

The Ghosts of Sprightly cemetery laughed until they cried.

"Is that what you're teaching these kids in that *Sexlective Thought Studies Program?*" asked Blaze, his laughter igniting small fires in nearby shrubs.

"*SE-LEC-TIVE Thought Studies,*" corrected Morblid, indignantly. "The good news is that Garby is learning to manifest what he wants."

Morblid patted Garby's back supportively.

Garby was surprised but obviously happy that Morblid stuck up for him this way.

The ghosts were now a bit wired whether from too much grandberry juice, soul cakes, or laughter, was hard to tell. They wanted us to play *The Game of Death* with them just like Morblid had said they would. We agreed but it was a sad experience. The game board was charred, the calling cards unreadable, the hearses and playing pieces melted beyond recognition. The ghosts were bummed. Morblid promised to make them a new heat-resistant version of the game and they were thrilled about this.

"Well – it's been more fun than a barrel of orbs but we must be on our way. I'll bring the new game next full moons!" said Morblid, holding the book we'd come for high into the air. He thanked Arctic Algor for returning it and thanked the others for a memorable evening.

We all returned to the auraplane. As I buckled myself in I felt something tighten around my forearm. When I looked I saw that a thin branch had coiled itself around my arm and was squeezing.

"That's a nice watch. You don't really need it. I'll trade you for one of these" said the Manipulating oak, presenting me with a bejeweled treasure box full of sparkling valuables.

In a quick glance I saw silver and gold watches, chunky decorative rings, pocket knives, chains and all sorts of strange and unusual treasures. But, nothing in that box could be nearly as valuable as my ESPY watch as far as I was concerned.

"Thanks – but no thanks," I said, attempting to unravel the branch that was twisted around my arm and causing it to turn blue.

The Manipulating oak persisted.

Finally, Morblid noticed it behaving badly and put an end to it. The auraplane lifted off and the ghosts flew beside us for awhile as we headed in the direction of Agrestalia's cottage. Just before he flew off into the night Algor called out to me, "Levi! Call me. I'll help you put that portal thingy in the tower."

"But – I don't have a phone!" I yelled.

"You don't need one. Just call me," he shouted."

"Put the *what* – in the *where?*" asked Garby, panic-stricken. It took him a good minute to process what Algor had said.

"Oh – no you don't. You're not going anywhere near that tower," said Garby, crossing his arms over his chest. Sticking his head out the window he shouted, "Hey, frosty! Don't wait around for a call from

Levi. He's not going to put that stupid portal in the tower if I can help it." Garby then turned to me and said, "You really need to stop hanging out with dead people. First there was the captain, then Suzanne – now these clowns. You know how they say you end up like the people you hang out with?"

CHAPTER TWENTY-EIGHT

TELEPATHY TEA

Soon we arrived at Agrestalia's followed by Mobert, Sner and Hemp whose presence was requested by Morblid.

Agrestalia didn't look anything like I thought she would. She was almost perfect and appeared to be close to my age. She wore a billowy pale pink dress and a band of wildflowers meandered through hair the color of sunlight. Dozens of orbs danced playfully around her.

She introduced herself to us. I stopped breathing momentarily as if breathing were no longer necessary. Garby didn't recognize her at first but when finally he did both he and I thanked her for saving us that day during solarshay practice.

"You're welcome. It's part of my job to intervene in P.B.E.'s – premature bodily evacuations," she said, gently squeezing our hands. "You both have a lot of life left to live."

"Aggie – good to see ya," said Sner, rushing in to hug her.

Several of the orbs that had been dancing around Agrestalia were now dancing around Sner. The orbs reminded me of the ones I'd seen at the museum except that those were mostly purple with faces inside them, some of which screamed.

"What are orbs, exactly?" I asked, touching one gently.

"Packages of energy filled with the essence of someone who has died but doesn't want to leave the dimension," said Sner.

"Why don't they want to leave?"

Sner shrugged. "They have their reasons. Usually because of some kind of unfinished business – like with Hiwinzin."

"I see. Why are they following you?"

"I don't know. Curious I guess."

Sner carried on a brief conversation with one of them.

"You can talk to them – and they can hear you?" I asked.

"Not just me – you, too! Anyone, really," said Sner.

"So – in addition to screaming – they also talk?"

"Not exactly. They communicate telepathically for the most part. You hear them in your head. Although – I once met an orb from *Dimension 10* that talked. It would mostly complain and pitch itself at anyone it found remotely annoying."

"Oh," I said, making a mental note to keep an eye out for that one.

As I listened to Sner I noticed that patches of pink now covered his body. It was the same pink as Agrestalia's dress. Sner told me that when they hugged earlier her essence rubbed off on him.

I looked down at my clothing. Her essence was on me, too. Agrestalia explained that this is the result of energy transference. She said it happens to everyone, every day, except that most can't see it.

We all playfully touched one another experimenting with this fascinating phenomenon. When we tired of this I looked around and noticed that the house, and everything in it, was devoid of color. It reminded me of the old black and white movies I once watched with my great grandmother.

My head boiled with questions. I wanted to ask Agrestalia why her house was in black and white. I wanted to ask her about the day Garby saw her at the river. I brought the hat I'd found the night I arrived hoping that she could tell me something about the boy to whom it belonged. But we'd just met and I felt it was too soon to ask her so many questions.

Everyone took a seat around the table. I scurried to take the one closest to Agrestalia. A silver flask floated between us pouring steamy spiced chai. It was a pleasant, familiar aroma that relaxed me.

I glanced at my ringless finger. I'd removed it at the cemetery and put it in the pocket of my jeans. Luckily for me it was still there. I chose not to put it on. I couldn't help wondering if Agrestalia could hear my thoughts.

While Sner regaled her with stories of their journey and close encounters with mad clawcons I noticed something strange happening in my teacup. Acting nonchalant, I pulled the cup and saucer closer for a better look. The tea swirled. The tiny whirlpool accelerated. I felt the resulting draft and caught a whiff of vanilla.

Random chatter erupted around the table. I listened as Morblid told Agrestalia about the day the Hiwinzin Gorman candle exploded. While hearing bits and pieces of muddled conversations I glanced around the table and soon realized that mine was the only cup with any activity.

Staring into the swirling taupe liquid I listened as Hemp told Agrestalia about his latest invention – the ESPY watch. I flushed with embarrassment as he credited me with the idea. I smiled appreciatively at him as he sipped his tranquil-as-a-puddle tea.

Looking down into my stormy tea I wondered if I could drink it. As I raised the cup to my lips Agrestalia turned toward me.

"Levi – tell me about your journey."

She rested her hand upon my shoulder leaving behind another patch of pink. I stopped breathing at her touch and returned the cup to its saucer.

"Which journey?" I asked, feeling a peaceful, easy feeling flow through me at her touch. I looked back and forth between her and the cup.

"Tell me about the journey from Earth to Ceres," she said, seemingly amused at my preoccupation with the tea.

"It was intense. I felt like I was slipping out of my skin."

"Really?" she gasped, sipping tea with her pinky extended.

Again, I wondered if she could hear my thoughts.

A few seconds later words floated in my tea:

Some. Not all.

Which ones? I studied the tea, waiting for an answer.

Only the ones you want me to.

I liked that answer. I looked around the table to see if anyone had noticed that Agrestalia and I were passing notes - mind to tea - but the others appeared too preoccupied with their own conversations to notice.

"I hope you're all planning on spending the night. I can arrange for color in your rooms if that would make you more comfortable," she said, looking at me.

I realized in this moment that she must have been listening to my thoughts about how depressing it must be to live in a house devoid of color. I hoped I hadn't hurt her feelings. But honestly, I couldn't help feeling like a character on the page of a coloring book with me being the only thing colored.

"I'm – I'm ok either way," I lied. "Although – some color would be nice."

Agrestalia's eyelashes flickered knowingly at my dishonesty.

Nonetheless, in a very dignified manner she showed us to our rooms. Later, we were to meet in the dining area to discuss her book.

I was the last to be led to my room. Agrestalia floated up the stairway beside me. She pointed to a panel on the wall inside a black and white room. The panel had more than fifty different color switches. She told me I could choose any color I want. I chose red. The only problem was that when I flipped the switch *everything* in the room turned red. Overcome with anxiety I stood grimacing in the center of the too-red room feeling as though I'd had too many shots of espresso.

"Oh – you don't like it?" she asked, regretfully.

She was being so accommodating. Wanting to be appreciative I tried to find a way to politely express how hyperactive I was feeling surrounded by the color. "Well – I like red. But – just not so much of it all at once."

"Hmm…well, I never could understand why anyone *needs* color. See if you like any of these better," she said, flipping switches.

The room changed color so fast I became nauseous. I placed my hand over my stomach. She understood the gesture and stopped flipping switches. The room was now light blue. This was definitely an improvement.

Agrestalia straightened her dress and floated out the doorway. She turned and said, "The assessment will take place at 11:11. Please be in the dining room by 11:00."

She floated down the hallway. I followed her, stopping to peek into one of the rooms along the way. Black and white photographs covered the walls, floor to ceiling. Before I could get a good look at the images Agrestalia slid in front of me, blocked my view and closed the door at once.

"That's *my* room," she said, locking the door with a silver key dangling from her rope necklace.

"I understand. It's a nice room. Who are the people in the photographs?" I asked.

"They're not photographs. That's my memory wall."

"Memory wall?"

"Yes. It's private," she said, as she walked away. I watched her disappear through the wall at the end of the hallway.

"What's a memory wall?" I asked, too late for her to hear.

I ran toward the wall through which she had just passed. I wanted to follow her. I recalled Sarabella having told me that nothing is really solid. That everything is just pieces of vibrating light. So, ignoring all common sense I tried to walk through the wall. My feet were the first to feel the resistance, followed by my hands and then the rest of me. *Vibrating light, huh? I'm pretty sure this is plaster.*

I turned and walked back down the hallway. Floorboards creaked beneath my weight. In between creaks I heard cries from Agrestalia's room. I paused to listen. A wave of sadness washed over me and the cries stopped. I assumed the sounds were coming from her memory wall. Curiosity got the best of me and I peeked through the keyhole to her room.

The impact to my forehead took me completely off guard. A bejeweled doorknob with a too-sweet voice apologized, "Oh my, hope you don't get a migraine. You startled me. I think I punched a little harder than usual. For the record – Agrestalia's memory wall is private."

"You don't look – or sound like Bonkrod," I said, rubbing the pain from the bump on my forehead.

"You know Bonkrod? We once monitored doors together at the museum – until Morblid gave me to Agrestalia for her birthday. Tell him Evokina said hello – will you? I miss him dearly."

"Right," I said, dazed and confused. I opened my mouth to speak but no words came.

By 11:00 p.m. everyone was gathered in the living room. I arrived early and spent time trying to convince Agrestalia to experiment with mixing colors. Although what she attempted wasn't quite what I had in mind it was a step in the right direction.

While the living room was still mostly grey Agrestalia had made the couch, a few scattered rugs, and the drapes, pink. The table for the upcoming book assessment was now lavender.

Morblid voiced his approval as Agrestalia mingled.

"It's great seeing you," she said, hugging Hemp. "I've looked forward to leads regarding my book for such a long time. It's my dream to see all caged minds free." A tear slid down her cheek. I rushed to her side and handed her a tissue.

"What did you just say – about caged minds?" I pressed, at

remembering having heard Airaldo say something similar. "Does everyone say that?"

"I don't know, Levi. I say it," she said, wiping away a solitary tear and motioning for us to join her at the table. We all took our seats.

When the timekeeper turned 11:11 Agrestalia closed her eyes and picked up one of the books. She held it for a moment, put it down on the table and did the same with the other. We all watched anxiously. The purpose of the meeting was to have her hold the books and glean whatever information she could from them. She closed her eyes and entered a deep state of relaxation. We all watched and waited anxiously. The tension in the air was suffocating. A few minutes later a wave of disappointment washed across the table - originating with her. She opened her eyes.

"These copies have tracking incantations on them," she concluded regretfully, as she handed them to me.

I sat there thinking, trying to make sense of this. Looking over at Garby it was apparent that he was, too.

"Tracking – incantation? As in knowing where it is? As in Orable knowing where it is?" barked Garby.

Agrestalia nodded, *yes*.

"Well – why'd you give them to me?" I fumed, tossing the literary hot potatoes to Garby who then tossed them to Penelope, and so on.

Agrestalia grabbed the books mid-air. She placed them on the table and poured a ring of sea salt around them. She then revealed that she sensed Orable's energy on them. As she ran her fingers across the covers more impressions came.

"I'm getting that Orable had his publisher print thousands of copies intended to deceive. Those copies are being distributed dimension-wide. Some are being sold at *Darvon's Thought Depot* as journals – but they're linked cognitively to Orable's etheric mind."

As I gazed around the table I couldn't help noticing how completely absent of understanding those faces looked.

"What does that mean?" asked Penelope anxiously.

"That means – not only can Orable track the location of the journal and its holder but – he can also hear the holder's thoughts."

"Wow! That's amazing," said Garby. "Not at all a good thing but definitely amazing."

Panicked chatter erupted around the table. Penelope, Garby and I worried that our own thought journals may be some of those linked to Orable. Luckily, we had them with us for Agrestalia to evaluate.

There was good news for all. None of our journals were linked to Orable.

My thoughts flashed back to the night I met Suzanne. She had at least a hundred copies of the book. I couldn't help wondering what role she plays in this demented drama.

"Hemp – we must inform the book doctor. She'll want to find and burn every copy in existence. It's less than a day's journey to her castle. It would be wise to leave in the morning and travel by daylight. She'll initiate the search and send her army of agents and publishers out to investigate," said Agrestalia.

Hemp glumly nodded agreement.

The silver flask floated around the table filling empty teacups. All agreed that in the morning we would journey to see the book doctor at her castle in the Mountains of Iam.

Meanwhile, Agrestalia recommended we bury the books in the garden and cover them with sea salt because this would interfere with Orable's tracking incantation.

I thought this was an excellent idea. I grabbed the books. Garby and I bolted. We ran around the living room in circles bumping into one another until finally I stopped beside Agrestalia.

"Where's the back door?" I asked urgently.

She pointed and held out a large crystal salt shaker.

"Right," I said, grabbing the shaker. Garby and I dashed into the garden to bury the duplicitous books.

The following morning a voice in my head urged me not to go to see the book doctor. It was a vague, gnawing sort of thought that kept popping up between other thoughts. I pushed it aside best I could and embarked upon the day's journey.

"Why are we walking? Can't we take an auraplane?" asked Garby.

"Too dangerous. *Sifter's Network News* reported sightings of a flock of wild clawcons," said Sner, elaborating about how sometimes they kick auraplanes causing them to crash into nearby mountains. Sner learned of two new casualties as he continued to watch the *SNN* report on his *T-View*.

"I'd rather face clawcons than the shady interdimensional beings coming and going by land," said Mobert, swinging a sickle at branches to widen the path.

"Great," I mumbled, bending branches out of the way as I reluctantly trudged onward. "That's just great."

Visibility was low even in daylight. Thick fog blanketed the ground. I couldn't see below my knees. As I looked around at the others I saw a bunch of legless journeyers seemingly floating across perilous territory.

We'd been walking for hours and we hadn't yet seen a sign. A few minutes later we arrived at a clearing. I noticed a pile of something shiny reflecting sunlight. I bent to scoop luminescent flakes from the ground.

Sarabella demanded that I give them to her. She took some of them from me and rolled her eyes. She started to complain about her career, her life, life in general – pretty much everything. Her hair turned tinsel silver. I was anticipating a bright shade of red. I didn't quite have this hair color mystery figured out, yet.

"He took them. I knew it. He took them," she said, angrily tossing the shiny flakes in the air.

"She's right. Look! There was a sign here. I think we've been walking in circles," said Mobert, snarling.

Sner bent to sniff the area.

"I just picked up the scent of Incantation Island," he said, with dread.

"What does Incantation Island smell like?" I asked.

"*That,*" said Sner, pointing to the soil.

Incantation Island was a good twenty miles southeast. One could reach it by water, air, or possibly a treacherous trip across the dilapidated bridge that once connected it to the mainland. Only Orable and his Virusian Soldiers live there. Finding a scent to the island on the trail couldn't be good.

"So – what exactly is the scent?" I asked. "Do you think it's the scent of a clawcon?"

"Doesn't smell like one to me," said Sner.

"OH – PA-LEASE! If you want to identify a scent you ask a *dog* – not a – whatever *that* is," said Alphia indignantly, pointing at Sner.

"I'm a nelf – and I welcome all opinions," said Sner, watching Alphia sniff the ground in small circles.

"Maybe it's a mouse, a chipmunk, or a raccoon," I suggested, as I watched Alphia sniff.

"We don't have any of those in Ceres. It smells like him," said Sner, taking several steps back, his eyes nervously raking the trees.

"Him who?" I asked, my eyes now following Sner's.

"Him – Orable."

"Smells like butt to me. And I know what butt smells like," bragged Alphia.

Sner stifled a laugh.

I looked at my ESPY watch. It was purple, just the way I like it.

"Best we stop wasting time talking and get out of this maze," said Hemp. "I'll call for directions."

Hemp closed his eyes and tilted his head skyward attempting to telepathically connect with Priscilla. As he did this a loud rustling sound skipped over the roots of the trees above us, similar to the way a tossed stone skips over the water's surface.

We all ducked as bits of dirt showered us.

"What was that?" I asked, keeping one eye on my watch.

Before anyone had a chance to answer it happened again. The forest's roof jiggled violently. There was another shower of dirt, followed by three loud skipping sounds. I looked skyward. There was now a gaping hole above where I stood. Before I knew what hit me I was caged and dangling beneath a sleek black parasike at least twenty feet in the air and gaining altitude. The cage rattled and shook.

"Who are you? Where are you taking me – and why?" I roared, at the back of what, to my dismay, could have only been a Virusian Soldier.

Higher and higher we flew. Below us flowed a winding river. It was the same river from my clawcon-filled nightmare. It was at this moment I realized my nightmares, like my dreams, are forecasts.

A flock of black clawcons surrounded me, just like in my nightmare. I was being abducted and taken toward an ominous crooked tower in the distance. I shook the rails of the cage as hard as I could. I jerked the bars but it was no use.

CHAPTER TWENTY-NINE

THE MAGIC MAKER

I craned my neck around trying to get a better look at the parasike's pilot. My heart dropped at recognizing his face.

"You? You! But why? Where are you taking me? Sarabella was right about you! You *are* a Virusian Soldier! And to think I was stupid enough to defend you to her," I yelled, grasping metal bars and kicking the cage until my foot ached.

"I see you found my hat. Looks like you're one of us now," said the boy.

I ripped the hat from where it was attached to my duffel bag and stuffed it through the narrowly spaced cage bars. It whizzed and spiraled toward the ground some two hundred feet below.

"Why'd you do that?" shouted the boy, jerking the parasike handle in frustration.

"I'll never be one of you. YOU'RE not one of you. You're being lied to. Your mind isn't your own!" I yelled.

"You don't know anything about me," snapped the boy, shooting venomous looks at me and kicking the cage with his muddied boot.

CRACK!

What just broke?

I looked at the river below. *Hmm – death by drowning in a cage, or death by brainwashing. I'd like a few other options, please.*

"I may not know everything about you but I know you just abducted me and that we're flying toward Orable's tower. I'm sure you didn't come up with this plan on your own. Kidnapping isn't a normal pastime. I'm your friend, not your enemy. But you're obviously too *stupid* to see that," I yelled, over gusts of wind.

"I'm not stupid. Don't ever call me stupid. Besides – *you're* the one in the cage," the boy yelled back caustically.

I reflected. He had a point. I snapped back nonetheless, "Well – physically yes. But mentally – it's you who is caged!"

"SHUT UP!" yelled the boy. He kicked the cage again, harder than before.

I heard a second snap. The hook connecting the cage to the parasike broke in two. Half of it landed on my lap. *Tell me this isn't happening.* Suddenly, my organs felt as though they were lodged in my throat. The cage plummeted toward the ground faster than the speed of fear. I could hardly breathe. This was worse than the day Garby lost his elevest.

Angry wind swept through my ears and yanked wickedly at my limbs. Every part of my body pounded against the cage as it tumbled. Back and forth I went like a ragdoll in a washing machine. There was a sudden impact and I was engulfed in water. I watched trillions of tiny bubbles rise as I sank deeper and deeper into the ever-darkening abyss. It happened so quickly I didn't have time to fill my lungs. *Have to ration oxygen. Must stay calm and escape. Why didn't the bloody thing fall apart on impact? I will not drown at the hands of a Virusian Soldier. Will I? Agrestalia! Help!*

River voices erupted around me like a party with dozens of people speaking at once. Overlapping laughter echoed through my head. The voices were uplifting and reassuring - some so brilliant I almost didn't mind dying in their presence - almost.

The vision of millions of tiny bubbles ascending through the water was breathtakingly beautiful. It was a bittersweet moment as air hunger argued with survival instincts cautioning me not to inhale. Unfortunately, the primal urge to fill my lungs overcame all logic. I inhaled. *This hurts. I'm drowning.*

The world fell dark and silent. I basked in nothingness until I felt water gush from between my lips. Coughing violently I opened my eyes to see a girl with a grey face removing her lips from mine. She twirled. Her vibrant, psychedelic dress was dizzying to the eyes.

"Ag-res-tali-ia," I choked. She smiled as her image faded. A pain hit me hard in the chest. Each breath burned wickedly. Freezing and wet I shook uncontrollably. As I twisted my t-shirt to wring water from it, both it and my jeans dried instantly. A peeling sensation rushed over me, toe to head. As I looked around I saw that I was lying on a patch of lilasuckle grass on the river bank. Beside me sat the still-in-one-piece, securely locked cage. As I contemplated my dry clothing, and the fact that I lived to lay my eyes upon that invincible cage, a sense of gratitude squeezed a bit of anger from me.

"Thanks, Agrestalia," I yelled, to no one there. "But really – what have you saved me for? More near-death experiences? And why haven't I saved myself. I'm much too proud for these magical handouts."

Agrestalia's voice popped into my head as though it were a thought of my own.

You're welcome. No time to talk. Been a busy day for P.B.E.'s – premature bodily evacuations. On my way to revive a visually impaired clawcon. Crashed into a tree. As for you, you have unfinished business, Levi. You're here for a reason – to make a difference in the dimensions. As for your pride, lose it or use it as a motivator because like it or not, until you master the magic in your own mind you're at the mercy of the minds of others. Soon you'll tire of the disconnection between your mind and your power. Oh, by the way, thanks for encouraging me to mix colors. I'm having such fun!

"You're welcome," I said, attempting to stand on shaky legs.

Which way should I go? If only I could fly. No – it's not about flying. It's about thinking. It's about feeling. It's about focusing my thoughts. Whatever I think about I get more of. Seems so simple, but it's not.

I decided to follow the river back to the compound. It was definitely the long way to go but it was a sure thing. I turned around for a final look at the tower, relieved to be free. I wondered if they had beds inside or if Orable makes his prisoners sleep on the floor, handcuffed.

As I turned away from the tower I felt a hard tug on my arm followed by several clicking sounds. I spun around to find myself handcuffed to my abductor. This time, instead of being caged I was forced to sit beside him on a parasike. We bickered as we flew toward the tower. When we landed the boy dragged the parasike on one side and me on the other.

I didn't like this at all. I stood and yanked my arm - the one handcuffed to the boy - and he was tossed to the ground.

"I don't know who you think you are – but you're not going to bully me and drag me around," I barked. My eyes felt dagger-like as I stared him down.

"I found our hat," said the boy, in a numb sort of way, rising and placing it on my head. "We really are two of a kind you know. Hey – my name's Justin. What's yours – friend?" he asked, extending his hand for a shake. As I looked at that hand I couldn't help feeling rage rise within me like I'd never felt before. For a moment I was frightened of myself, my thoughts – of what I might do. I knew I had to get it under control fast.

"My name's Levi. But, I don't imagine you have any friends if this is how you treat them." I tore the hat from my head with my free hand and practically squeezed the embroidered lettering from it.

"That was quite a fall. I didn't expect to find you alive. You're a lucky guy," said Justin, gazing skyward.

"Is that what this is – *luck?*" I said, as I shoved my cuffed hand in front of Justin's face.

Justin pulled his arm down – hard. Along with it came mine.

"I've got orders to take you to Orable. I'm just following instructions or there'll be consequences."

My eyes locked venomously with his.

"Really? And what *are* the consequences of a failed kidnapping?" I asked icily.

"Too graphic – trust me. You don't want to know," said Justin, his face leaching fear.

"Well, I'm not a sheep. I'm not going to let someone monopolize my thoughts and dumb me down. I won't carry out his missions or follow his ridiculous, self-serving instructions. I think for myself."

"Orable can fix all that. You'll get to the point where you won't even want to think. He'll do it all for you. Life's easier that way. Just do as you're told. Don't ask questions. Orable's really helping you – protecting you from yourself," said Justin, through blank sort of eyes.

I laughed spontaneously and for the first time ever a bit sardonically.

"Oh, Justin – you've been misinformed. Let me get this straight. If Orable told you to kill me, right now – you'd do it – no questions asked?"

"He knows best. I don't question instructions. He represents *The Order*."

"The ORDER? What ORDER?"

"The cosmic order. He's a chosen one. He can talk to the magic maker."

"The magic maker?" I repeated, feeling my eyebrow arch skeptically.

"You know – the one who puts magic in the wands," said Justin.

"You're joking, right? Please tell me you don't actually believe that."

"I believe whatever Orable tells me."

"How sad for you. Magic isn't in a wand. It's here," I said, pointing to my head. "You're the magic maker. We're all magic makers."

"That's just silly. Everyone knows there's only one magic maker and he's the only one with any magical power," said Justin, urging me to walk faster. Justin yanked my cuffed arm. I yanked back harder. We exchanged challenging glares.

"Hmm. So – does Orable have magical power?" I asked, stopping abruptly and causing Justin to fall.

"Well – he's been asked to speak on behalf of the magic maker which gives him a lot of power," said Justin, from where he lay on the ground brushing dirt from the knees of his raggedy grey uniform.

"Yeah – I bet it does. At least in the eyes of those whose minds aren't their own," I said.

Justin stood and pulled me in the direction of the tower. Every time he pulled, I pulled back harder.

"Have you ever seen the magic maker?" I asked.

"No."

"Well then – how do you know she exists?"

"She? It's not a she. It's definitely a he. There are a lot of books written about him."

"There are a lot of books written about a lot of things. Just because there's a book about something doesn't mean it's true," I said sharply.

Justin stopped fast in his tracks. A look of grave perplexity fell across his face like a black velvet curtain at the surprise ending of a play.

"Look at that. You're actually thinking," I said caustically.

"Stop it! You're going to get me in trouble. We're not allowed to think on our own. It's too dangerous." Justin jerked his cuffed arm forward deliberately, causing me to stumble.

"What's *dangerous* is not thinking for oneself," I said, clamping my hands over my ears at once. "Oh – what's that *dreadful* sound?"

"What sound?" asked Justin, stopping for a moment to listen. His cuffed wrist dangled in the air beside my face.

"Oh – that's *so* annoying. I feel – I feel suddenly depressed. It's draining."

"What does it sound like?" Justin tilted his head in anticipation.

"Like the Thinking River – but the exact opposite."

I heard self-defeating thoughts, voices of doom and self-doubt. I felt lethargic, hopeless, and heavy.

"What's the Thinking River?"

"The river I nearly drowned in. It's a place where every great thought ever thought can be heard."

"How do you know if a thought's great?"

"Careful. You're thinking again," I said teasingly.

Justin pointed toward the moat.

"You must be hearing the Quote Moat. I don't even notice it anymore. Just blends in with my thoughts."

"Of course – the Quote Moat! We learned about that in class. Yeah – well, I don't like it. It makes me feel worse than awful."

"Just excerpts from Orable's teachings," said Justin.

"No wonder! Ok. NO! – I'm not going any closer to that tower. Either you unlock these handcuffs *immediately*, or one of us will soon be missing a hand – and it won't be me!" *Did I really just say this* ? I thought.

Justin's eyes grew two sizes at hearing this. He looked down at the place where our wrists were cuffed. Our eyes locked like predator and prey.

"Where's the key? I'm growing impatient. Unlock them," I demanded, as I reached inside Justin's jacket pocket with my free-reigning hand.

Voices from the Quote Moat grew louder and more degrading.

Justin pushed me. I pushed back. I didn't want to fight, or rip Justin's hand off but I would do either, or both, if left no other option. I refused to accept a fate as Orable's prisoner.

There was a struggle. We toppled over the wooden railing of the drawbridge. Standing waist deep in mind-numbing moat water we punched one another with our free hands.

"I'm free and I'm not going to lose my freedom to you – or anyone!"

Just then the handcuffs warped and became pliable. It was as if they were made of rubber. I imagined that Justin was cuffed. In less than a second it was so. *Did I do that? I did that. I DID THAT! How did I do that?*

With all the splashing and punching that had been going on before this historic moment, neither of us had noticed the dozens of clawcons honking and flapping their wings wildly above. Black ones, large and small, circled the tower; their gazes curious as they looked upon the two odd creatures that had just battled beneath them in the shallow moat.

A buzzing sound, the kind one hears in the presence of something traveling faster than fast, grew louder. Before I knew what had hit me I was swept out of the moat and high into the air. I grabbed Justin at the very same moment the clawcon grabbed me. We were now dangling precariously from the back of the monstrous beast.

And just when I thought things were improving.

CHAPTER THIRTY

THE BEGINNING

Sharp fangs clamped my spine as if I were a block of wood in a vice grip. Flames shot through the air burning my eyes and scorching my eyebrows. My face felt as though it were melting. Coughing, I turned toward the ghastly creature. I wanted to look into the eyes of the beast who could at any moment take my life.

"Rupert?"

"Are you talking to a clawcon?" yelled Justin, through gusts of wind.

"Yes. Yes, I am," I smiled drunkenly.

"I've never heard of a talking clawcon," he yelled a bit louder.

"I imagine there's a lot you haven't heard of."

As I smiled I felt a pinch of madness wash across my face. Rupert placed me ever so gently on her back and released her grip. I quickly pulled Justin to safety. Rupert flapped her wings proudly.

I replayed the whole Quote Moat incident in my head.

How did I get the cuffs off? How did I put them on Justin? I visualized the outcome I wanted but I've tried this hundreds of times before and it never worked. I don't understand.

326

Little did I know that it was my conviction that made the difference. I hadn't struggled to free myself from the handcuffs. I just knew I was free and refused to accept any other reality.

As I lay there basking in a sense of accomplishment Rupert honked madly. I turned and saw that we were surrounded by dozens of black clawcons, each at least twice the size of Rupert. Rupert's flight became erratic. Unfortunately, her white feathers made her stand out target-like against the darkened sky.

Here we go again. Ok – how did I do that earlier? Can I do it again? Yes. I can do it again. I will do it again. I must.

As I was focusing my thoughts one of the clawcons swung its hind end around fast and hard. It kicked Rupert - hard. This sent Justin catapulting through the air with one of Rupert's feathers still clutched in his hand. I knew that without a parasike, he didn't have a chance of surviving the fall. So, I dove into the abyss after him.

Rupert flew in the opposite direction. The remaining clawcons trailed her. Rupert coughed erratic ribbons of fire at them. One by one, blinded and screeching they dropped out of sight. Rupert headed back toward me.

My flight was swift and smooth with the precision of a well-programmed missile. Once I got my hands on Justin I flew to Rupert with him clutched in my arm. Rupert nodded her head and honked approvingly as I mounted her.

"You saw that – huh?" I asked proudly.

Rupert honked again and pulled something from under her wing. It was Spelzig's portal. Before I could say a word Rupert sped toward the tower. Higher and higher we flew. She landed on the rooftop and looked at me expectantly.

Spelzig appeared within the canvas dressed in black, head to toe. Against the black background it was difficult to see anything except for his face and hands.

"I KNEW you could do it, Levi! Spectacular manifestation. Absolutely spectacular," said Spelzig, applauding.

"But – I didn't do it. I didn't thought propel here," I said, feeling like a complete failure.

"Levi – it's the end result that matters – not the how of it. You set your mind to placing me in the tower and one way or another you've achieved it. Simply magnificent."

Spelzig looked around the rooftop.

"There," he said, jumping up and down. "Put me over there beside the Bin of Joy. I'll investigate all discarded happy thoughts and begin my investigation."

I darted across the roof with Spelzig's portal and placed it beside the *Bin of Joy*.

"This is just the beginning my boy," said Spelzig, extending his tiny hand for a shake. "I've arranged for an auxiliary portal to be delivered to your cottage so that I can travel between the tower and your place. I'll be in touch soon."

We shook hands. Rupert honked.

I ran to Rupert at lightning speed and mounted her just seconds before a black clawcon blew a twenty foot blast of fire at the very spot I'd occupied seconds ago.

"Why'd you save me? I'm your enemy," said Justin looking baffled but grateful.

"We don't have to be enemies. I try to make everyone my friend," I said, wishing we were all somewhere else. I wanted to be back at the *Downstream Diner* with Garby, Hemp, Penelope, Sarabella, Morblid, Mobert, Sner and Alphia..."

On and on I went happily envisioning us all at the diner. In my imagination I filled in every detail down to the color of Hemp's toe socks.

A thunderous sound shook me back into the moment. I clutched onto Rupert and yelled for Justin to do the same.

What's happening? Is someone shooting at us? Was that a bomb?

A flash of golden light blinded me. As it faded I saw myself seated on a stool beside Penelope, her arms wrapped around me just as I'd imagined they would be. This vision flashed in and out. It was disorienting because I wasn't at the diner but yet I saw myself seated there beside her. I considered the possibility that somehow I was in two places at once.

Then suddenly, I was back inside my body but unable to speak, feel, or move. It was as if my body and soul had travelled separately. When the two reunited I found myself seated at the *Downstream Diner* on a stool beside Penelope with her embracing me just as I'd visualized.

Balloons and streamers were strewn across the walls and ceiling. Bubbles floated through the air. A layer of colorful confetti peppered the floor and tables. A whopping organic carrot cake with thick cream cheese frosting sat waiting with just one very large orange candle in the center.

Hmm. A party? They can't possibly be celebrating my abduction. Can they?

Everyone stood and applauded.

I flushed as my eyes fell upon a sparkling neon banner floating above the table:

Levi Levy = HERO!

"How'd you know I'd be here?" I asked, accepting a fat piece of cake from Penelope.

"Priscilla predicted it. You were on *Sifter's Network News*. Lilith Chatters played a clip of you and some boy fighting in a moat. Then it flashed to a scene of the boy being knocked off Rupert and you diving after him. Wicked sick it was. Should've seen you. Right before the kid hit ground you grabbed him – and levitated! Then you ripped up into the sky, found Rupert and flew up to the tower. It was awesome! How'd you do that?" asked Garby, all the while using his hands to mimic my movements in a very dramatic way.

"I – I really have no idea. I just knew what I wanted and wanted it so badly that I couldn't – wouldn't accept any other outcome."

It wasn't until I said this that I realized how I'd done it.

Penelope cut a piece of cake for Justin. As I was about to hand it to him I saw that he was still cuffed.

"Let's get those off. Sorry I put them on you in the first place. I was just protecting you from yourself and all that *thinking* you were doing back there," I joked. "Are you going to tell me where the key is now?"

Justin nodded and eyed the pocket of his shirt.

I reached in, got the key and removed the cuffs.

"You're one of us now – friend," I said, handing him a juicy veggie burger, basket of Fickle chips, and piece of cake. At first he was afraid of the Fickle chips but once I explained them he was quite entertained.

He ate ravenously. Between swallows he thanked me for saving him earlier.

I nodded humbly. "That's what friends are for."

Morblid, Mobert, Sner and Maya rushed toward me and took turns hugging me. Mobert growled approvingly. Maya applauded. Morblid asked a million questions all of which were missing the final word. Sner tossed me several Coconut Cosmos candy bars - all of which I caught.

"Welcome back," said Hemp, with a knowing twinkle in his eyes as he stood before me looking as if he were watching a rerun of the day's events through my eyes.

"Who is he and why is he wearing your hat?" whispered Garby.

"Wasn't that in the news, too?" I asked, winking.

"No – Lilith said he was underage so they withheld his identity."

"Well – it was *his* hat all along."

"Noooo way. That was his? But he's a – I mean – isn't he – holy crap! Did you? Oh – you did! You freed a Virusian Soldier!" said Garby, grabbing my shoulders and shaking me. "Who would have thought it possible? Hoo ha!" Garby punched at air.

"Me. Remember? I thought it was possible," I said.

Hemp turned to Justin.

"Justin – your body's free now but your mind – well, that's an entirely different matter. A challenging road lies ahead.

Hemp poured Justin a tall glass of green lemonade then slapped me on the back and whispered, "Well done, lad."

I felt my cheeks flush. "One down. Hundreds to go," I said, as I turned toward Sarabella who was pointing to a message she crafted with sesame seeds on the tabletop:

NOT BAD, HERO BOY

"Thanks – but I'm no hero. I'm just a boy remembering who I *really* am."

"You're a hero. But don't let it go to your head, pet," said Alphia, licking the cream cheese frosting from my slice of cake.

"And – who are you – *really?*" came a voice that seemed vaguely familiar.

"I'm a sifter," I answered proudly, as I looked around the room for the person to whom the voice belonged.

Then the music stopped playing – at least in my head. It was like a scene from a scary movie when the bad guy appears unexpectedly out of nowhere. There she was standing in front of me.

"Dr. Oblivia?" I gasped.

Can't be. I must be hallucinating. Please tell me that's not really her. Is the cake enchanted? Is that a commune cake? There's no way I'm going back now.

I hurried to check the cake box for a warning label.

Dr. Oblivia burst into mad laughter. She then explained that I wasn't the only one who'd received an invitation. A girl had brought an invitation to one of her sessions and left it there for she had no interest in leaving her family behind.

"Naturally, with both of you receiving one of those things I was curious. I burned it myself. That crater drop was a trip – huh?" she said, laughing wildly.

"So – you're not here to try to make me go back?" I asked, finding no warning label on the cake box.

"Goodness – NO! Hemp offered me a job at the compound. I'll be Ceres' first ever interdimensional psychologist. I'll meet and greet new sifters and help them prepare for crossovers. I'll deprogram Virusian Soldiers as you free them. We'll make a *magnificent* team! And — we're going to find Agrestalia's book. This is just the beginning, Levi!"

I wasn't sure how I felt about all this.

After apologizing for having doubted me during our sessions Dr. Oblivia slid her eyeglasses down the slope of her delicate nose. Peering over them she said, "Thank you for helping me to see beyond my beliefs and understanding of things." And as she said this her hand instinctively searched her neck and throat for her silver diamond-encrusted cross. When she found it she held it and rubbed it between her thumb and index finger.

We smiled and nodded knowingly at one another.

END OF BOOK ONE

ABOUT THE AUTHOR

C.G. Rousing resides in southern California. She earned an A.A in Music Performance and a B.A. in Liberal Arts. In addition to being an author Rousing is a talented pianist, songwriter/composer and medium. Her passion for metaphysics, psychology, philosophy, the paranormal, and astrology - along with the ideology contained in books like *The Secret, Ask and It is Given, Three Magic Words,* (and countless others like them) is woven into a universally relatable tapestry that will enlighten and inspire readers of all ages, for decades to come, in - *THOUGHTS TO DIE FOR.*

To order signed copies in bulk, at a discounted rate, to schedule an author talk, interview, or book signing – or, if you are interested in optioning film rights for *Thoughts To Die For* please email the author at:

cgrousing@gmail.com